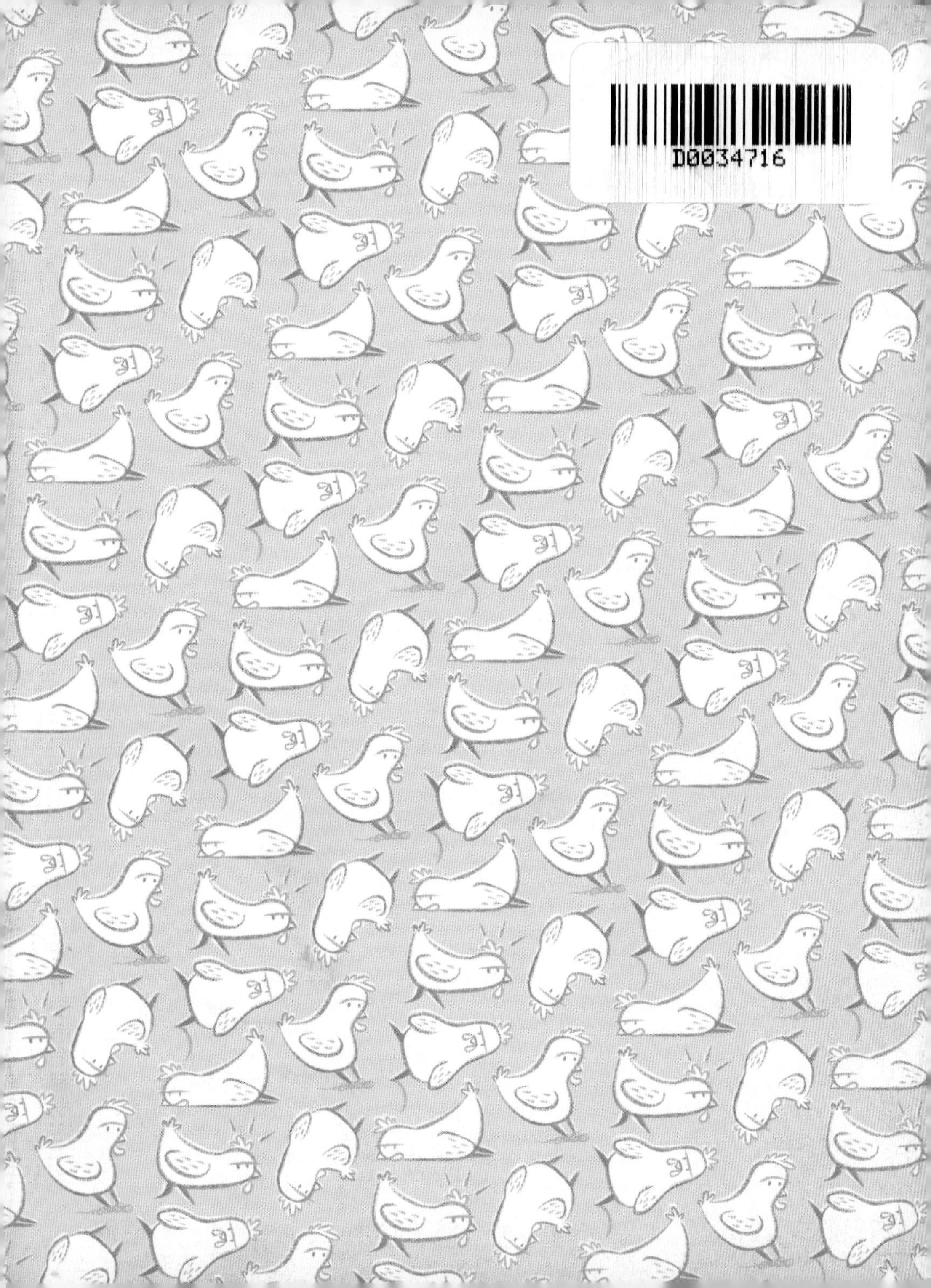

CRANKY CHICKEN

CHICKEN

PARTY ANIMALS

CRANKENSTEIN

KATHERINE BATTERSBY

MARGARET K. McELDERRY BOOKS

NEW YORK   LONDON   TORONTO   SYDNEY   NEW DELHI

For the Magical Weirdos,
the best (and least cranky)
illustrator group a girl
could ask for

MARGARET K. McELDERRY BOOKS

An imprint of Simon & Schuster Children's Publishing Division

1230 Avenue of the Americas, New York, New York 10020

© 2022 by Katherine Battersby

Book design by Rebecca Syracuse © 2022 by Simon & Schuster, Inc.

For information about special discounts for bulk purchases, please contact

Simon & Schuster Special Sales at 1-866-506-1949 or business@simonandschuster.com.

The Simon & Schuster Speakers Bureau can bring authors to your live event. For more information

or to book an event, contact the Simon & Schuster Speakers Bureau at 1-866-248-3049 or

visit our website at www.simonspeakers.com.

The illustrations for this book were rendered digitally using

custom chalk, pastel, and watercolor brushes.

Manufactured in China | 0322 SCP

First Edition | 10 9 8 7 6 5 4 3 2 1

Library of Congress Cataloging-in-Publication Data

Names: Battersby, Katherine, author, illustrator.

Title: Party animals / Katherine Battersby.

Description: First edition. | New York : Margaret K. McElderry Books, 2022. | Series: Cranky Chicken | Audience: Ages 6–9. | Audience: Grades 2–3. | Summary: A curmudgeonly chicken and a cheerful worm explore what it means to be best friends while sharing three adventures.

Identifiers: LCCN 2021044759 (print) | LCCN 2021044760 (ebook) | ISBN 9781534470217 (paper-over-board) | ISBN 9781534470231 (ebook)

Subjects: CYAC: Chickens—Fiction. | Worms—Fiction. | Best friends—Fiction. | Friendship—Fiction. | Mood (Psychology)—Fiction.

Classification: LCC PZ7.B324376 Par 2022 (print) | LCC PZ7.B324376 (ebook) | DDC [E]—dc23

LC record available at https://lccn.loc.gov/2021044759

LC ebook record available at https://lccn.loc.gov/2021044760

CONTENTS

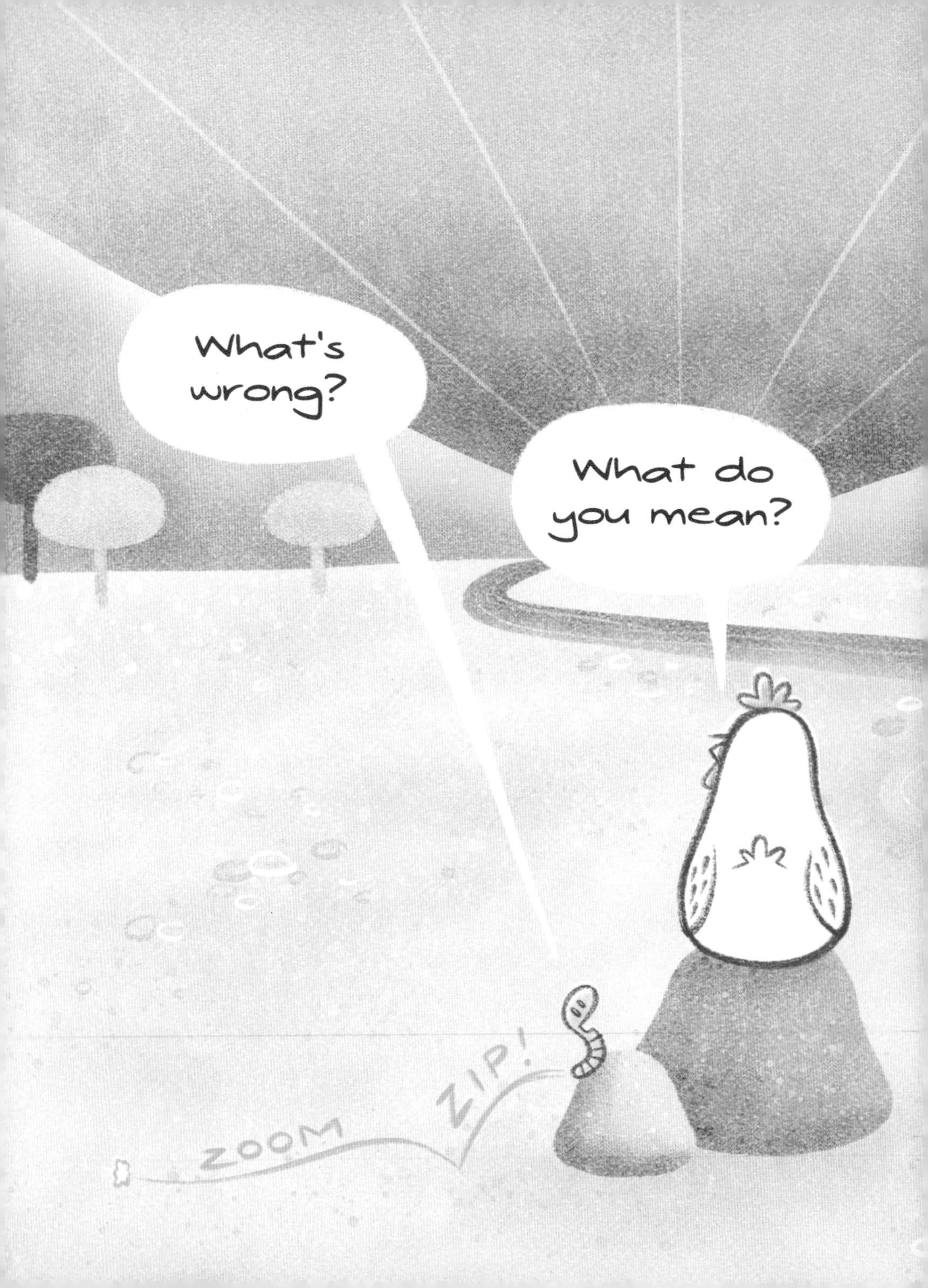
What's wrong?
What do you mean?
ZOOM
ZIP!

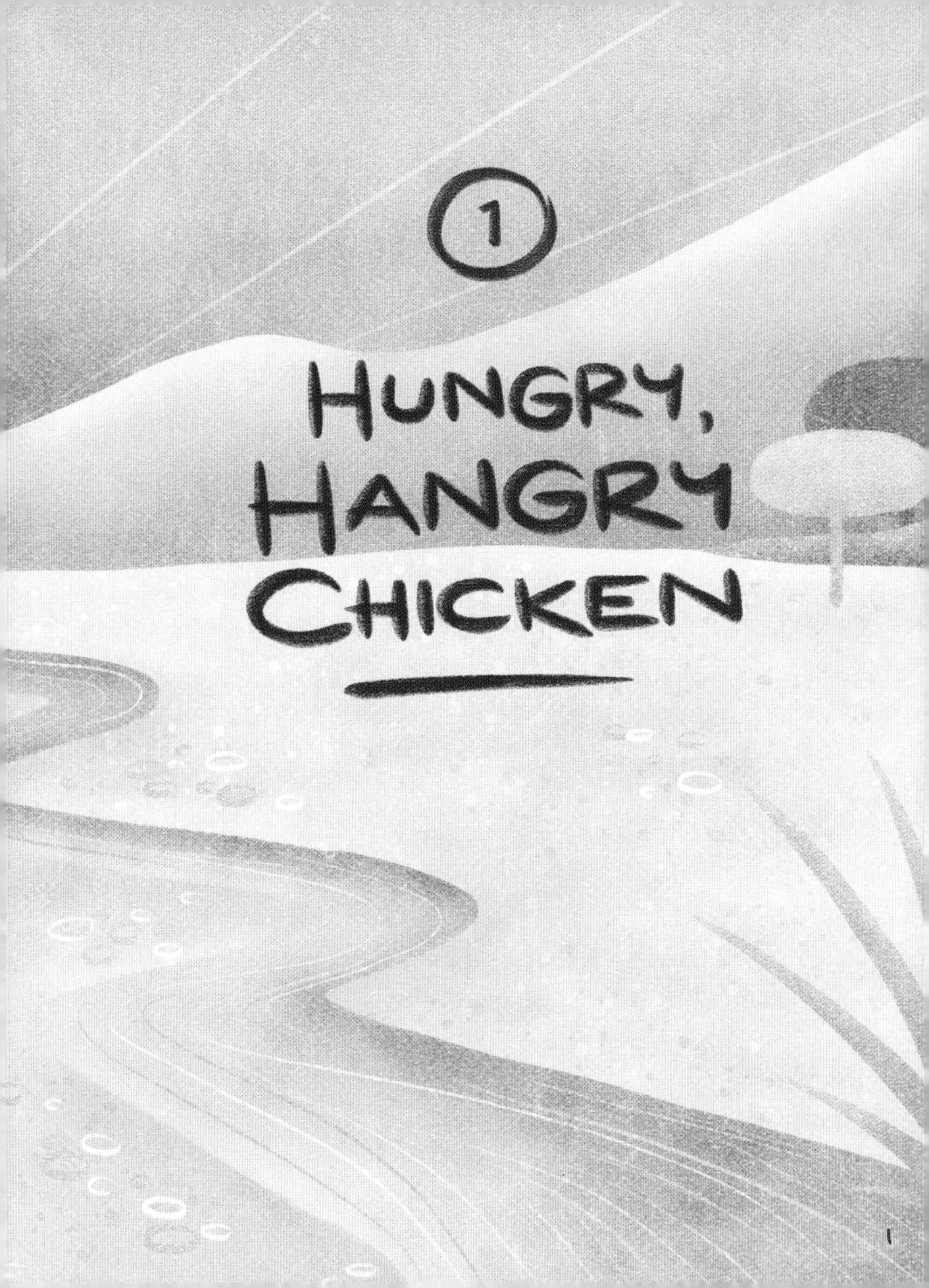

1
Hungry, Hangry Chicken

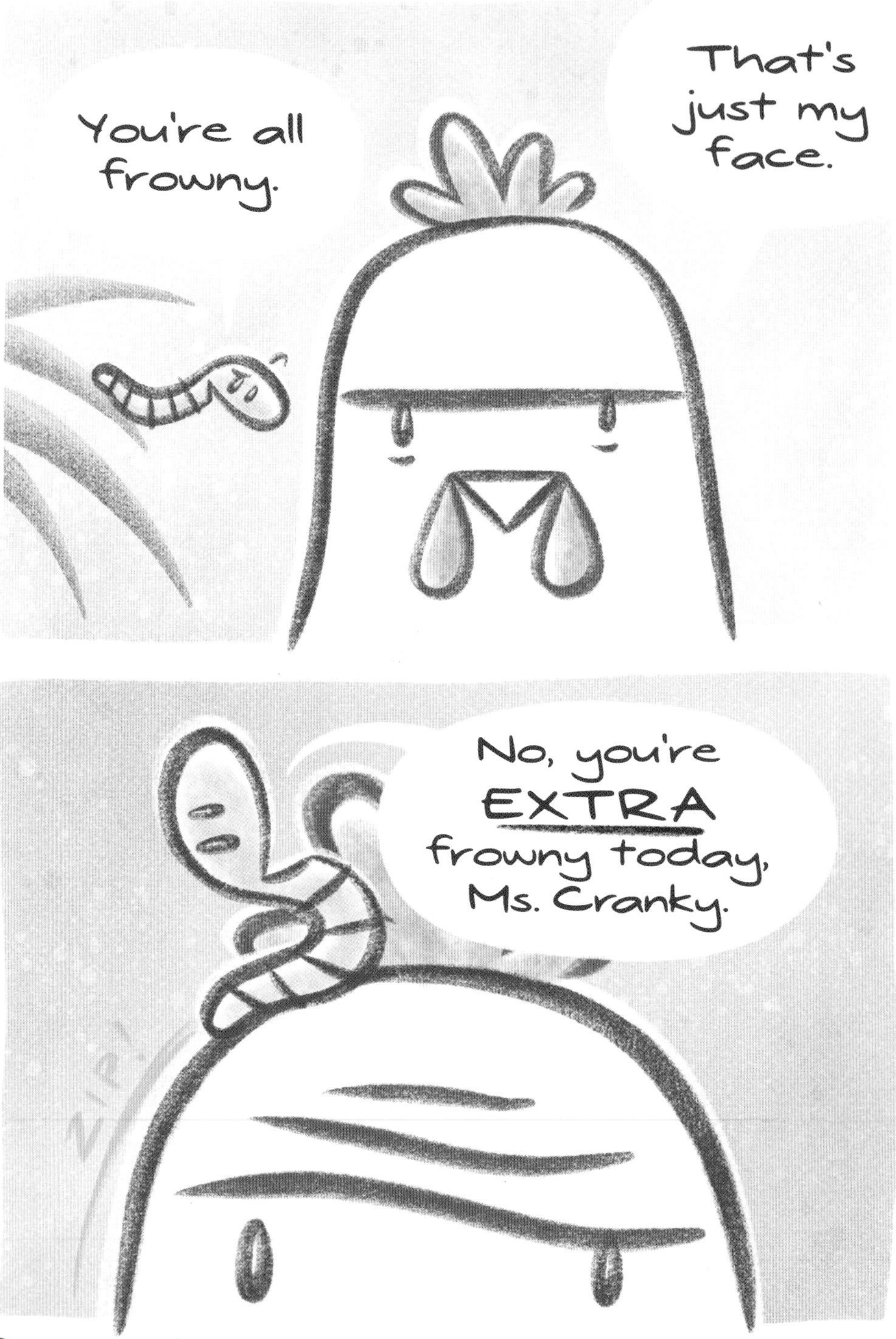
You're all frowny.
That's just my face.
No, you're EXTRA frowny today, Ms. Cranky.
ZIP!

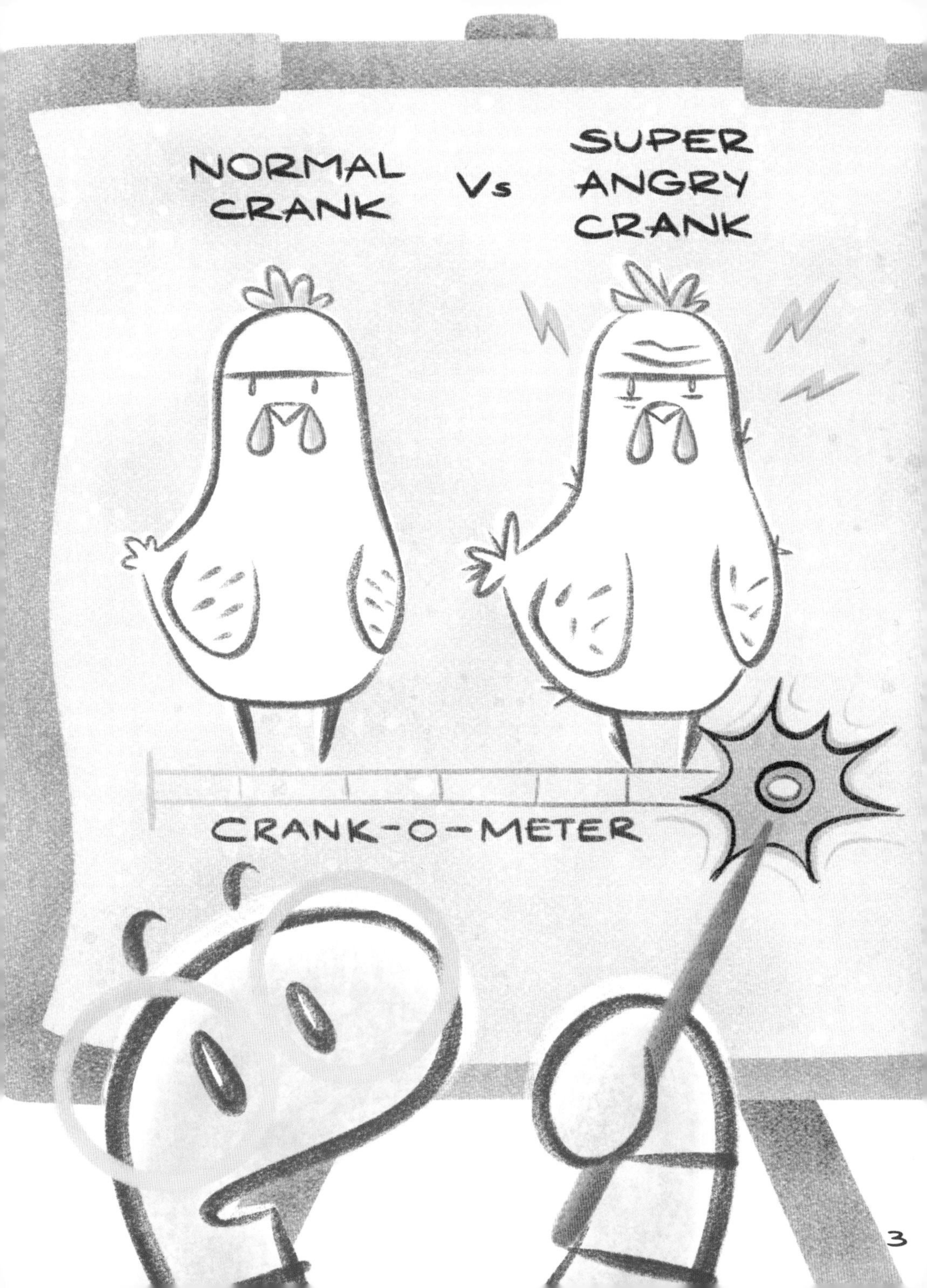
NORMAL CRANK
Vs
SUPER ANGRY CRANK
CRANK-O-METER

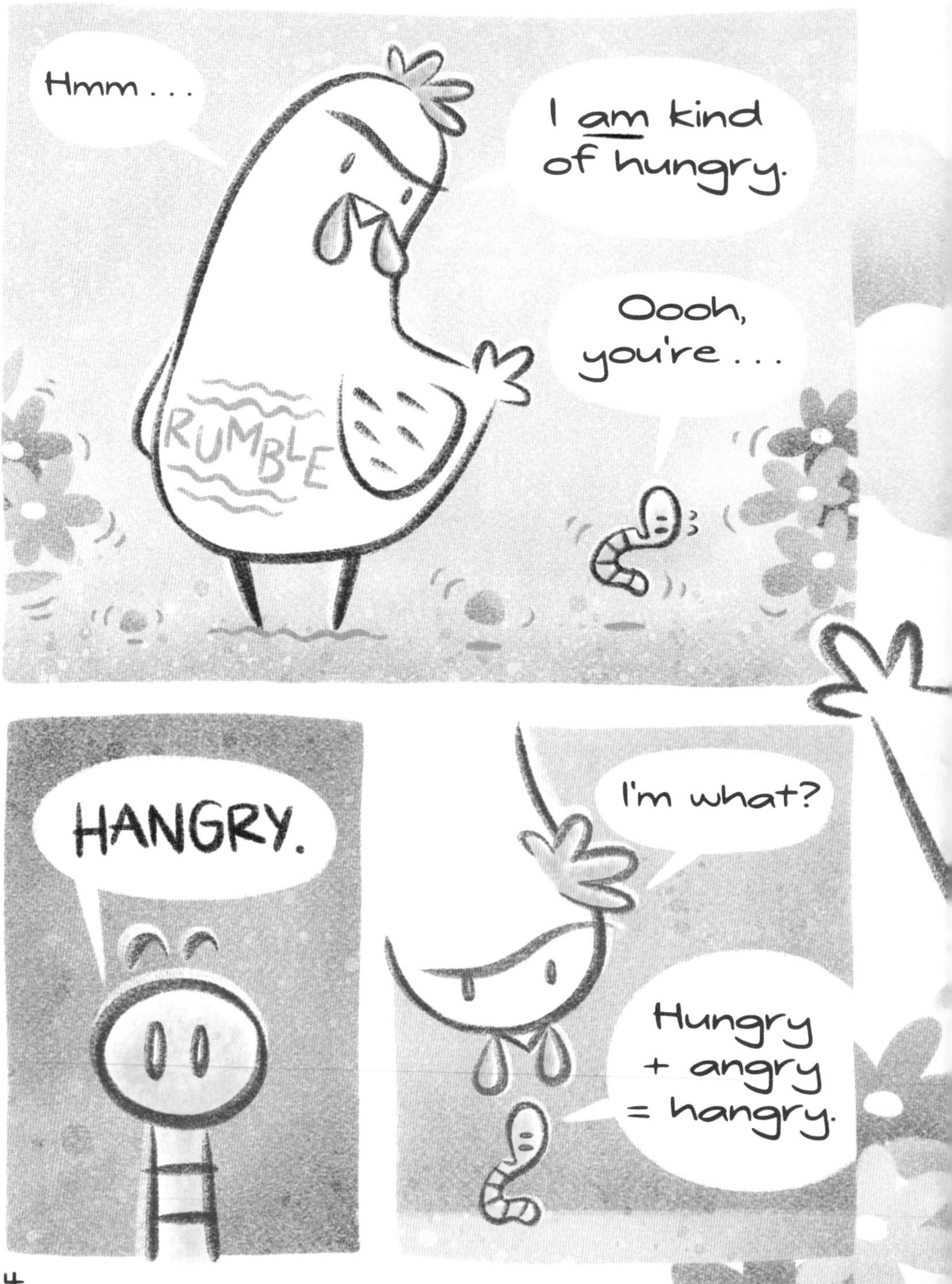
Hmm . . .
I am kind of hungry.
RUMBLE
Oooh, you're . . .
HANGRY.
I'm what?
Hungry + angry = hangry.

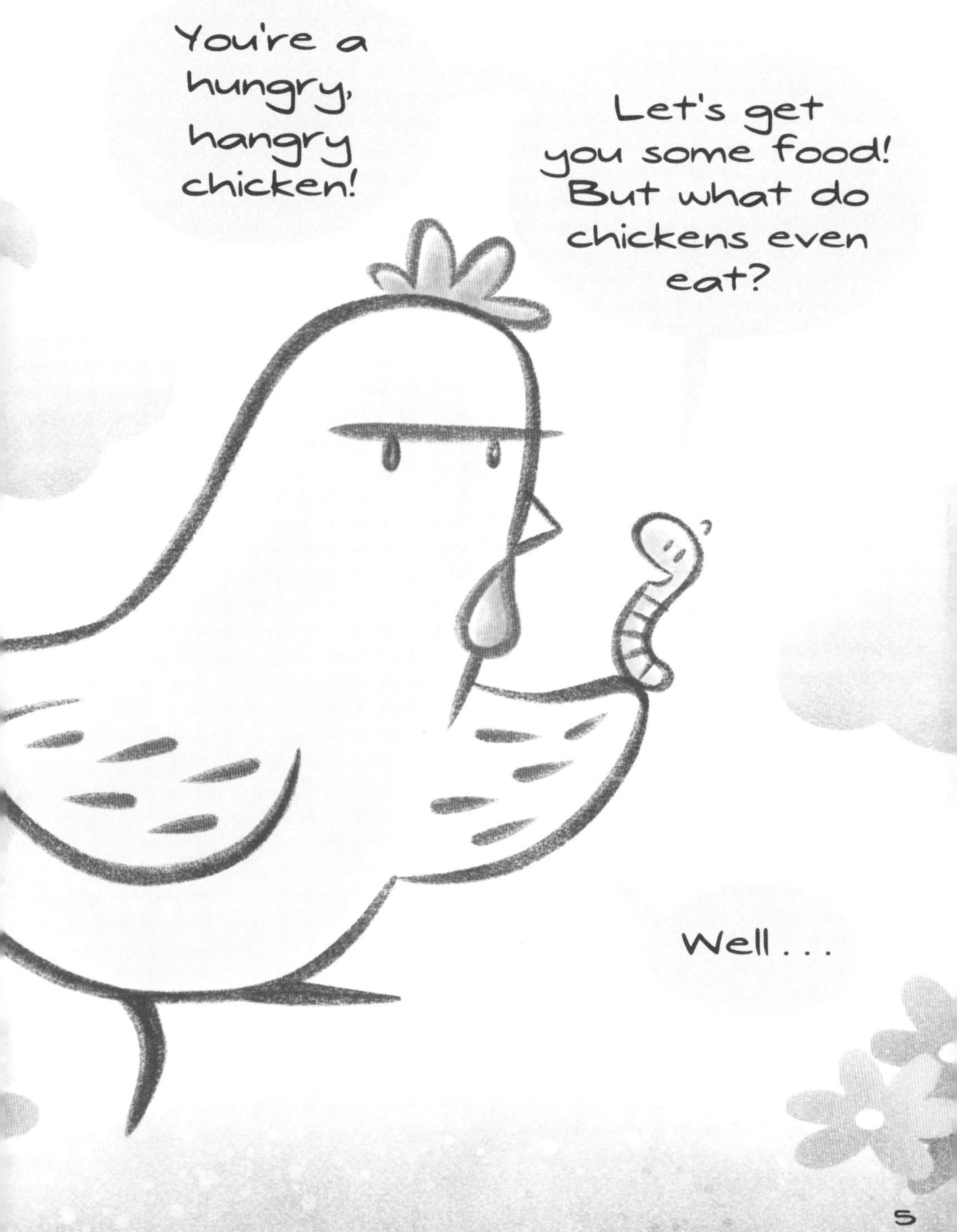
You're a hungry, hangry chicken!
Let's get you some food! But what do chickens even eat?
Well . . .

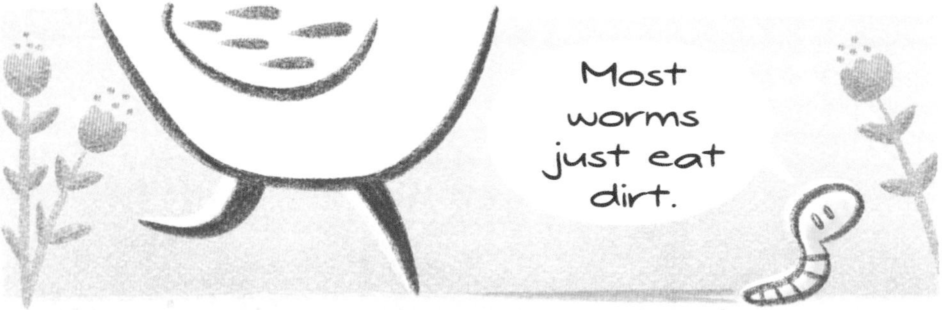
Most worms just eat dirt.

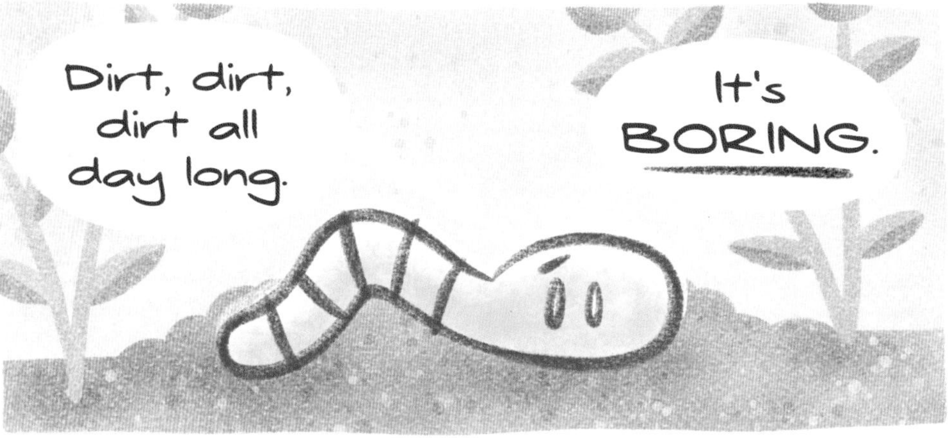
Dirt, dirt, dirt all day long.
It's BORING.

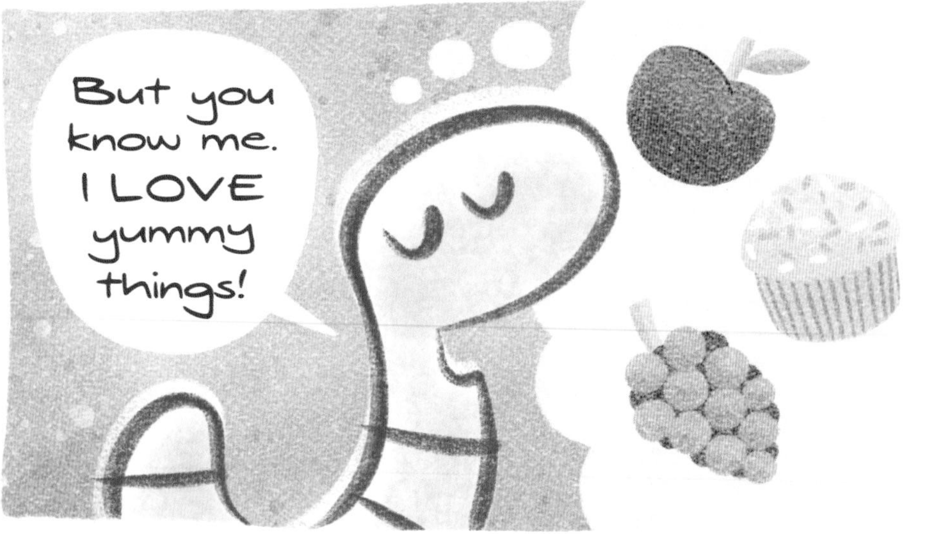
But you know me. I LOVE yummy things!

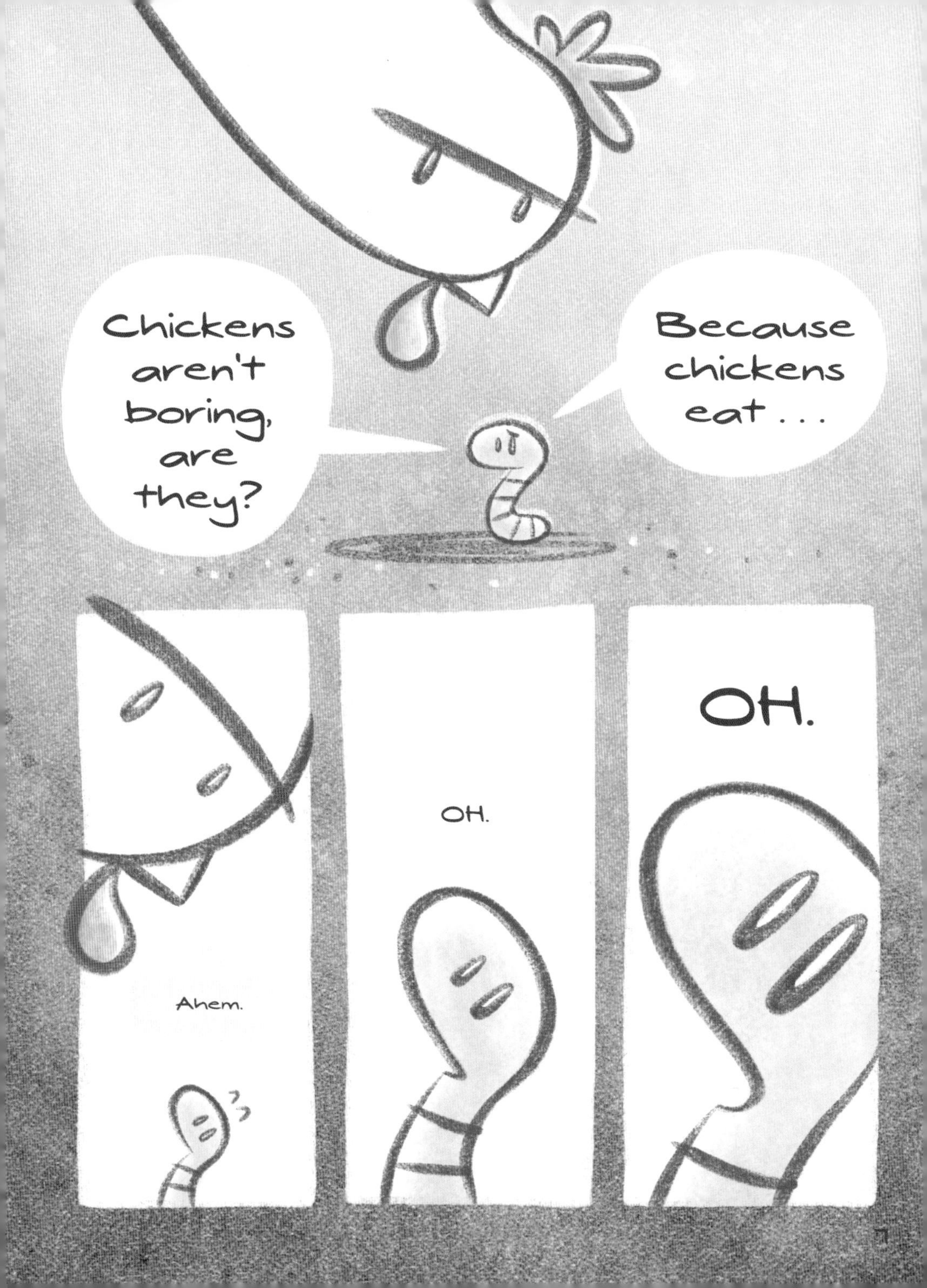
Chickens aren't boring, are they?
Because chickens eat . . .
Ahem.
OH.
OH.

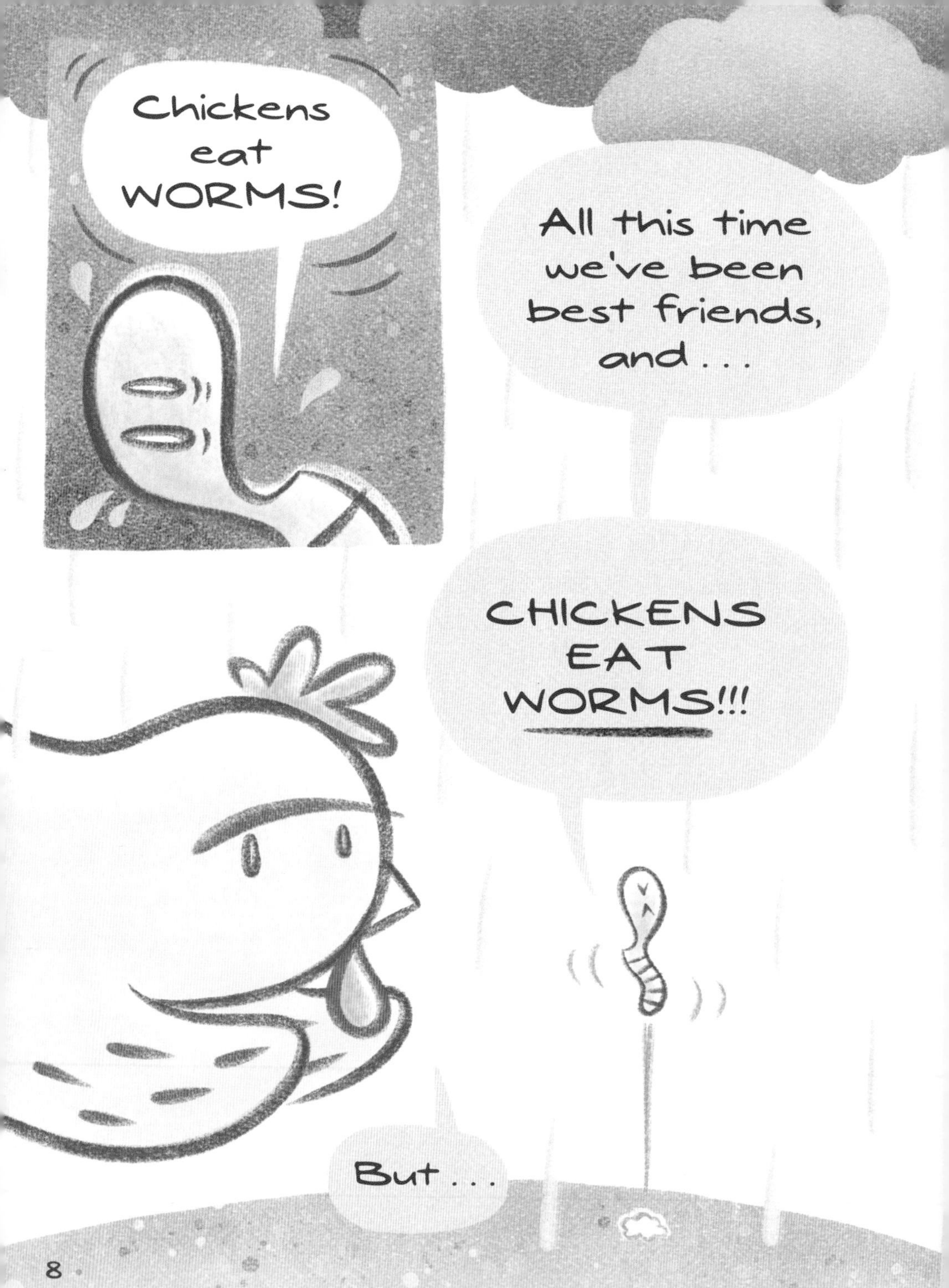

Chickens eat WORMS!
All this time we've been best friends, and . . .
CHICKENS EAT WORMS!!!
But . . .

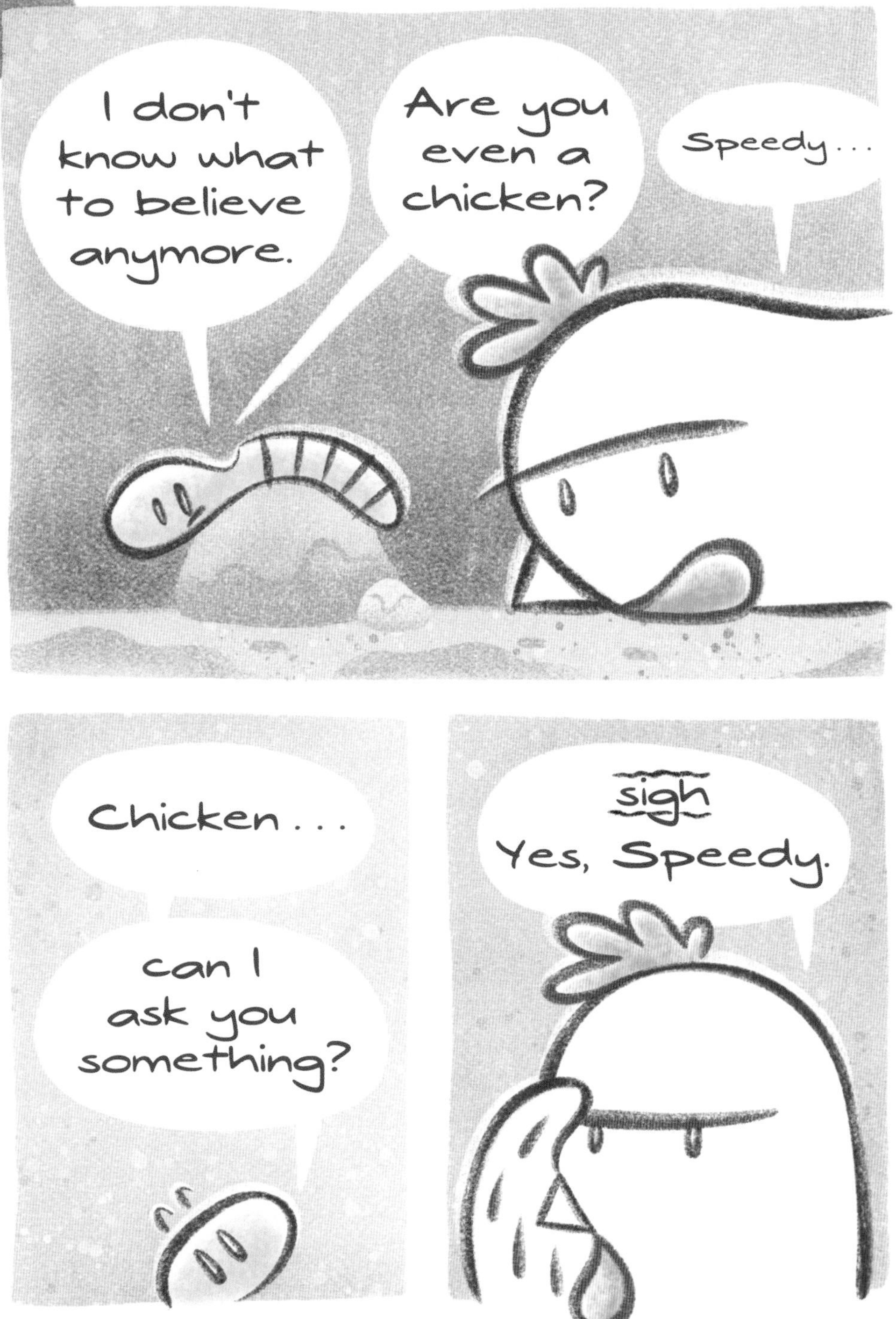
I don't know what to believe anymore.
Are you even a chicken?
Speedy . . .
Chicken . . .
can I ask you something?
sigh
Yes, Speedy.

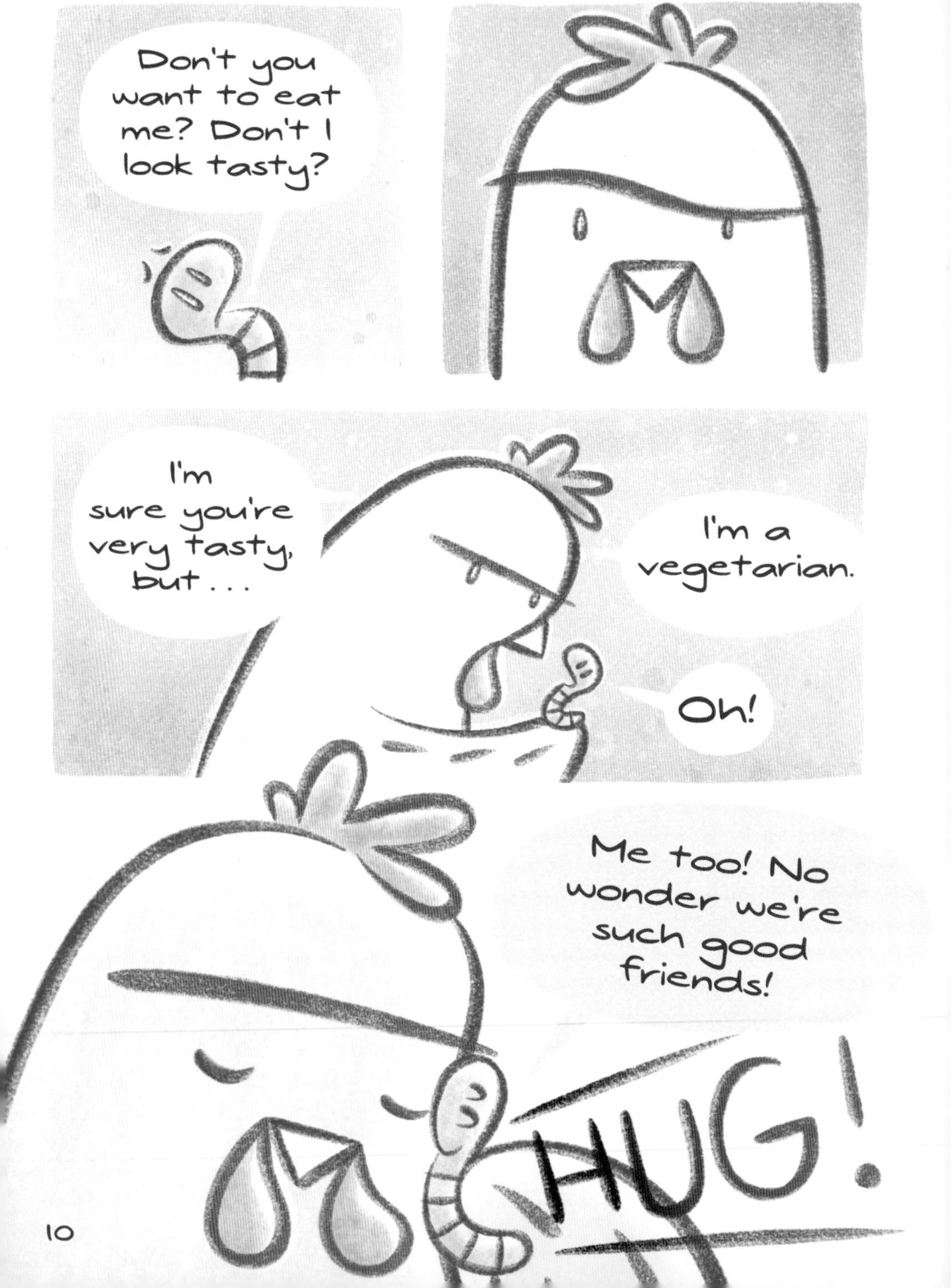
Don't you want to eat me? Don't I look tasty?
I'm sure you're very tasty, but . . .
I'm a vegetarian.
Oh!
Me too! No wonder we're such good friends!
HUG!

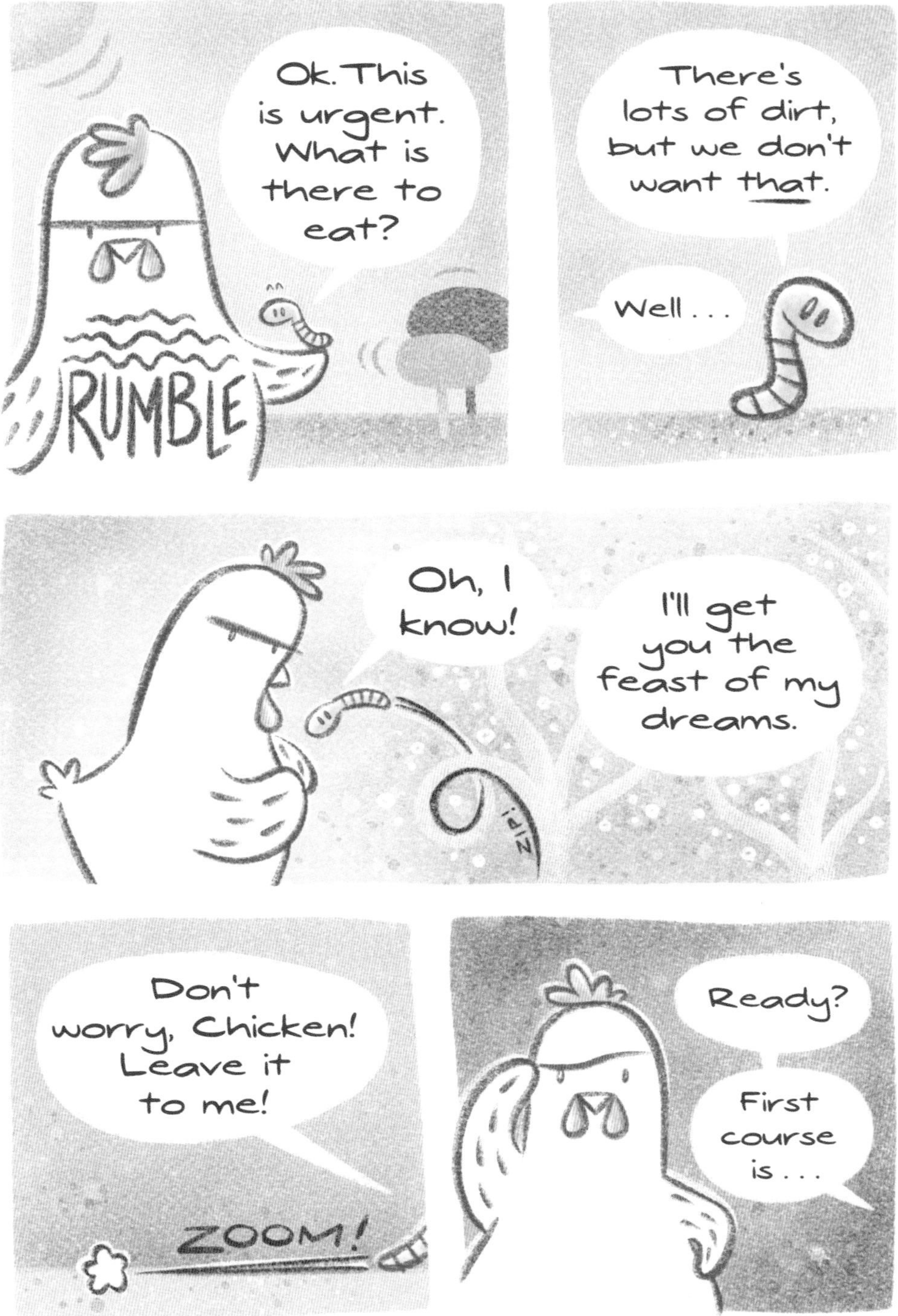
Ok. This is urgent. What is there to eat?
RUMBLE
There's lots of dirt, but we don't want that.
Well . . .
Oh, I know!
I'll get you the feast of my dreams.
ZIP!
Don't worry, Chicken! Leave it to me!
ZOOM!
Ready?
First course is . . .

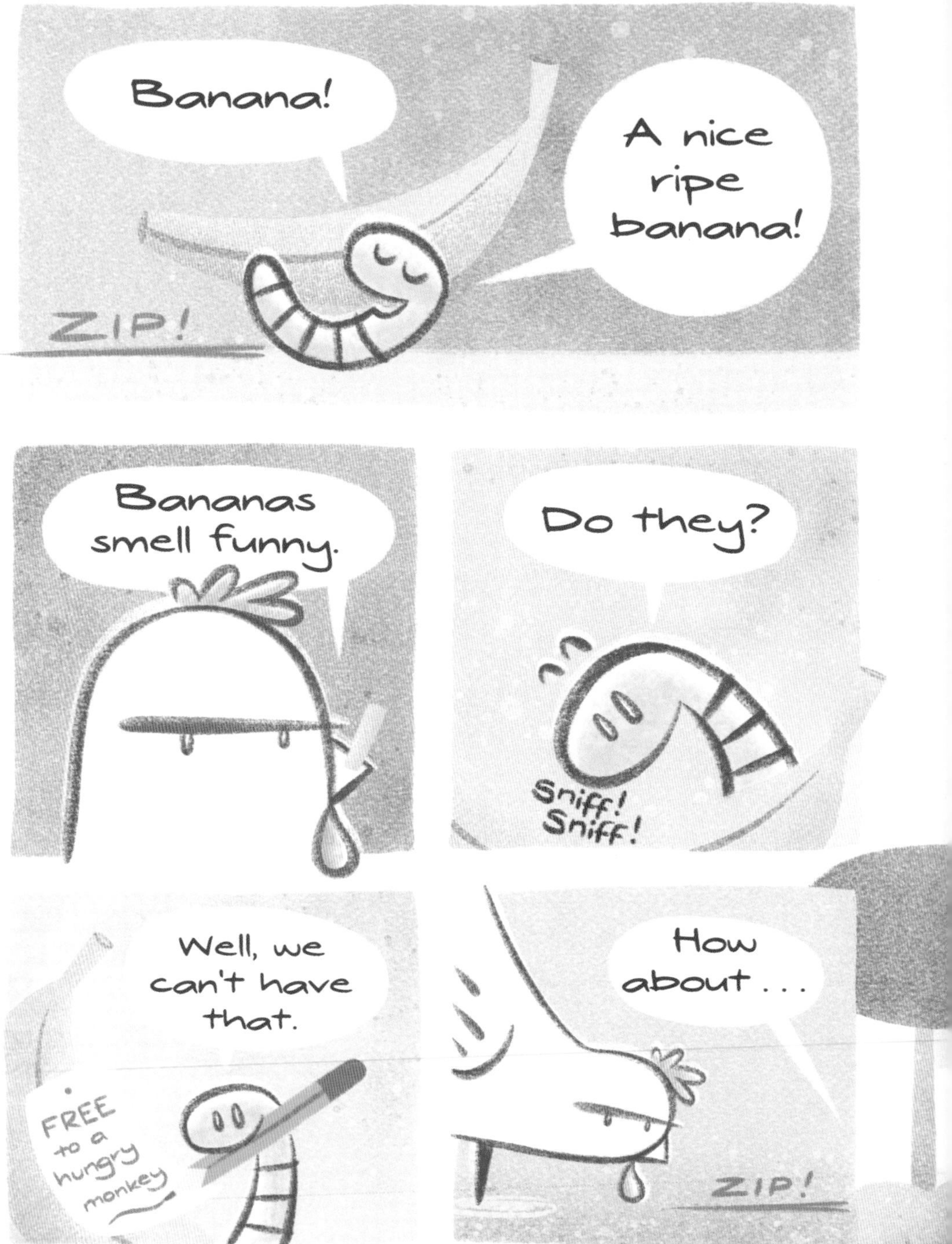

Banana!
A nice ripe banana!
ZIP!
Bananas smell funny.
Do they?
Sniff! Sniff!
Well, we can't have that.
FREE to a hungry monkey
How about . . .
ZIP!

Jell-O!

Everyone loves Jell-O!

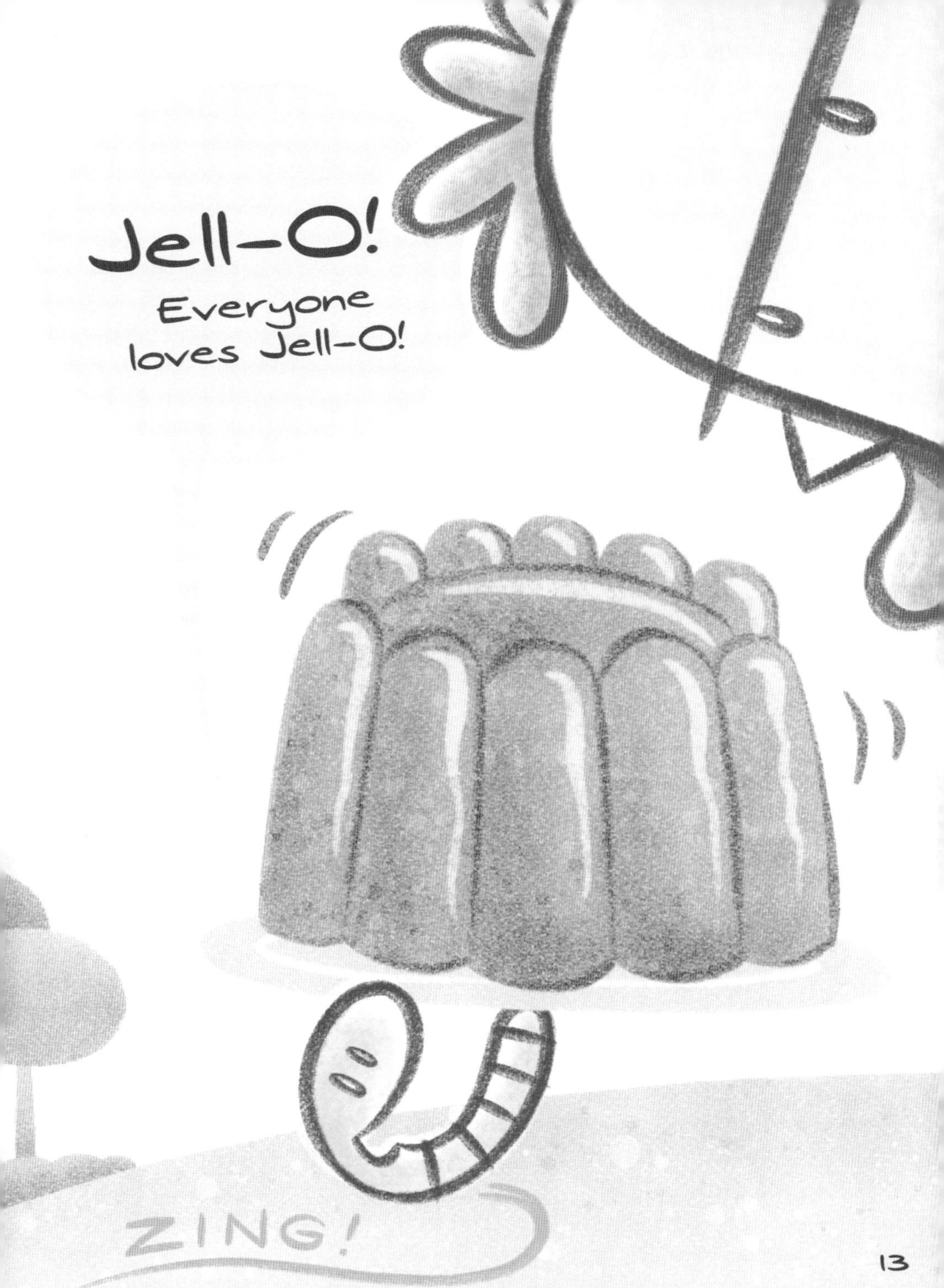
ZING!

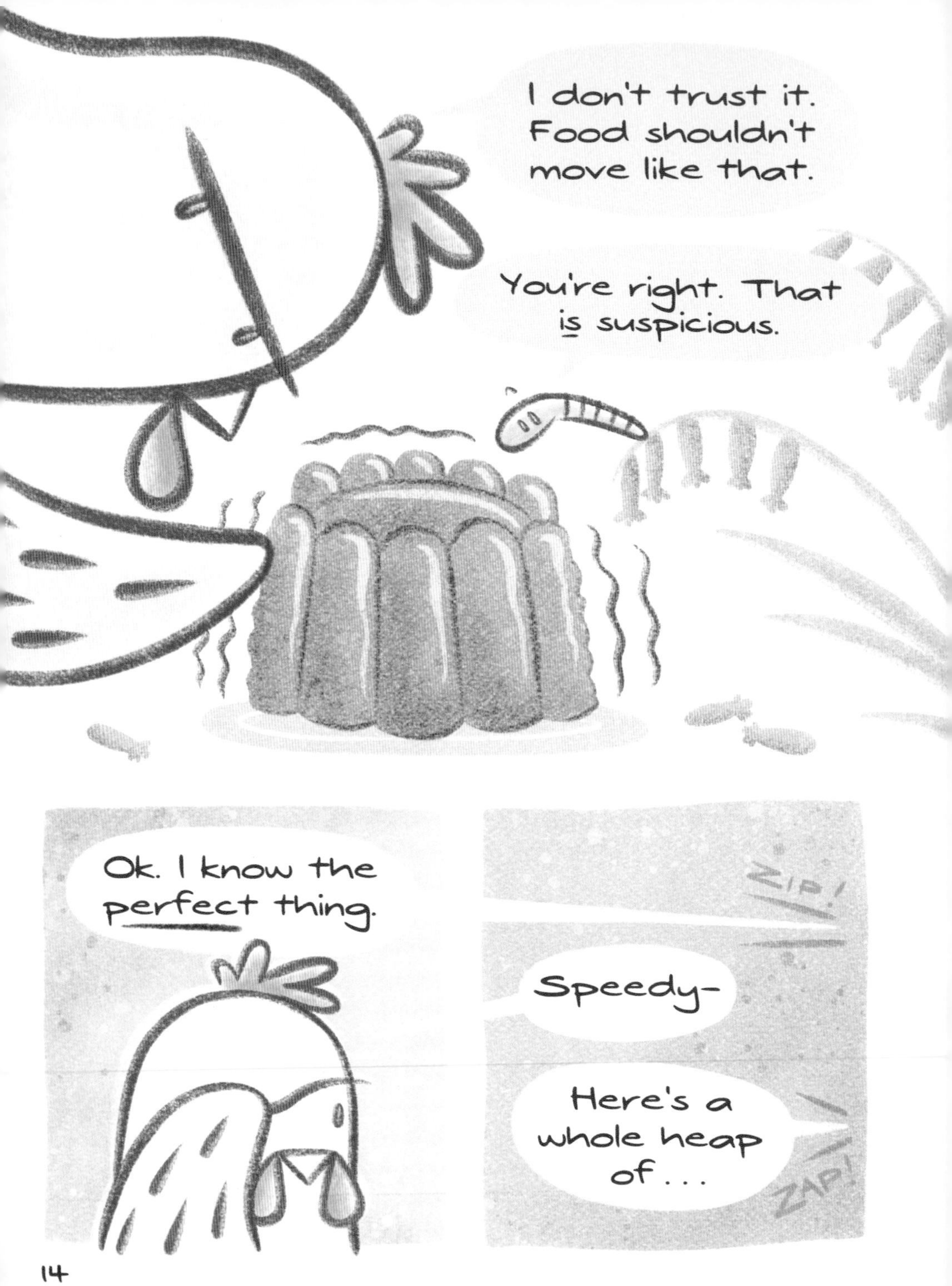
I don't trust it. Food shouldn't move like that.
You're right. That is suspicious.
Ok. I know the perfect thing.
ZIP!
Speedy-
Here's a whole heap of . . .
ZAP!

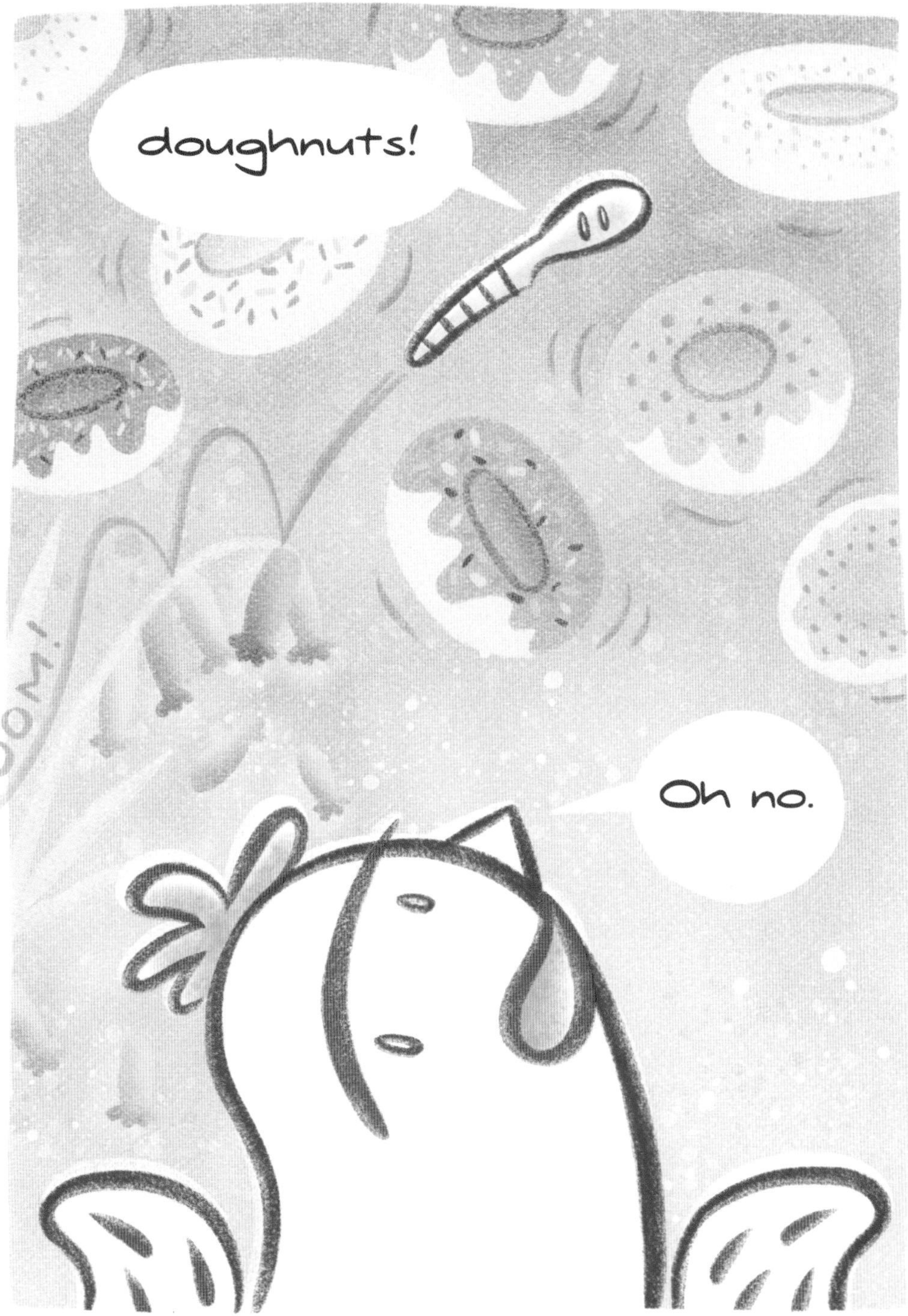
doughnuts!
ZOOM!
Oh no.

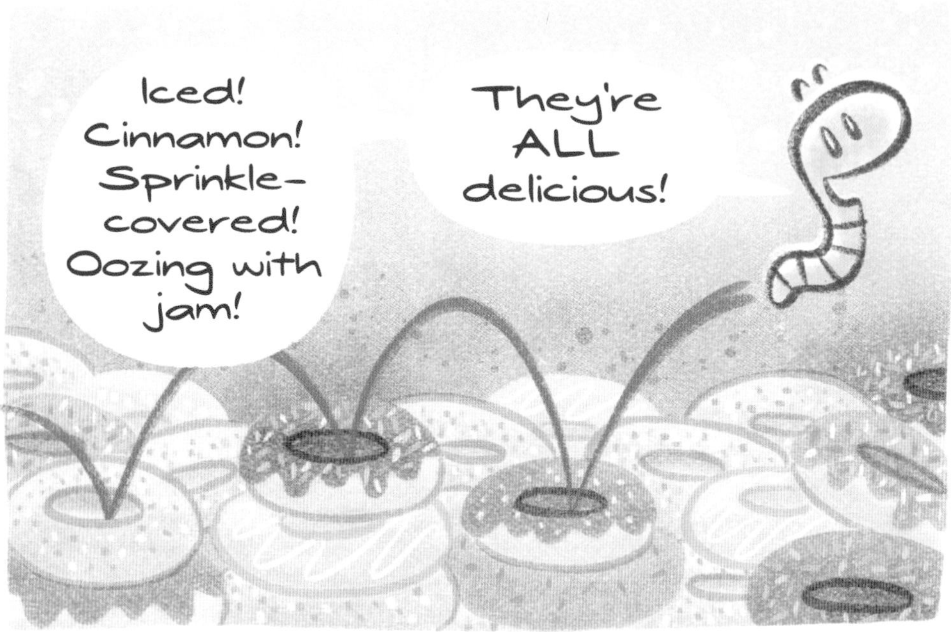
Iced! Cinnamon! Sprinkle-covered! Oozing with jam!
They're ALL delicious!

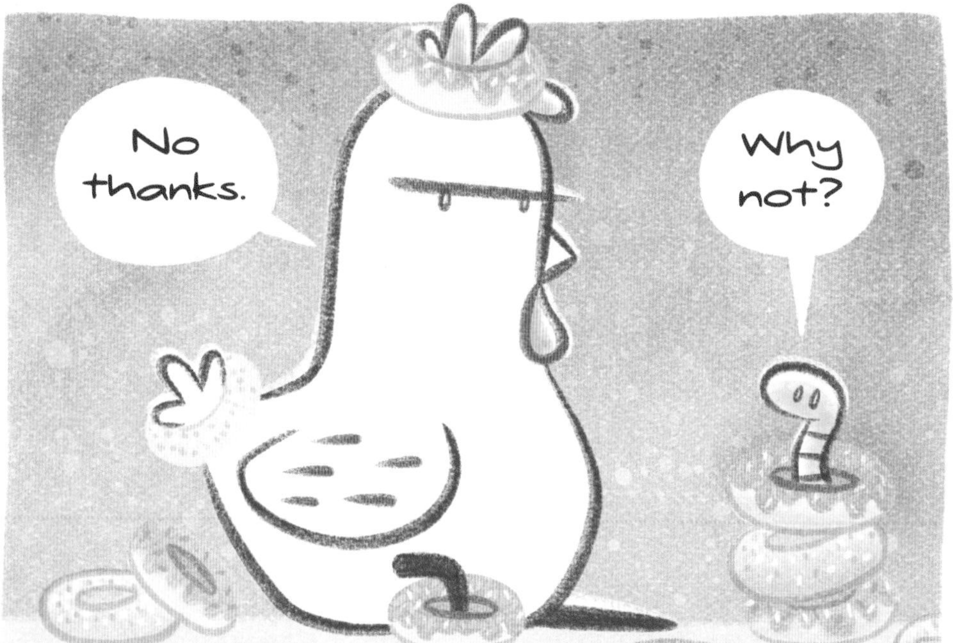
No thanks.
Why not?

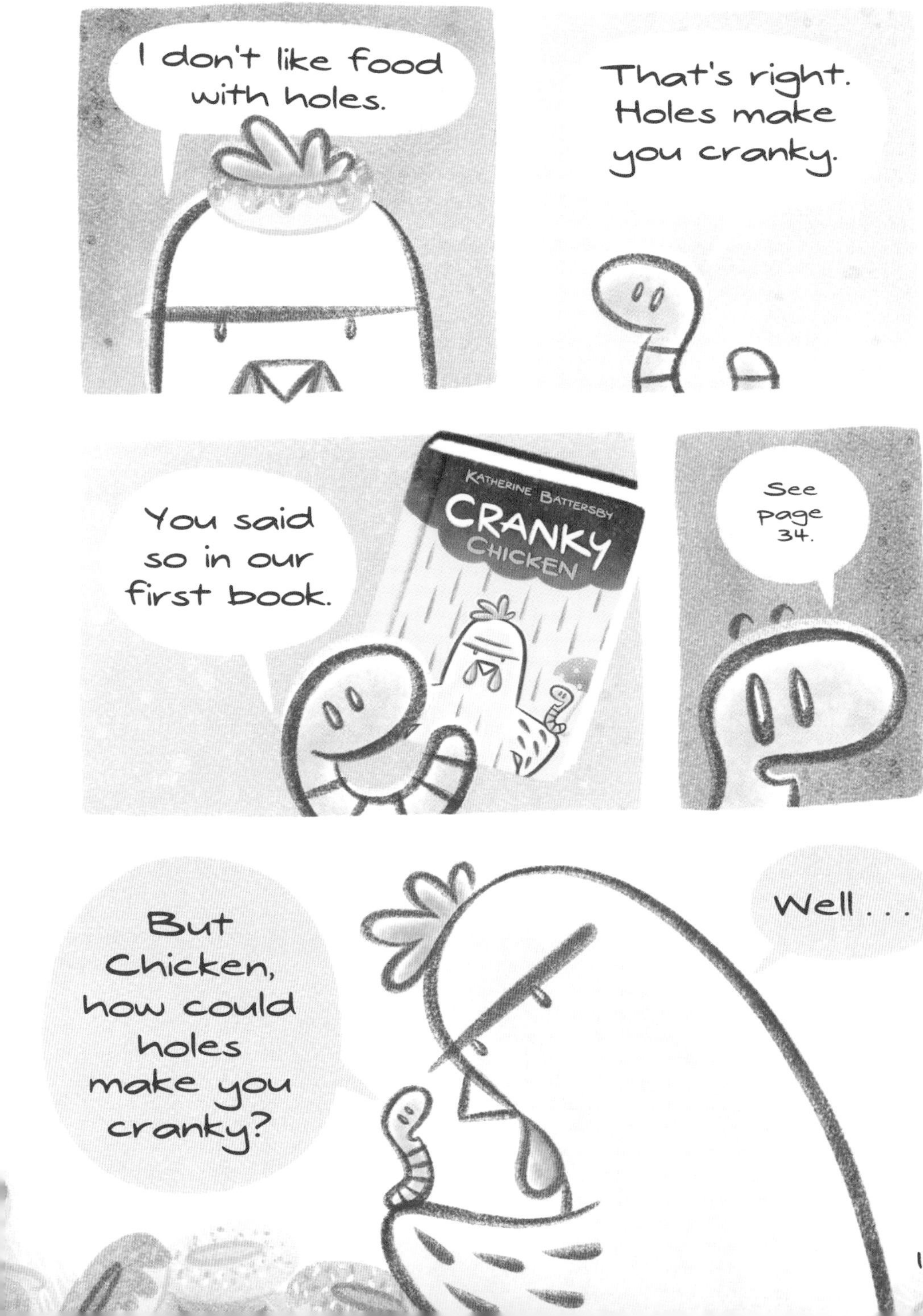
I don't like food with holes.
That's right. Holes make you cranky.
You said so in our first book.
KATHERINE BATTERSBY
CRANKY CHICKEN
See page 34.
But Chicken, how could holes make you cranky?
Well . . .

WHY FOOD WITH HOLES MAKES CHICKEN CRANKY

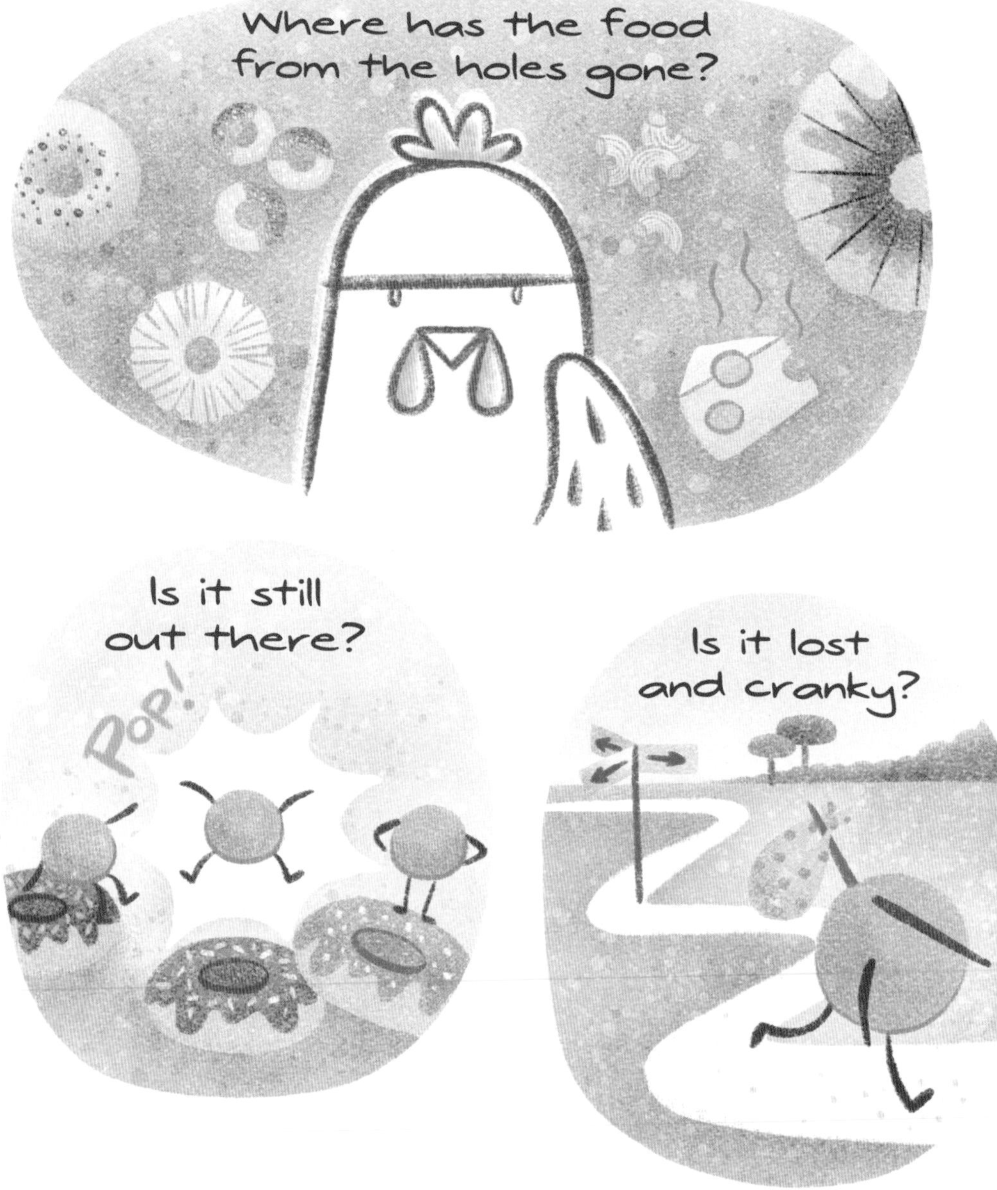

Where has the food from the holes gone?
Is it still out there?
POP!
Is it lost and cranky?

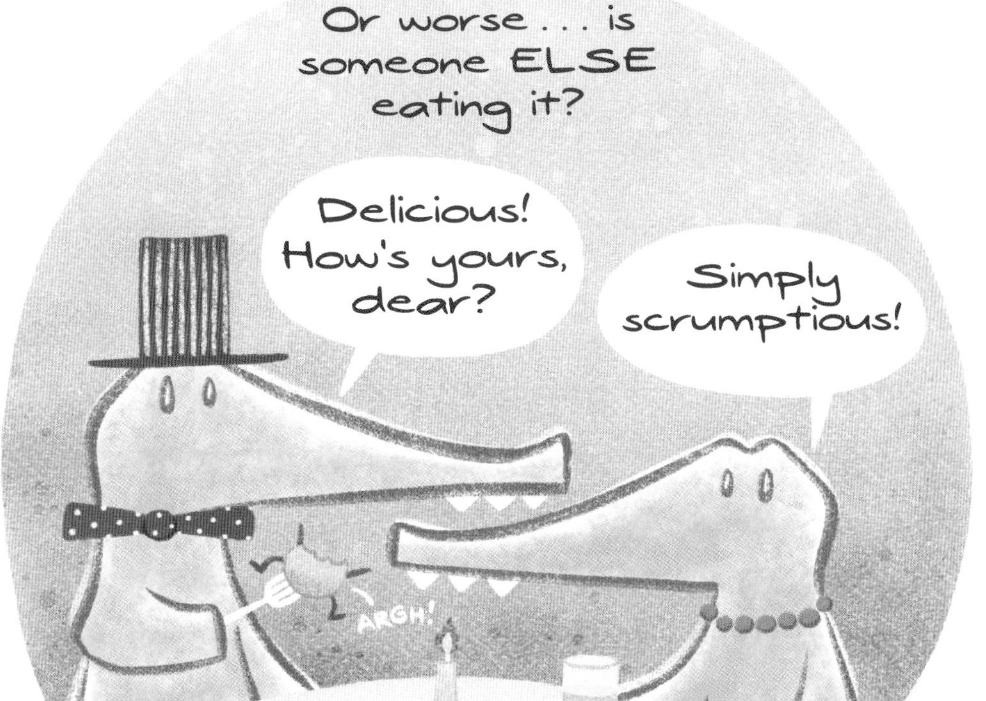
Or worse . . . is someone ELSE eating it?
Delicious! How's yours, dear?
Simply scrumptious!
ARGH!

Holes raise too many questions.

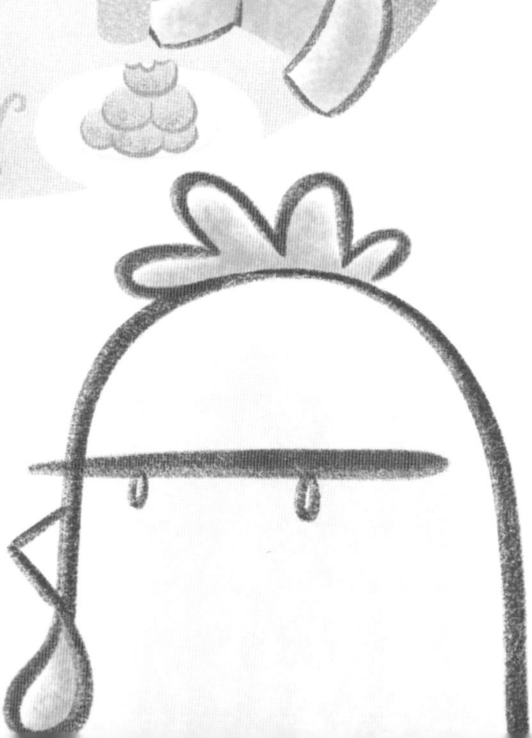

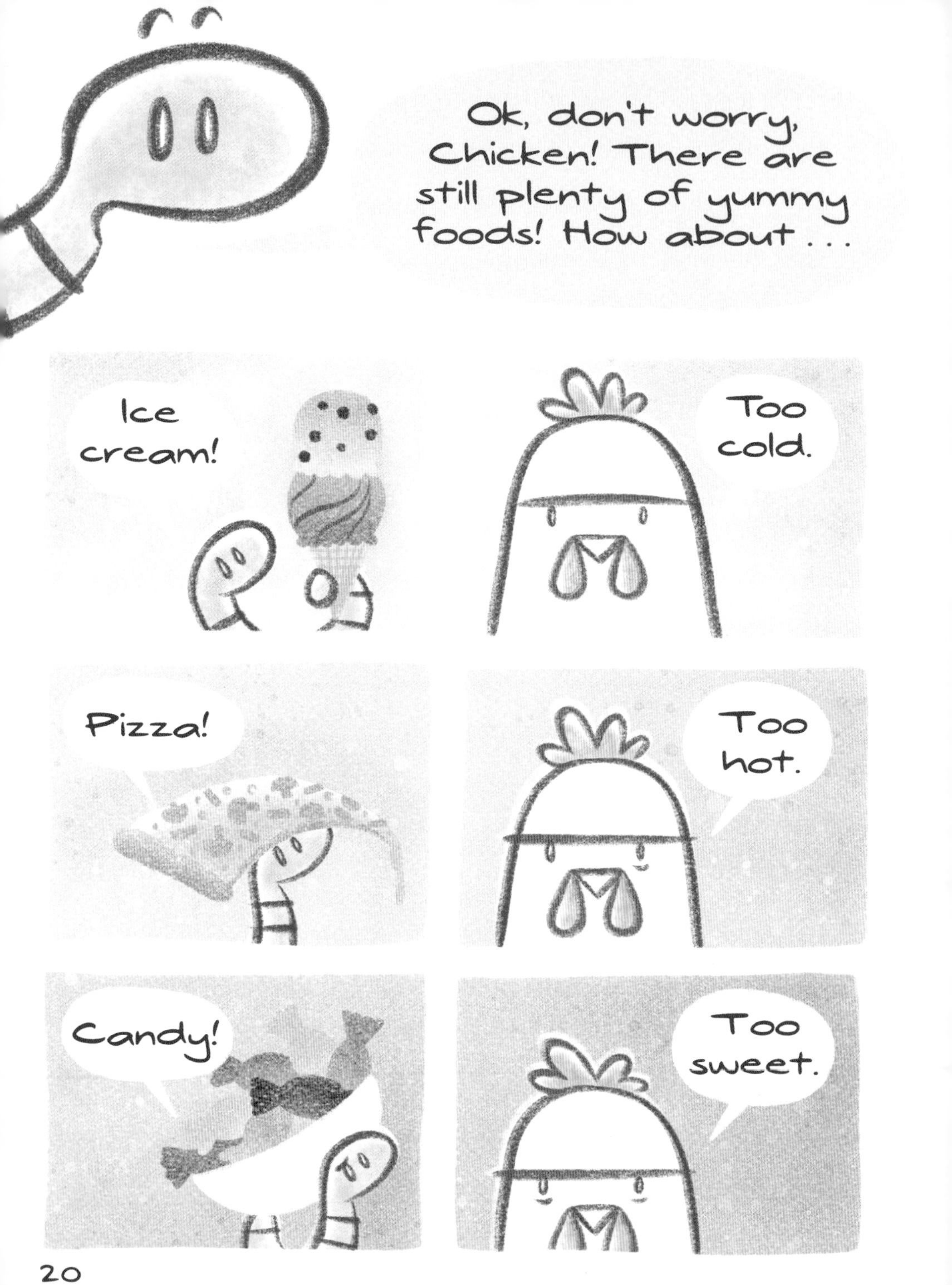
Ok, don't worry, Chicken! There are still plenty of yummy foods! How about . . .
Ice cream!
Too cold.
Pizza!
Too hot.
Candy!
Too sweet.

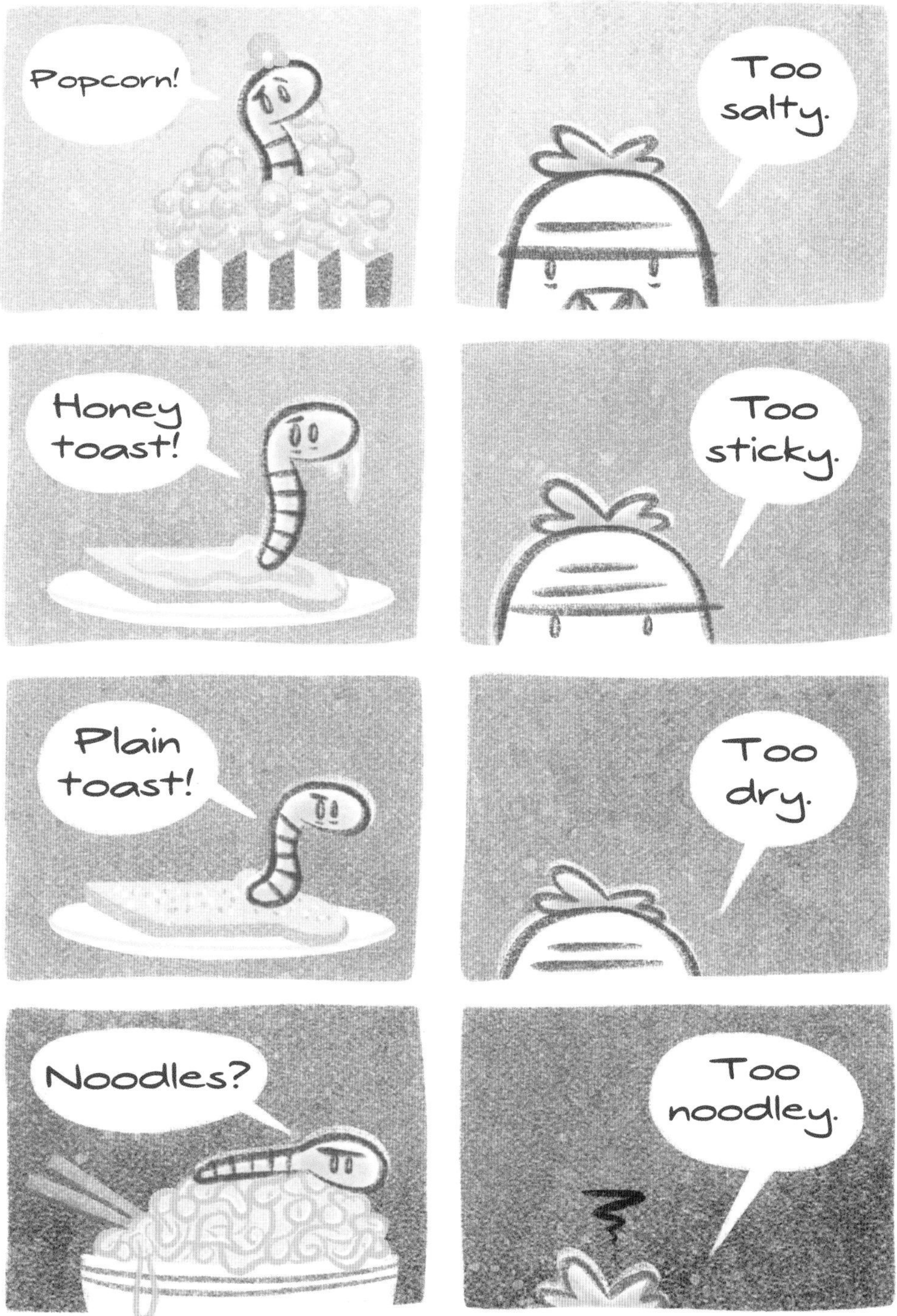
Popcorn!
Too salty.
Honey toast!
Too sticky.
Plain toast!
Too dry.
Noodles?
Too noodley.

Uh,
Speedy?

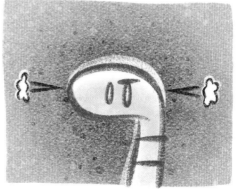

RUMBLE!

I don't
know what
to do!

You're
hungry, but
you won't
eat!!

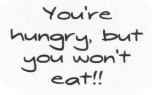

22

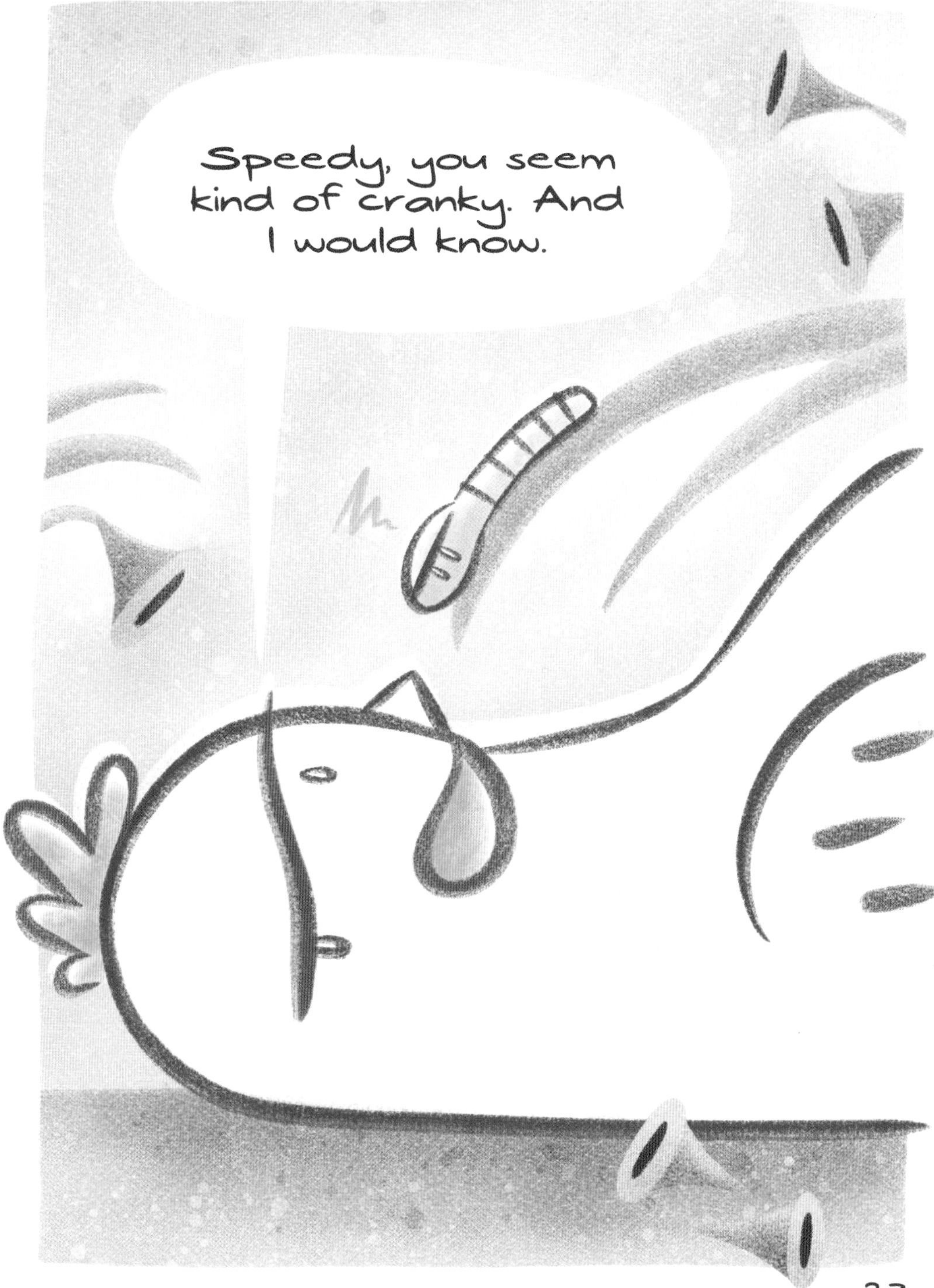
Speedy, you seem kind of cranky. And I would know.

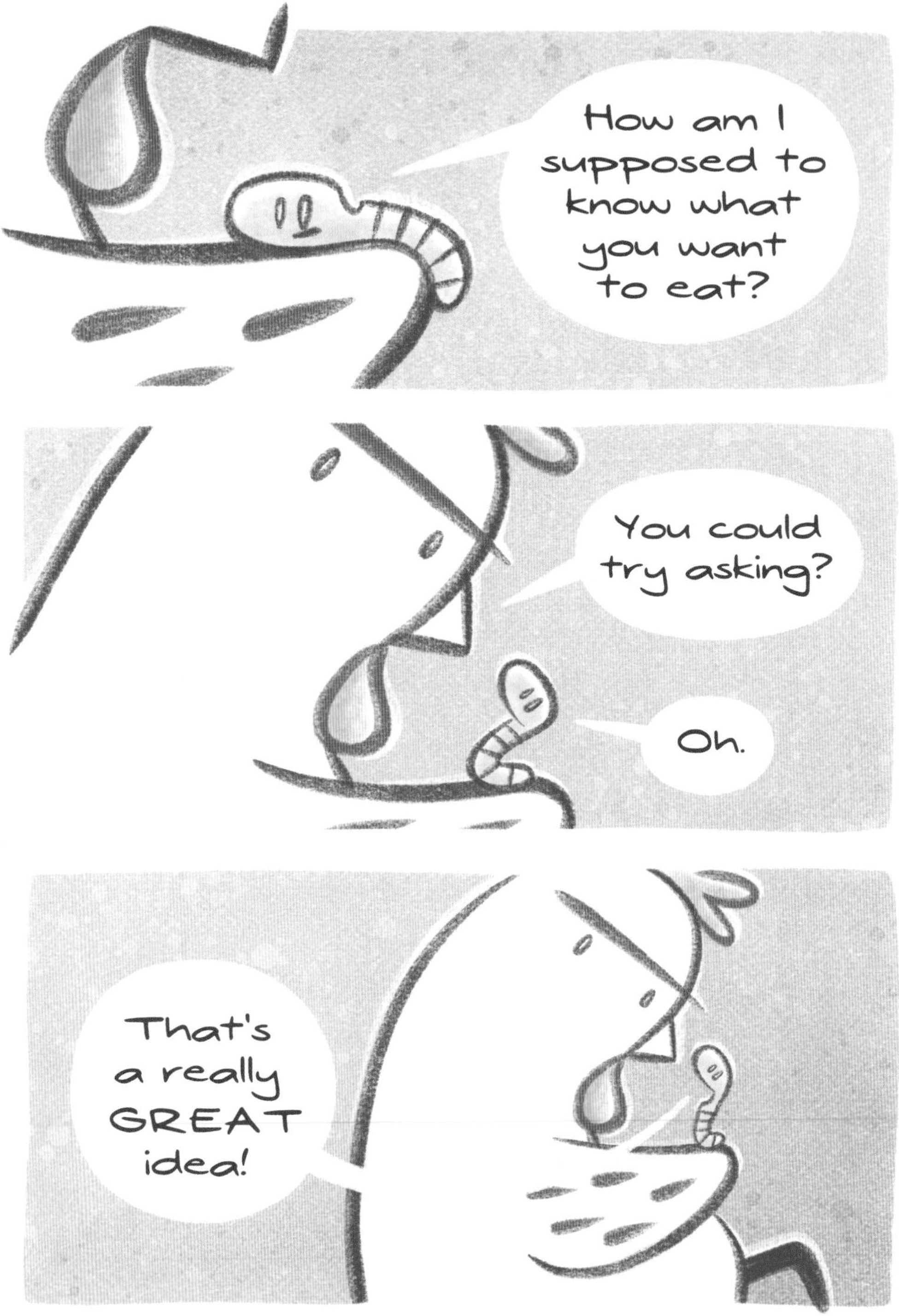
How am I supposed to know what you want to eat?
You could try asking?
Oh.
That's a really GREAT idea!

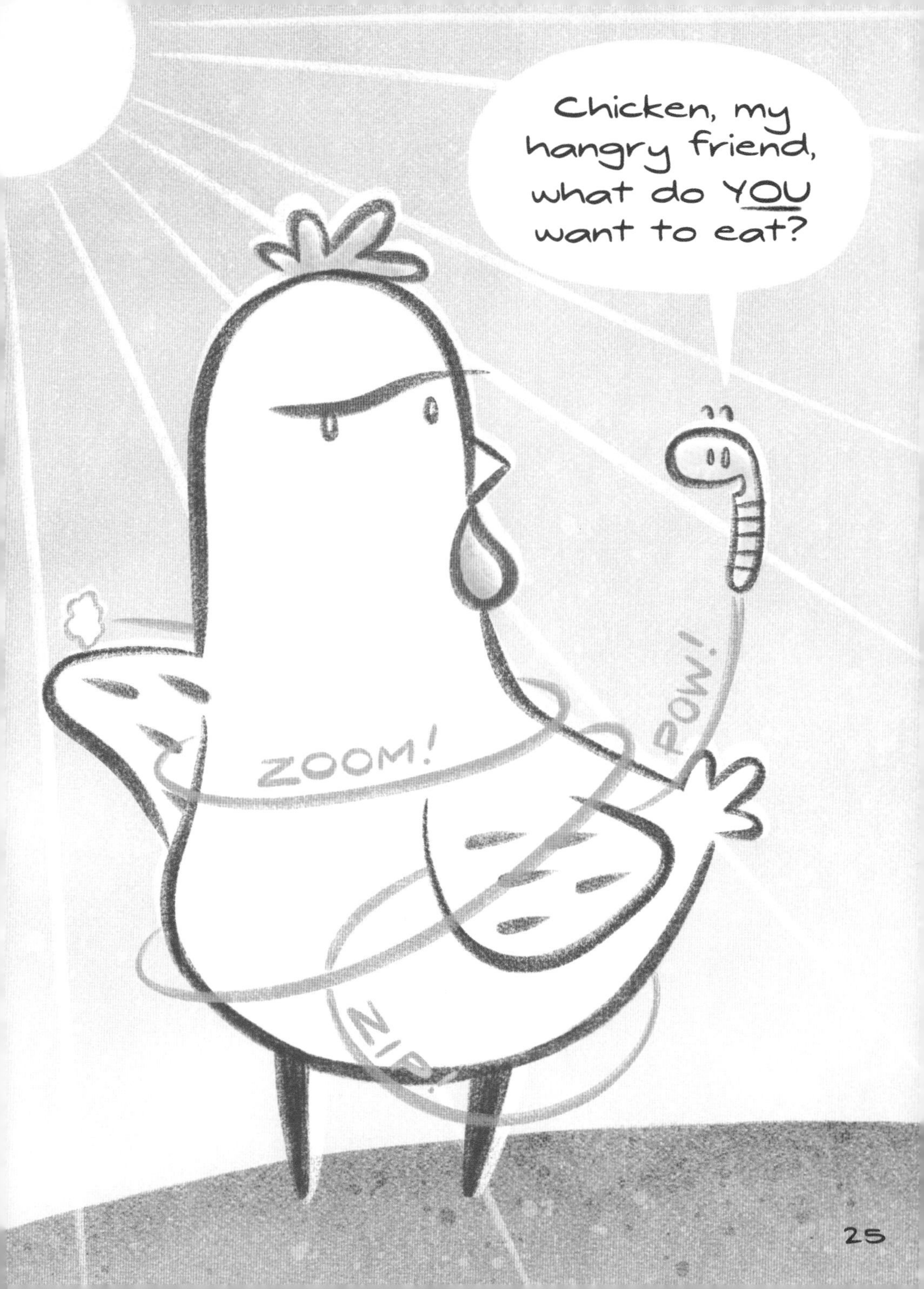
Chicken, my hangry friend, what do YOU want to eat?
ZOOM!
POW!
ZIP!

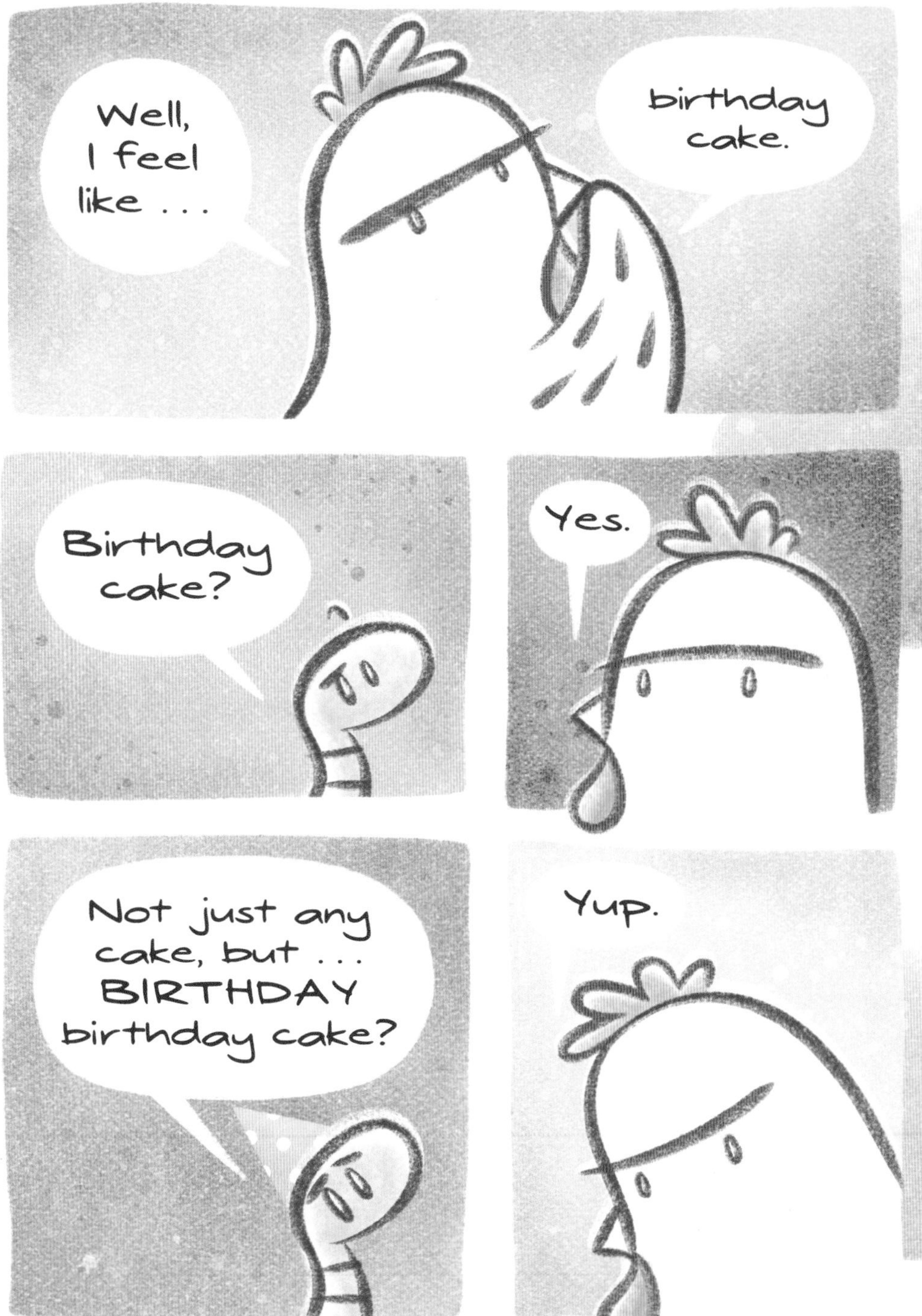
Well, I feel like . . .
birthday cake.
Birthday cake?
Yes.
Not just any cake, but . . . BIRTHDAY birthday cake?
Yup.

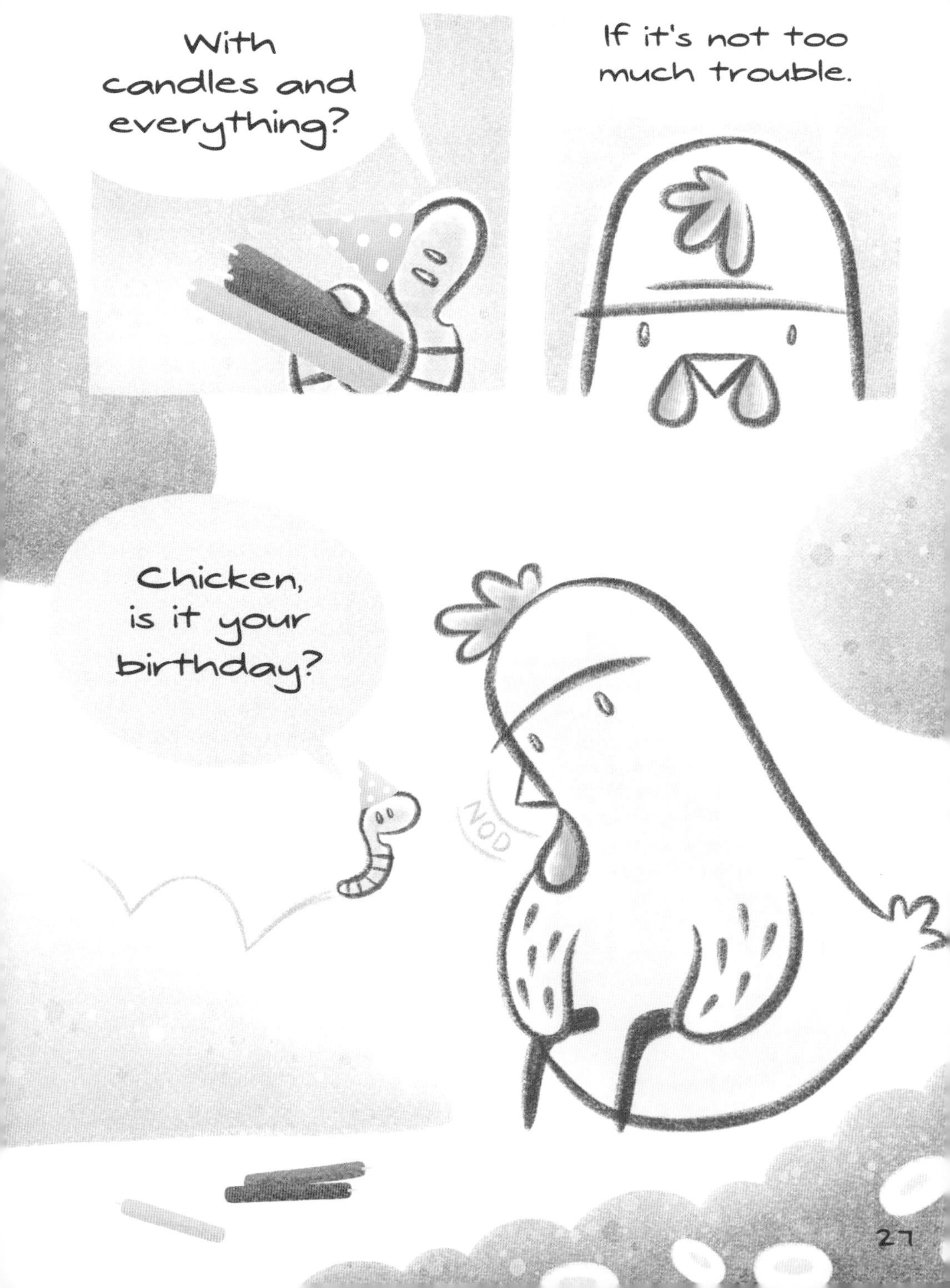
With candles and everything?
If it's not too much trouble.
Chicken, is it your birthday?
NOD

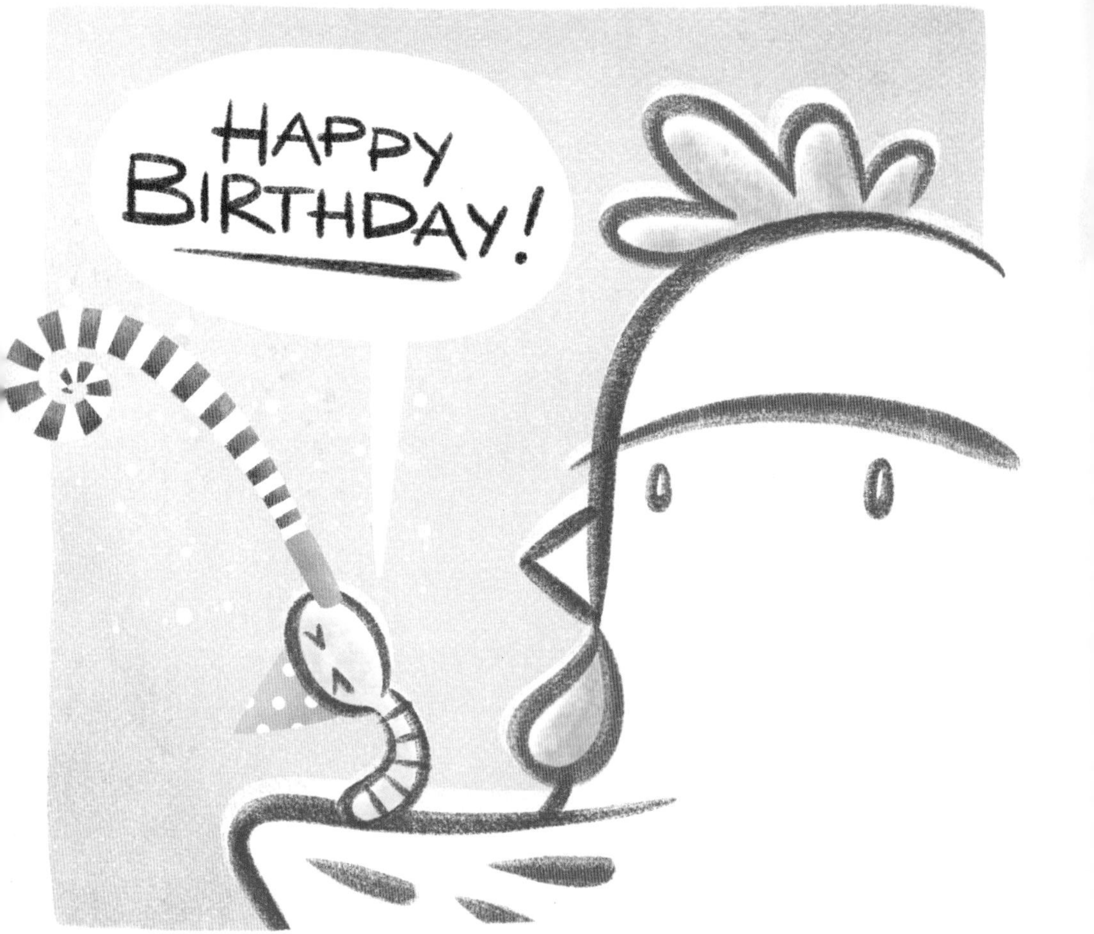
HAPPY BIRTHDAY!

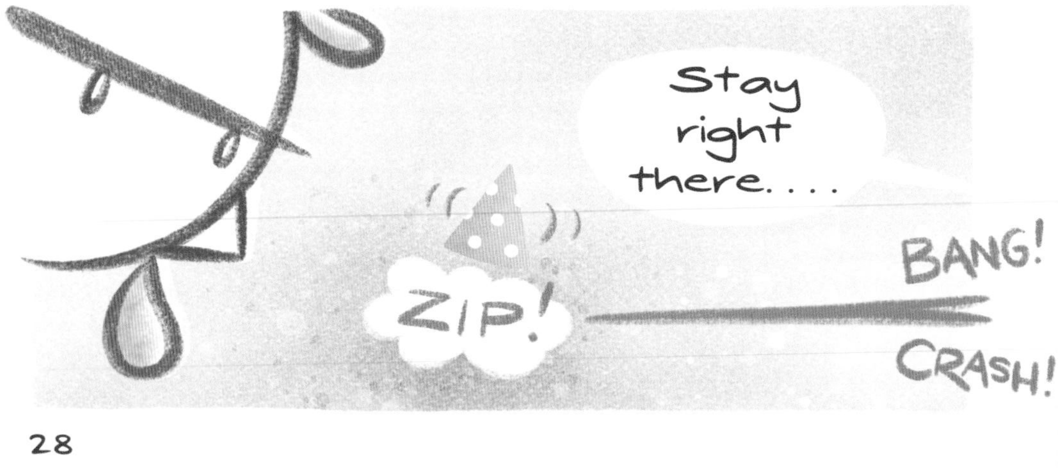
Stay right there....
BANG!
ZIP!
CRASH!

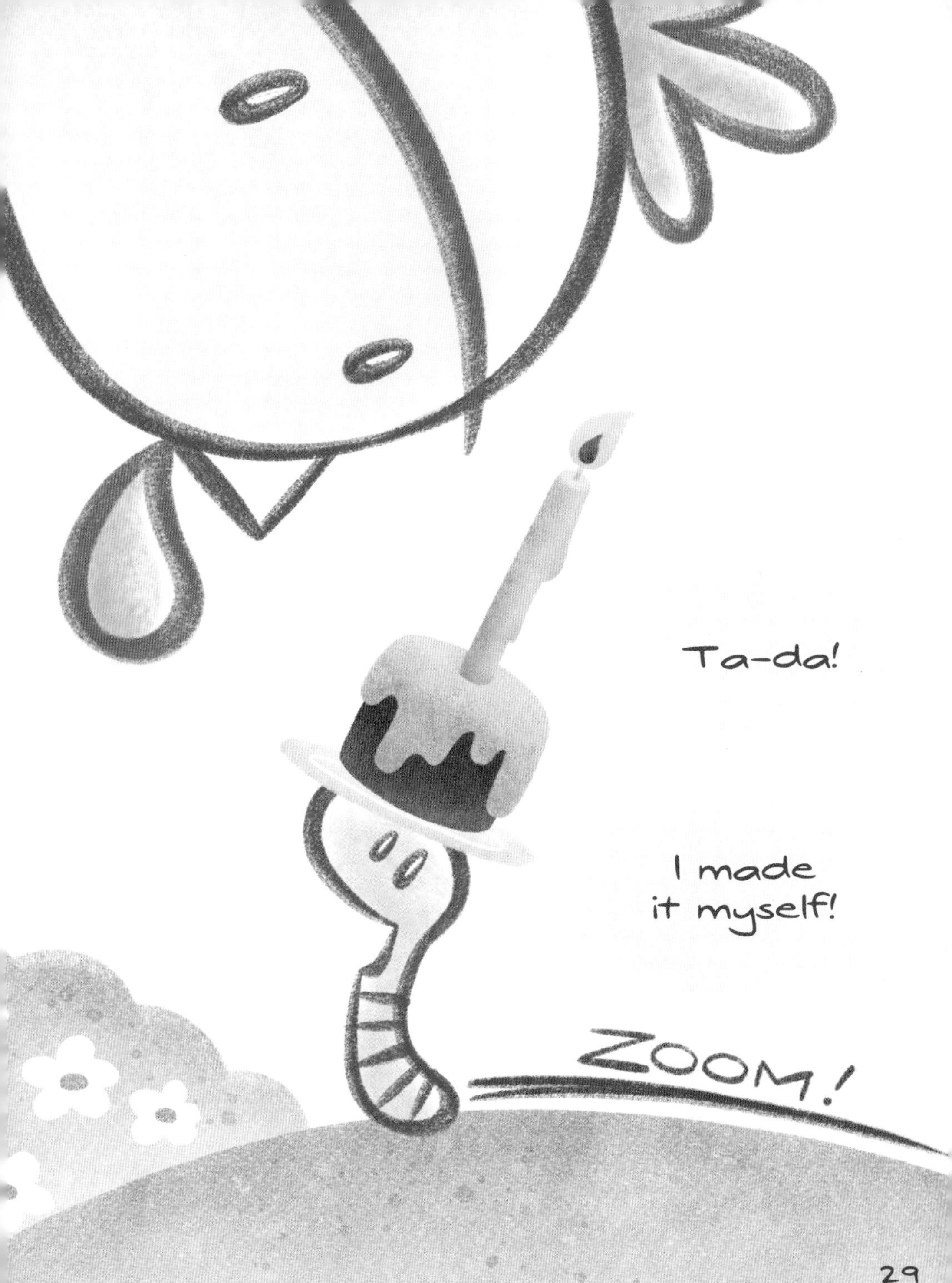
Ta-da!
I made it myself!
ZOOM!

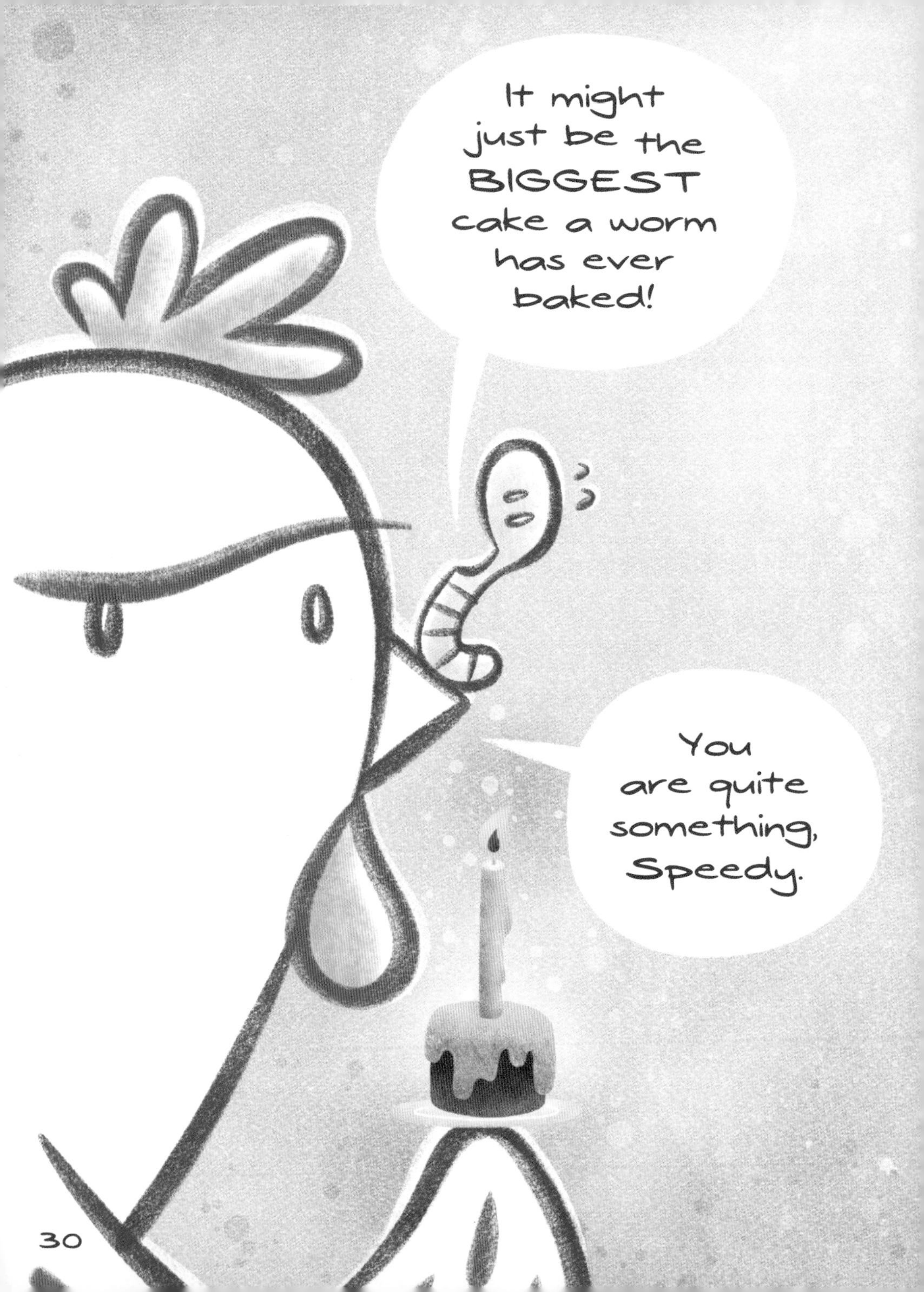
It might just be the BIGGEST cake a worm has ever baked!
You are quite something, Speedy.

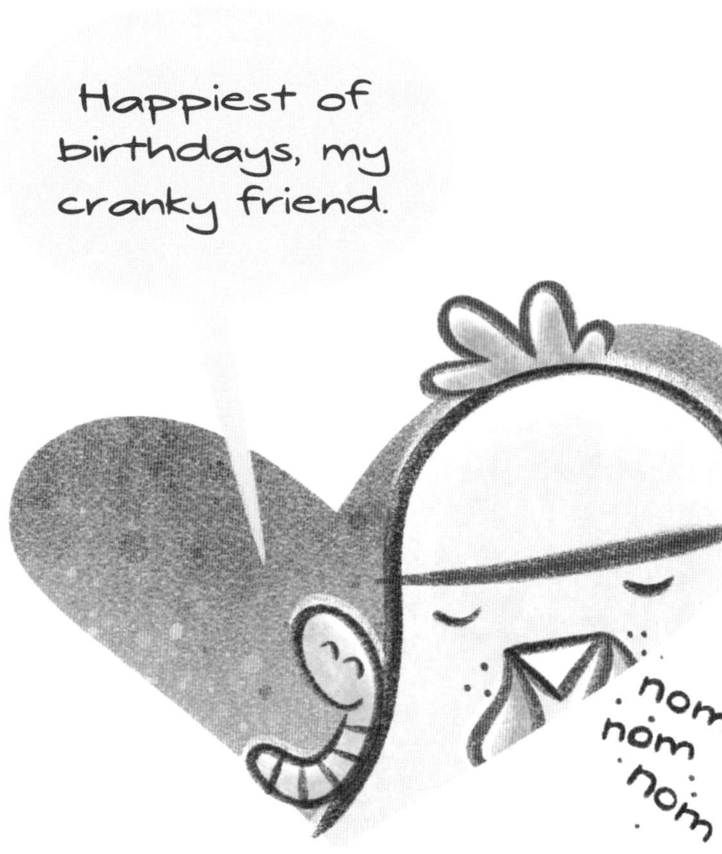
Happiest of birthdays, my cranky friend.
nom nom nom

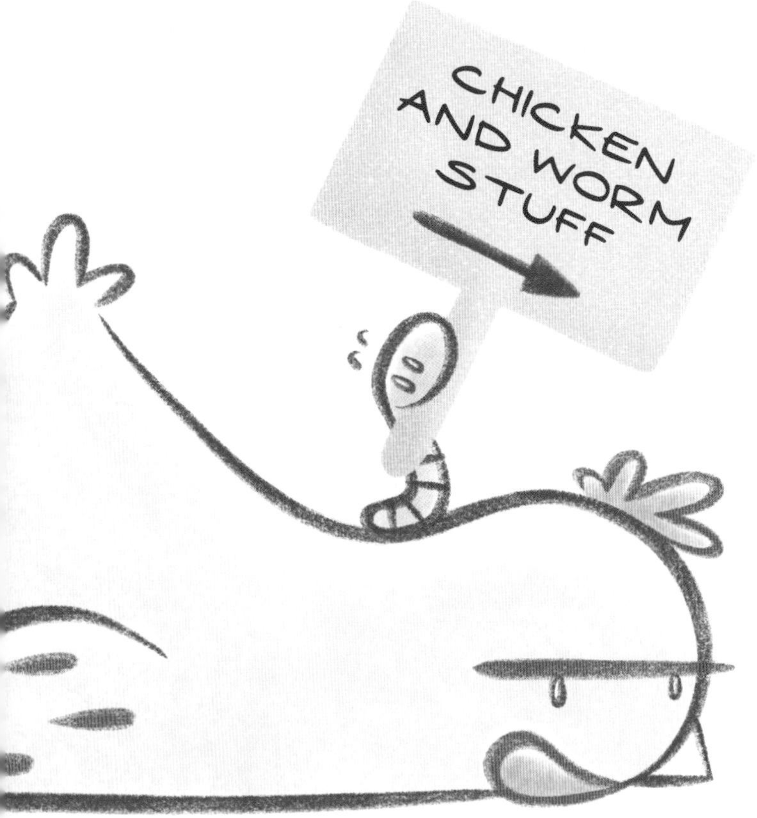
CHICKEN
AND WORM
STUFF

Chicken's Cranky Pants and Speedy's Party Pants

Riding pants

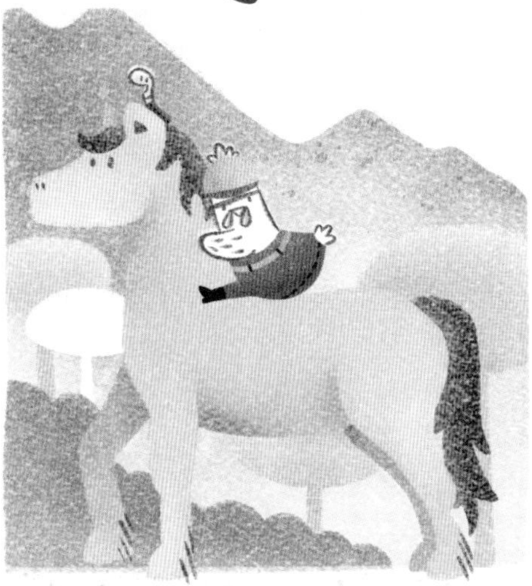

Circus pants

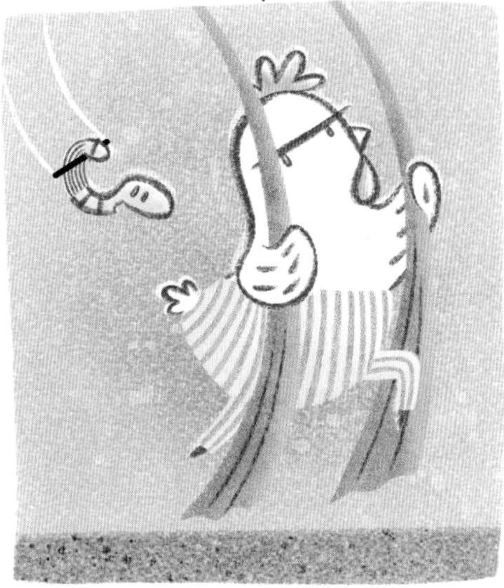

Space pants

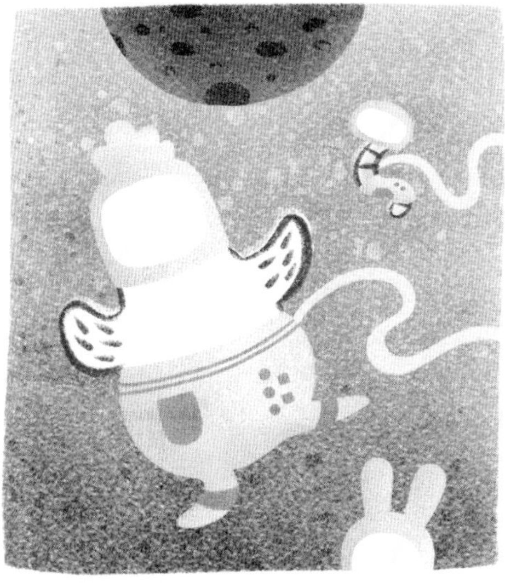

Disco pants

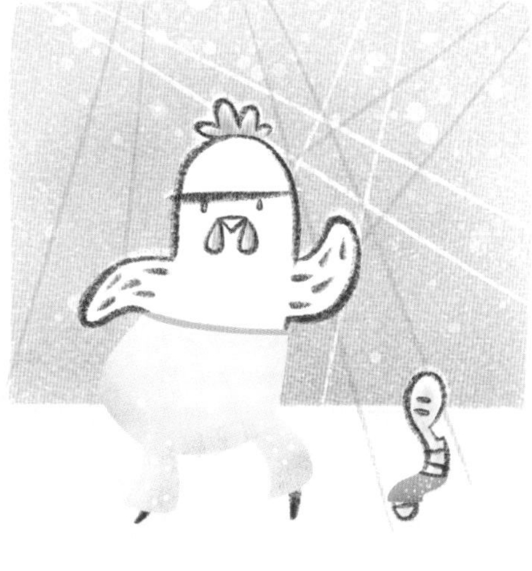

Things That Make Chicken Cranky

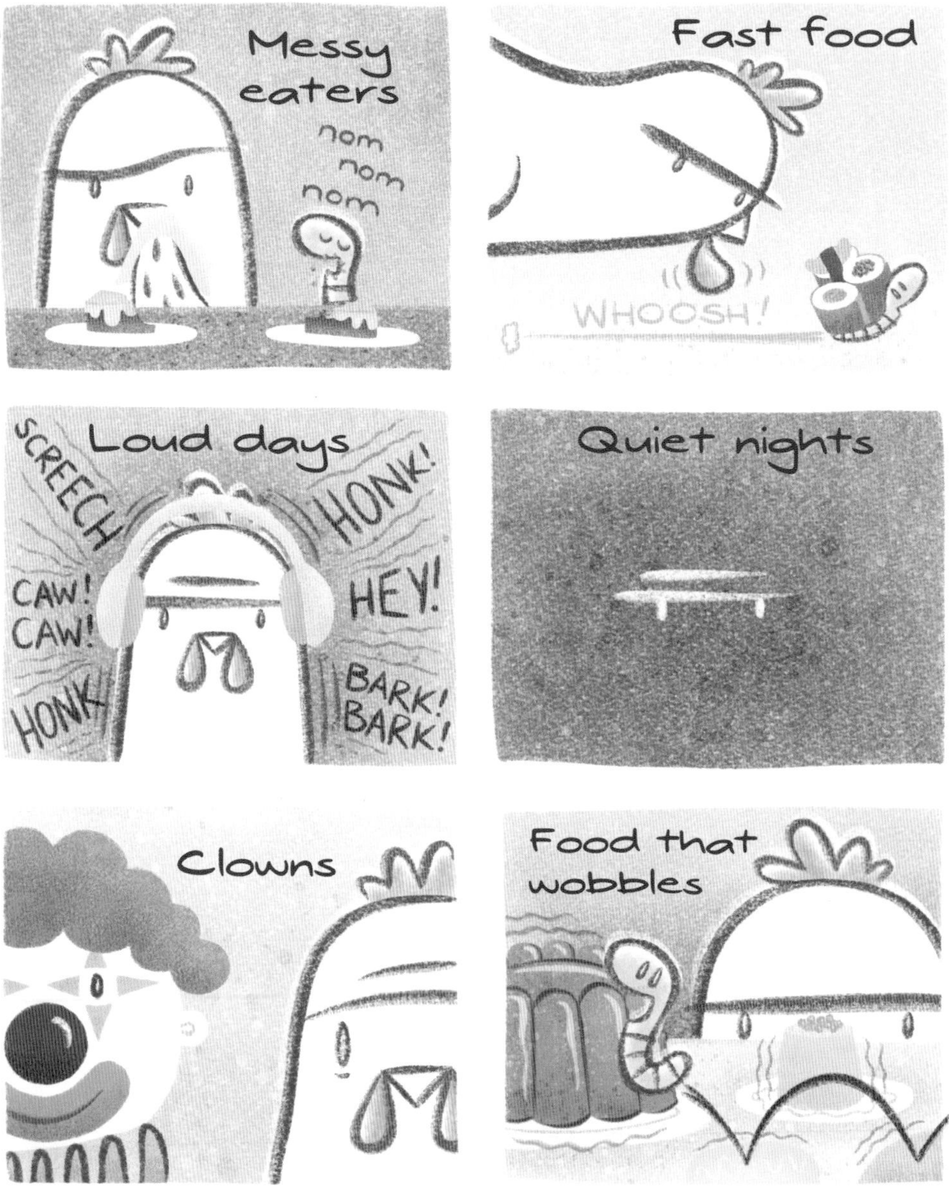
Messy eaters
nom nom nom
Fast food
WHOOSH!
Loud days
SCREECH
HONK!
CAW! CAW!
HEY!
HONK
BARK! BARK!
Quiet nights
Clowns
Food that wobbles

Things That Don't Make Chicken Cranky

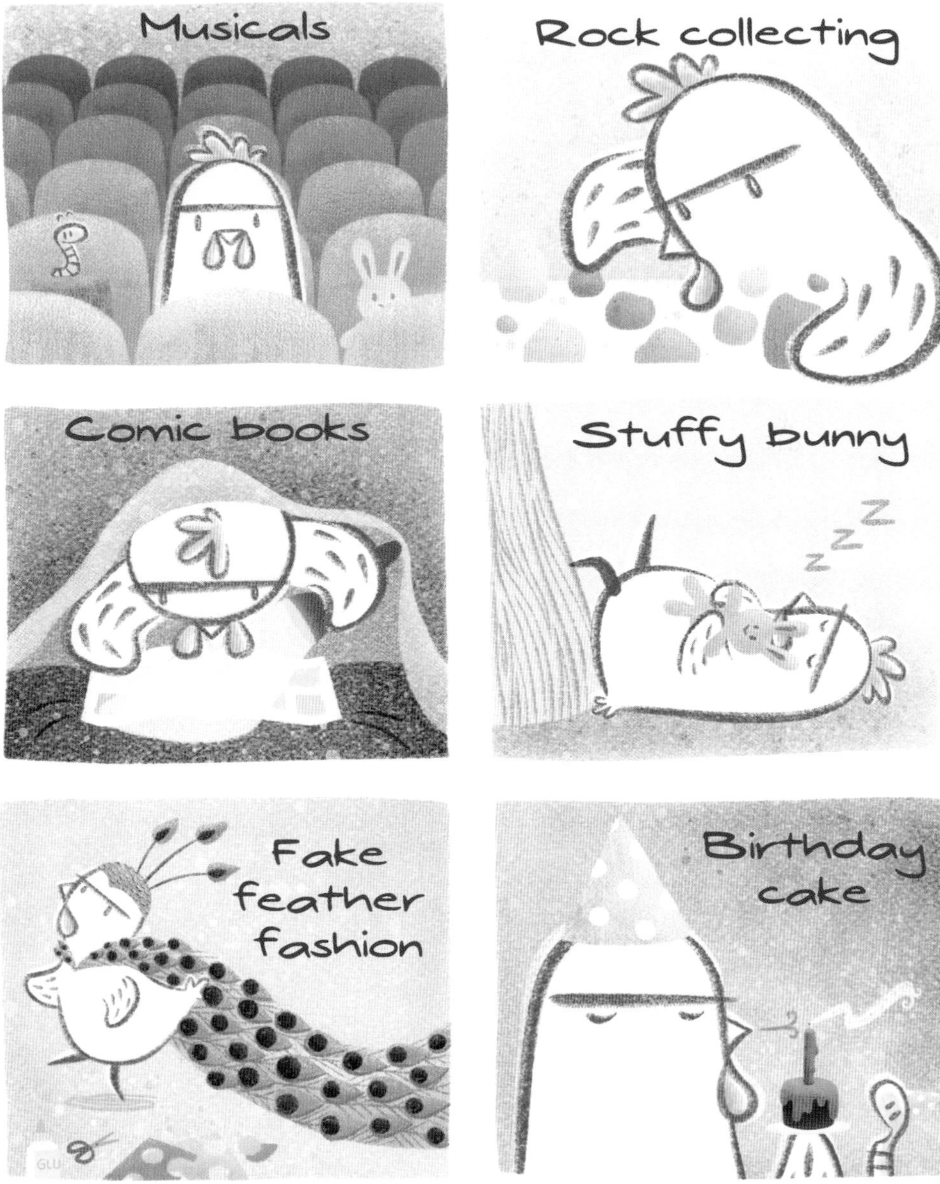
Musicals
Rock collecting
Comic books
Stuffy bunny
Z Z Z
Fake feather fashion
GLU
Birthday cake

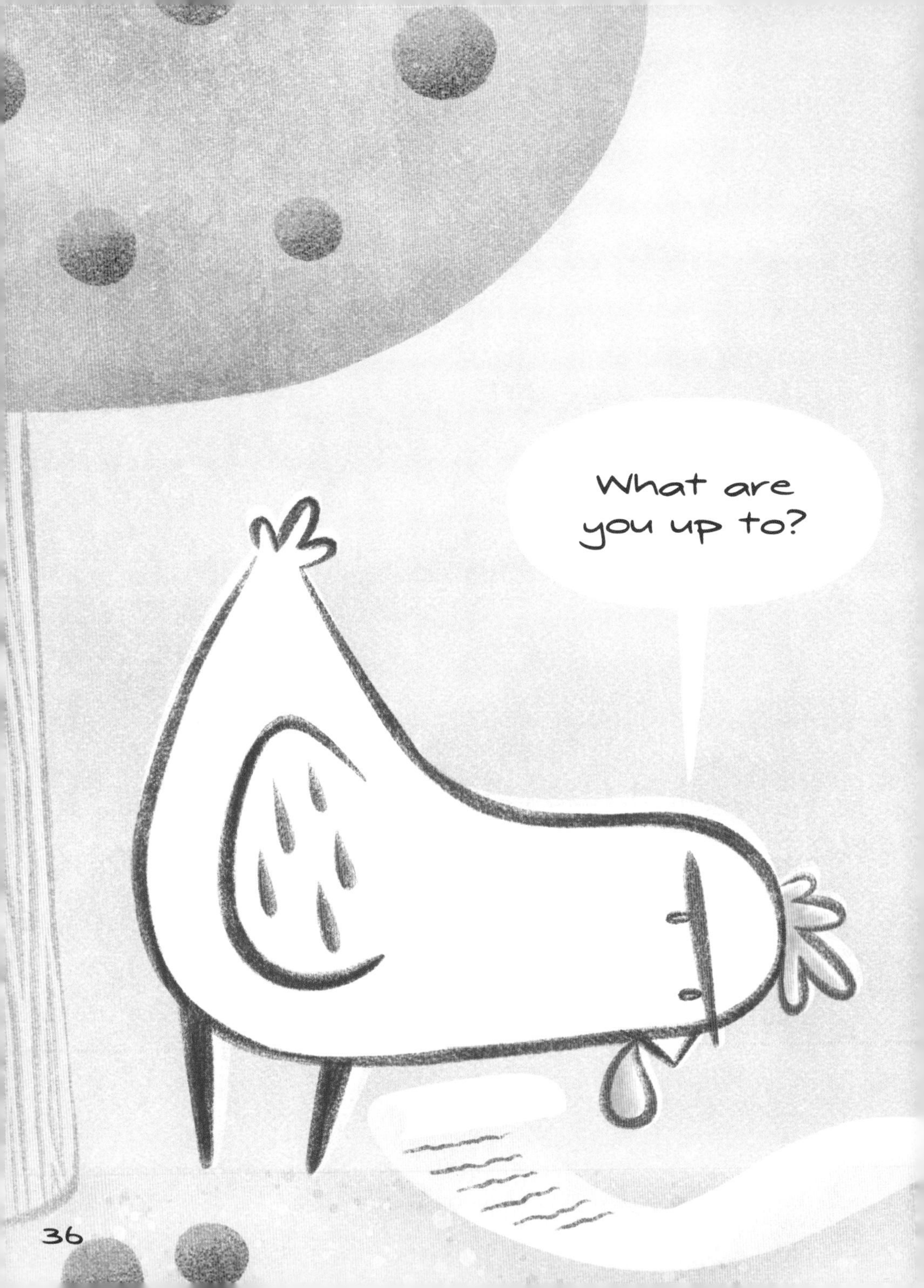
What are you up to?

② THE UNSURPRISING PARTY

scribble
Scribble
Scribble

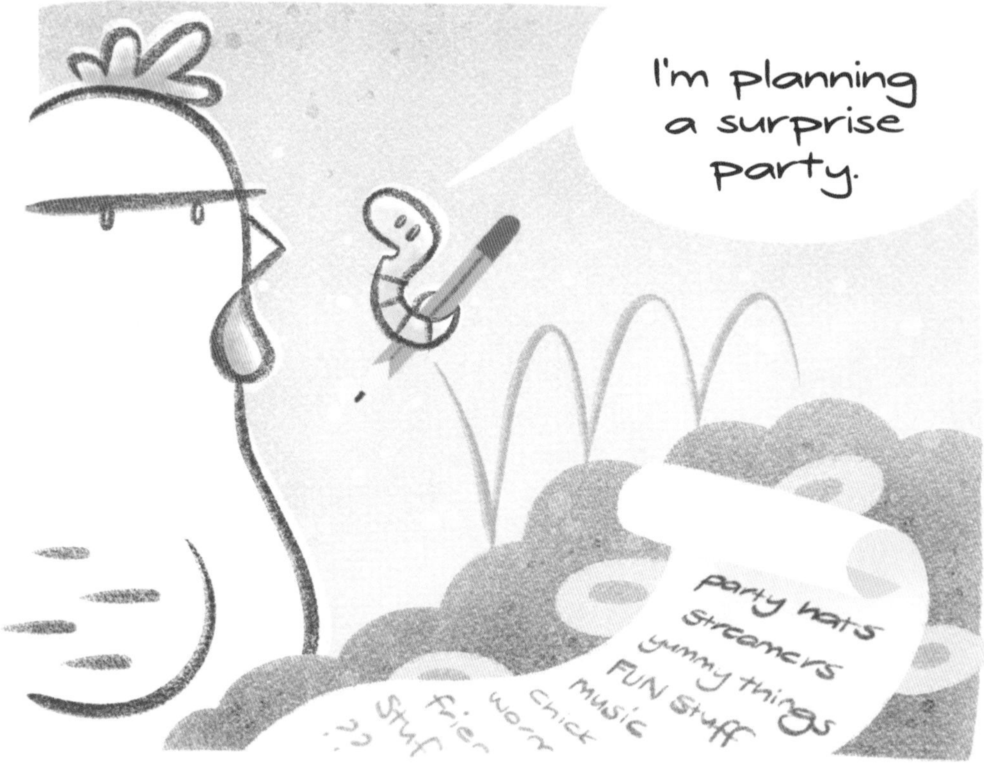
I'm planning a surprise party.
party hats
streamers
yummy things
FUN stuff
music
chick

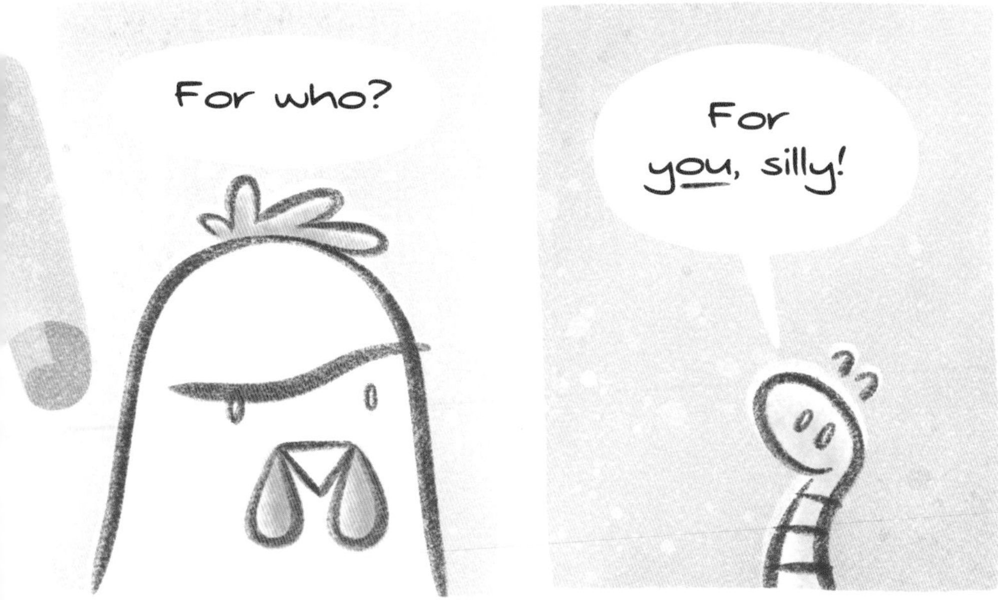
For who?
For you, silly!

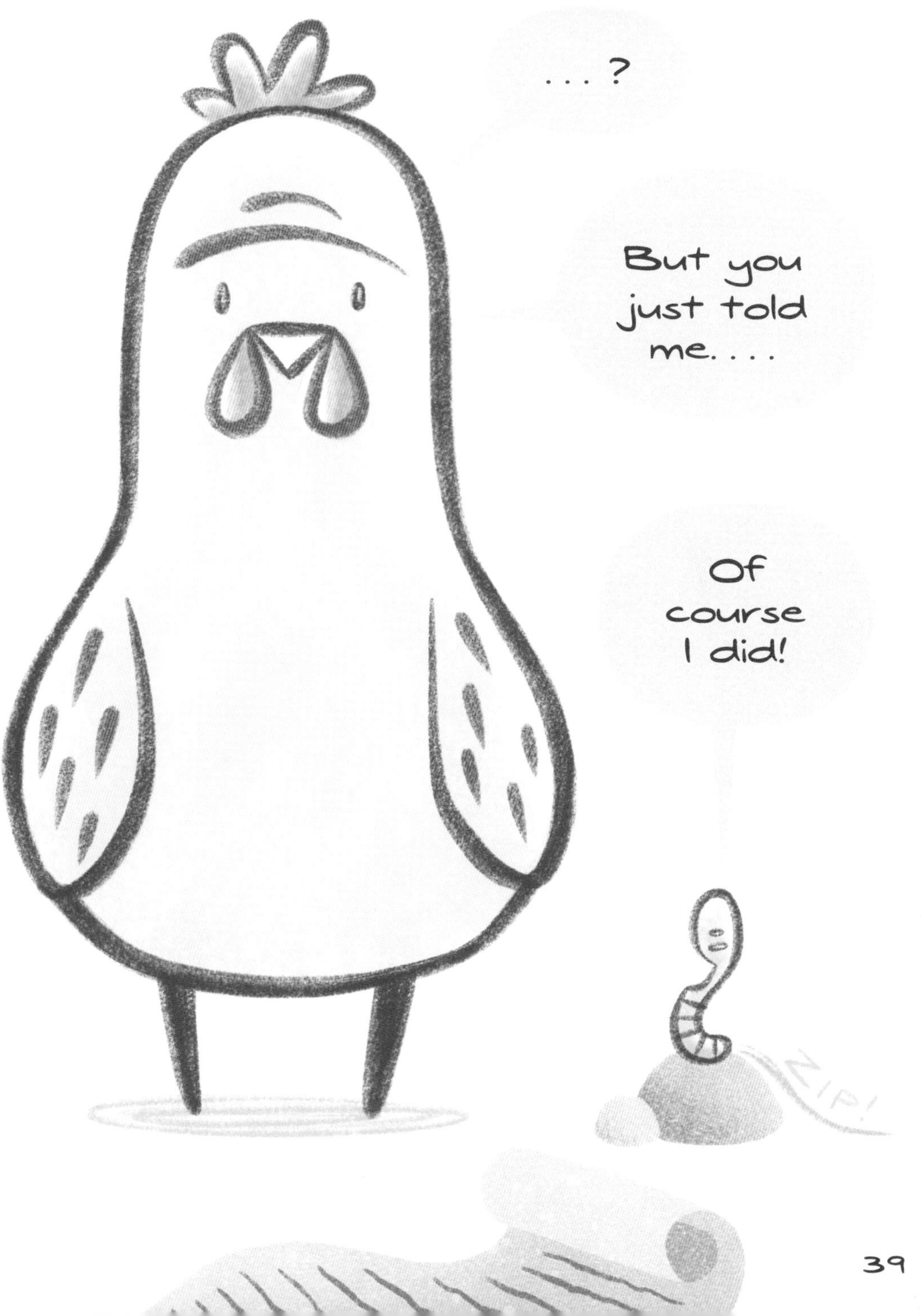
. . . ?
But you just told me. . . .
Of course I did!
ZIP!

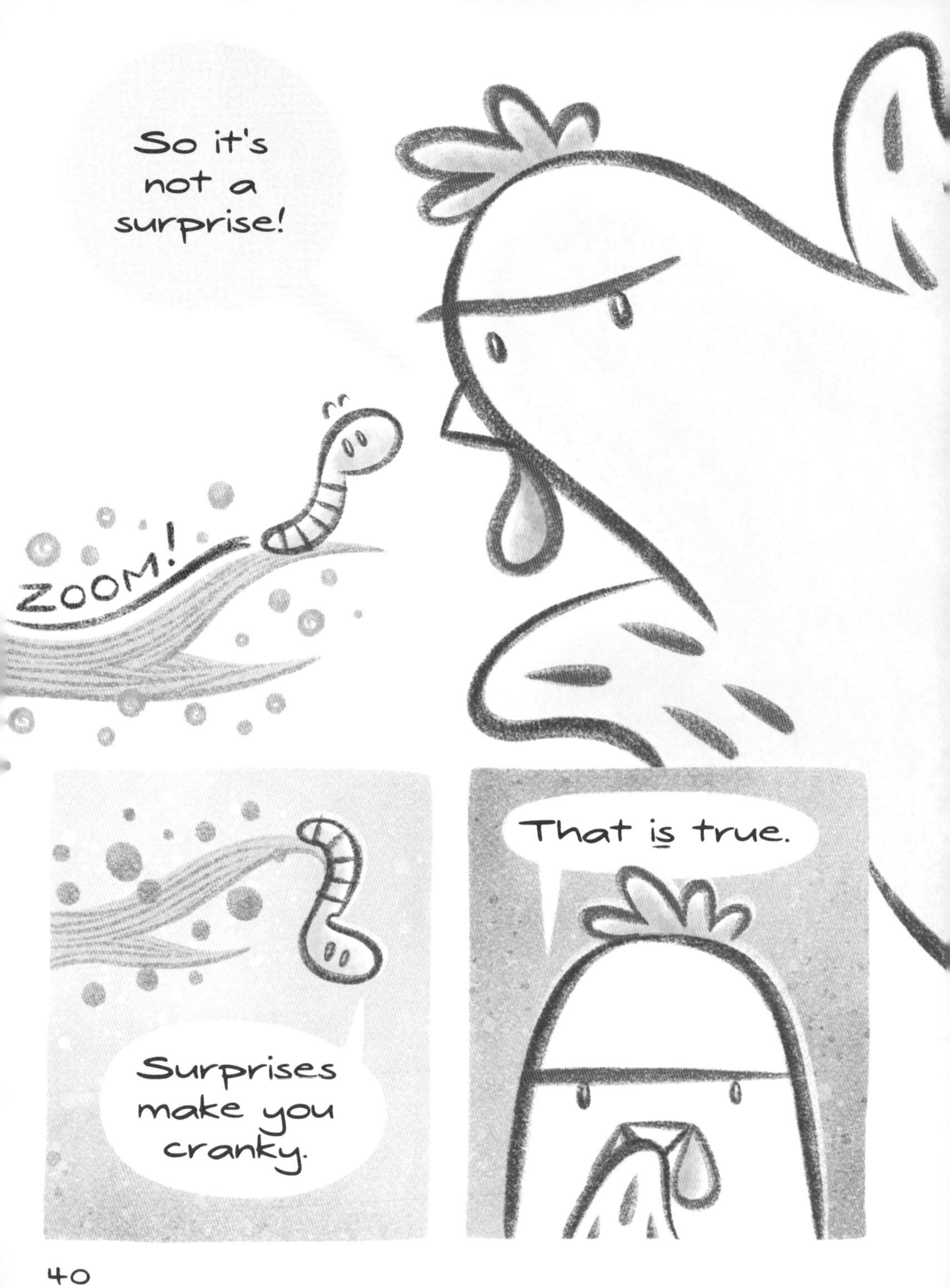
So it's not a surprise!
ZOOM!
Surprises make you cranky.
That is true.

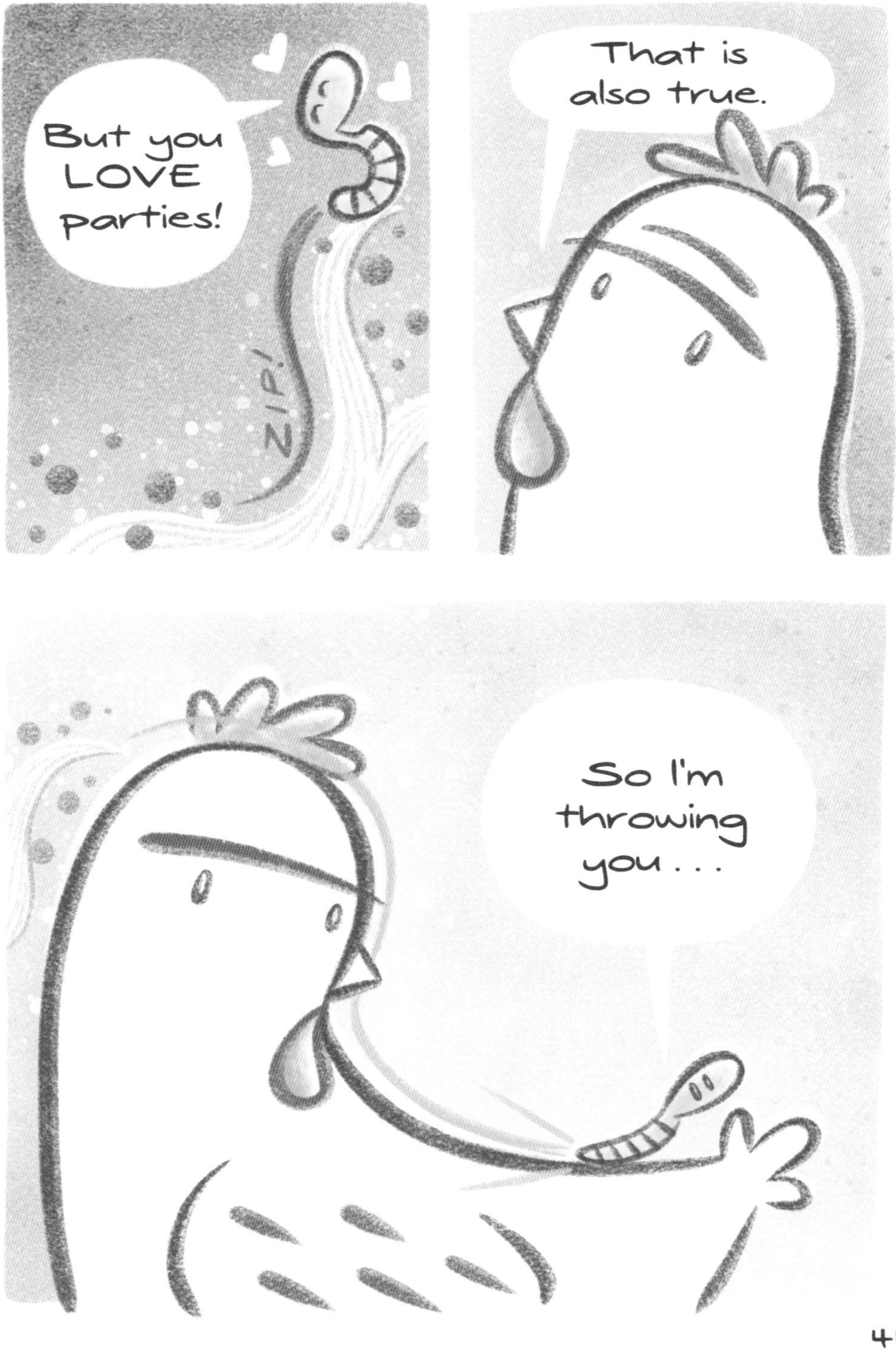
But you LOVE parties!
ZIP!
That is also true.
So I'm throwing you . . .

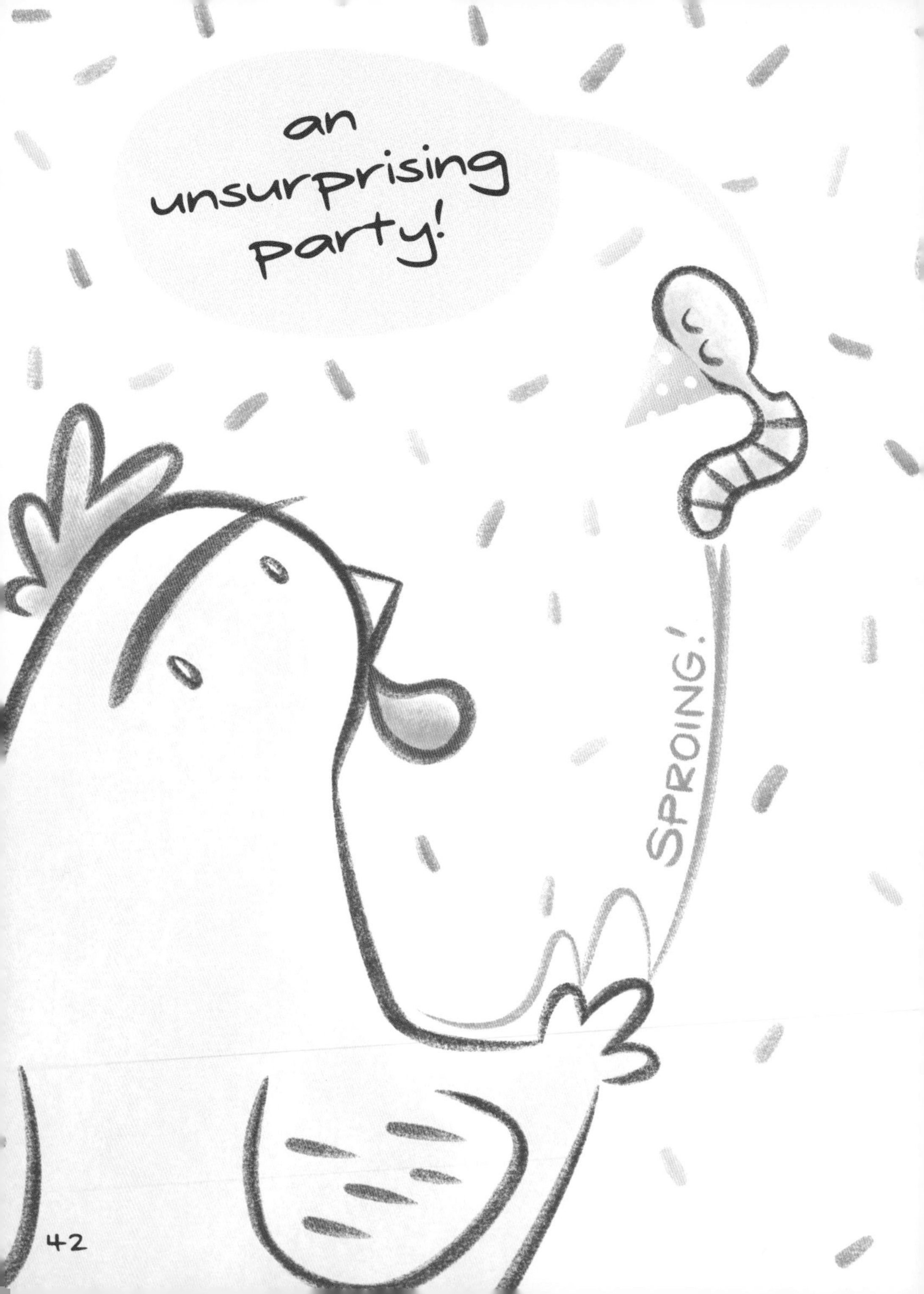
an unsurprising party!
SPROING!

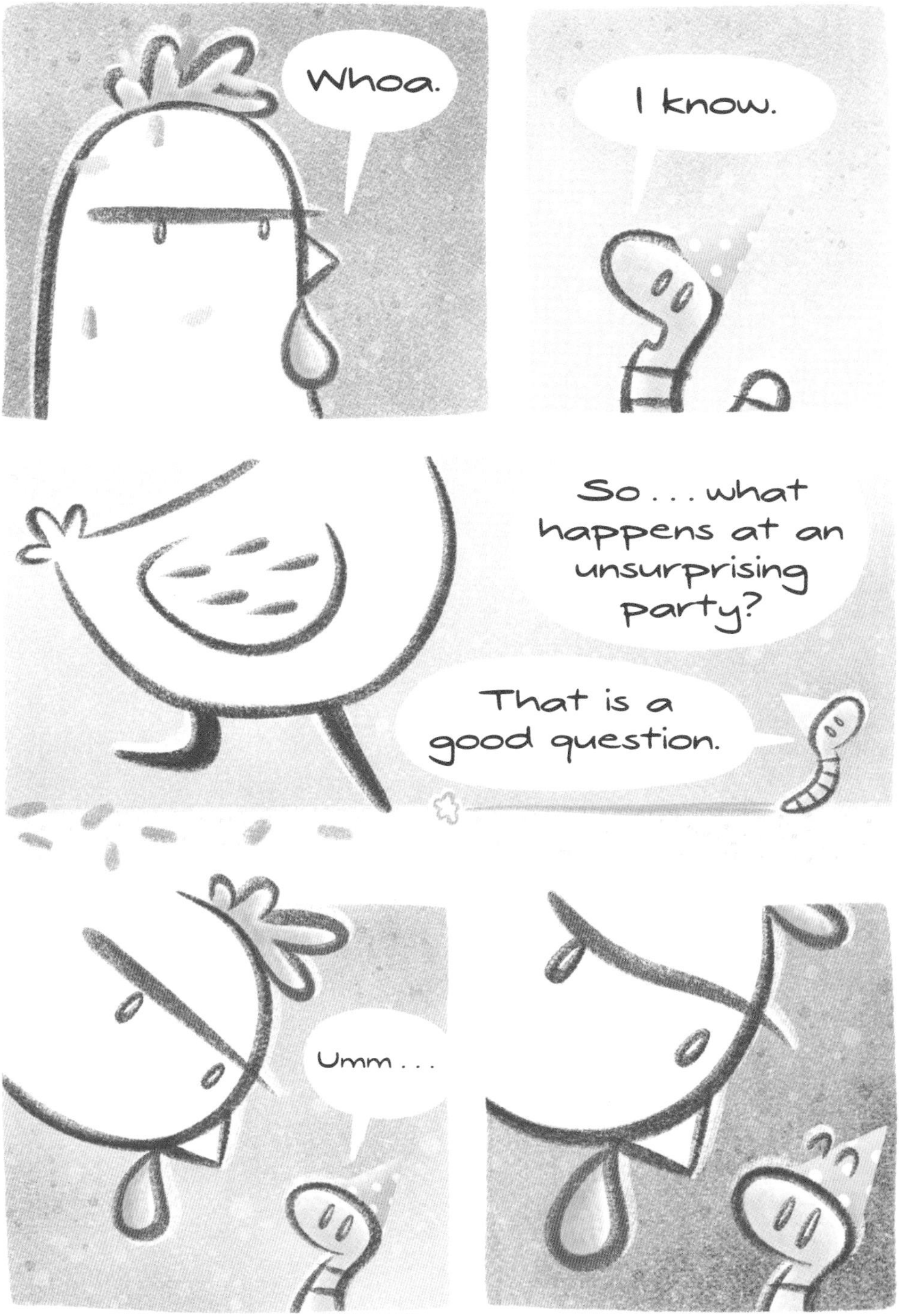
Whoa.
I know.
So . . . what happens at an unsurprising party?
That is a good question.
Umm . . .

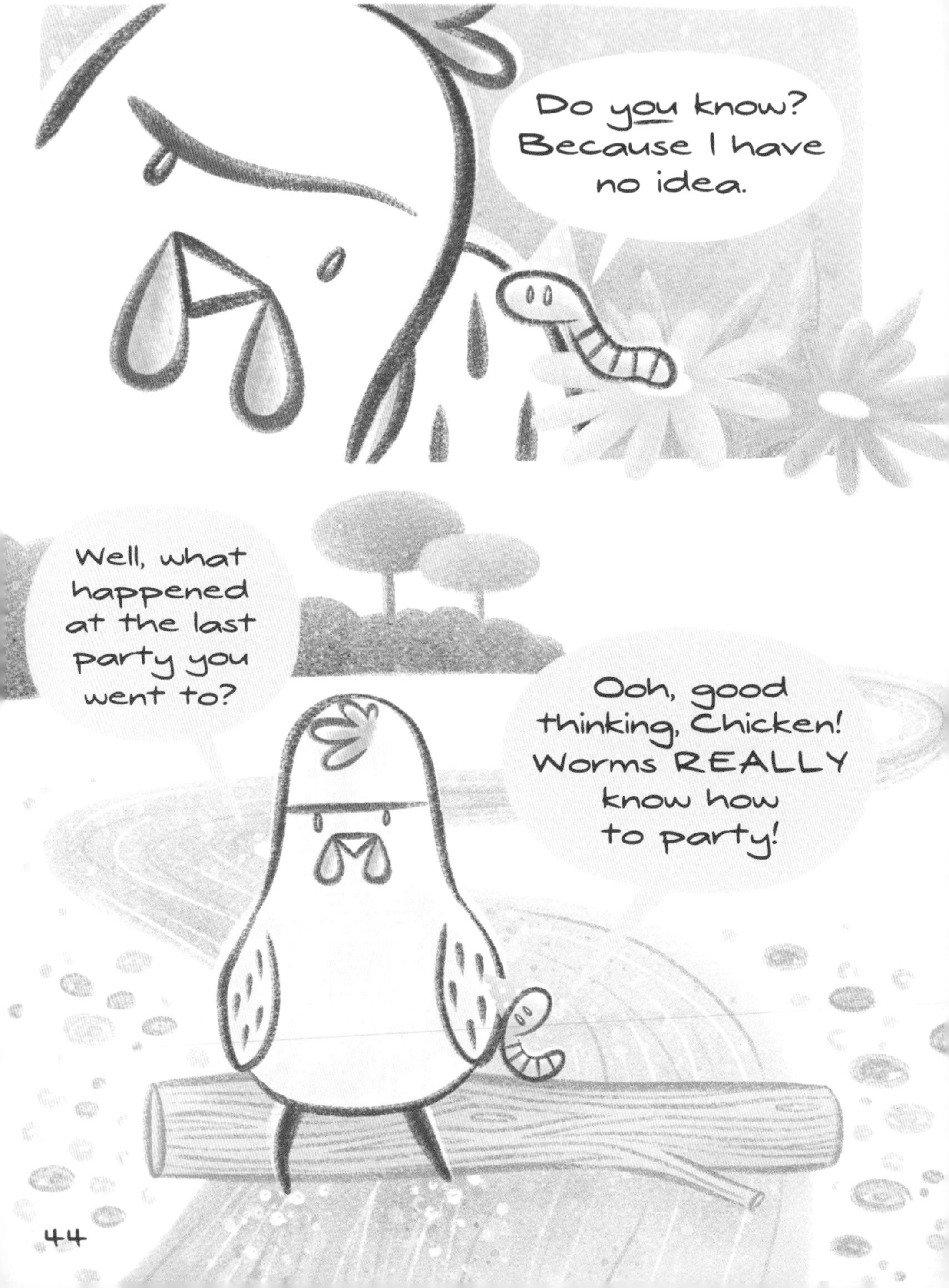
Do you know? Because I have no idea.
Well, what happened at the last party you went to?
Ooh, good thinking, Chicken! Worms REALLY know how to party!

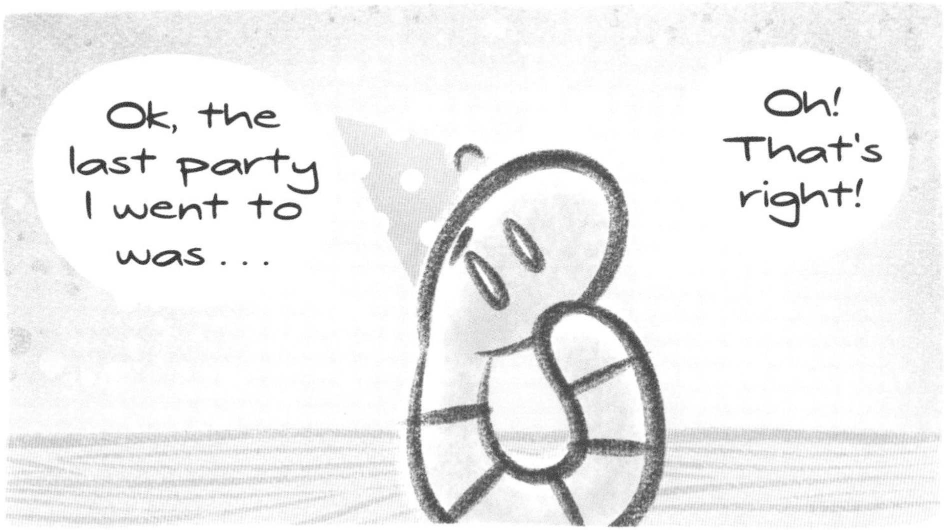
Ok, the last party I went to was . . .
Oh! That's right!

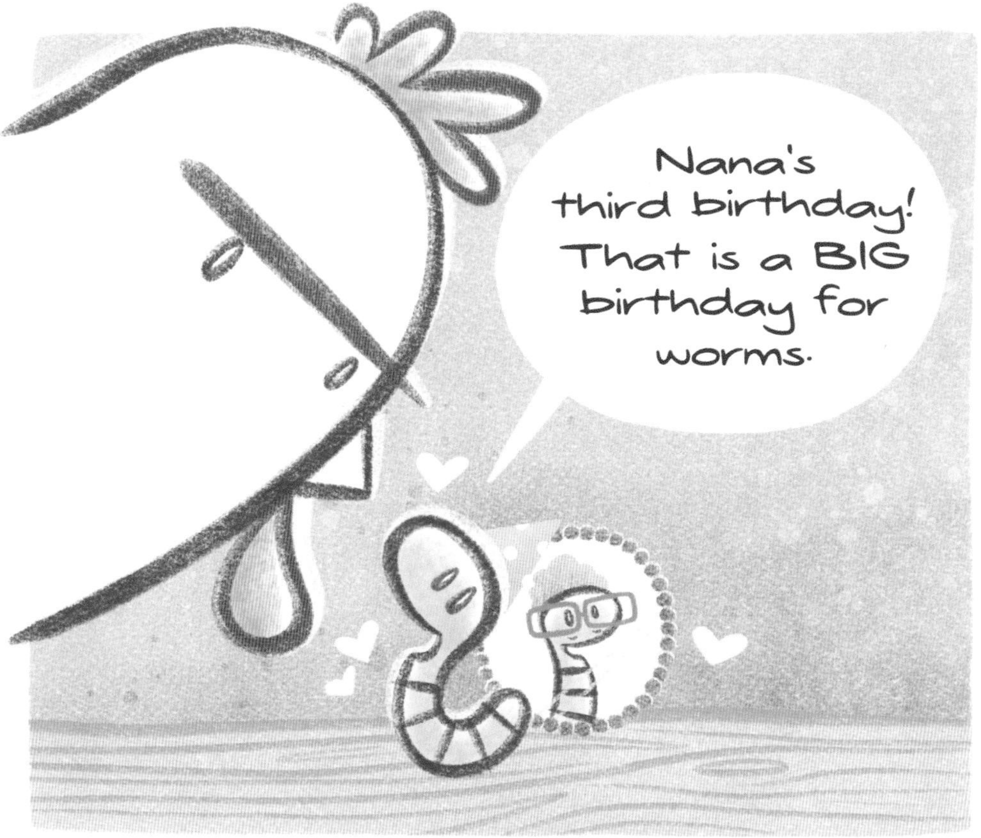
Nana's third birthday! That is a BIG birthday for worms.

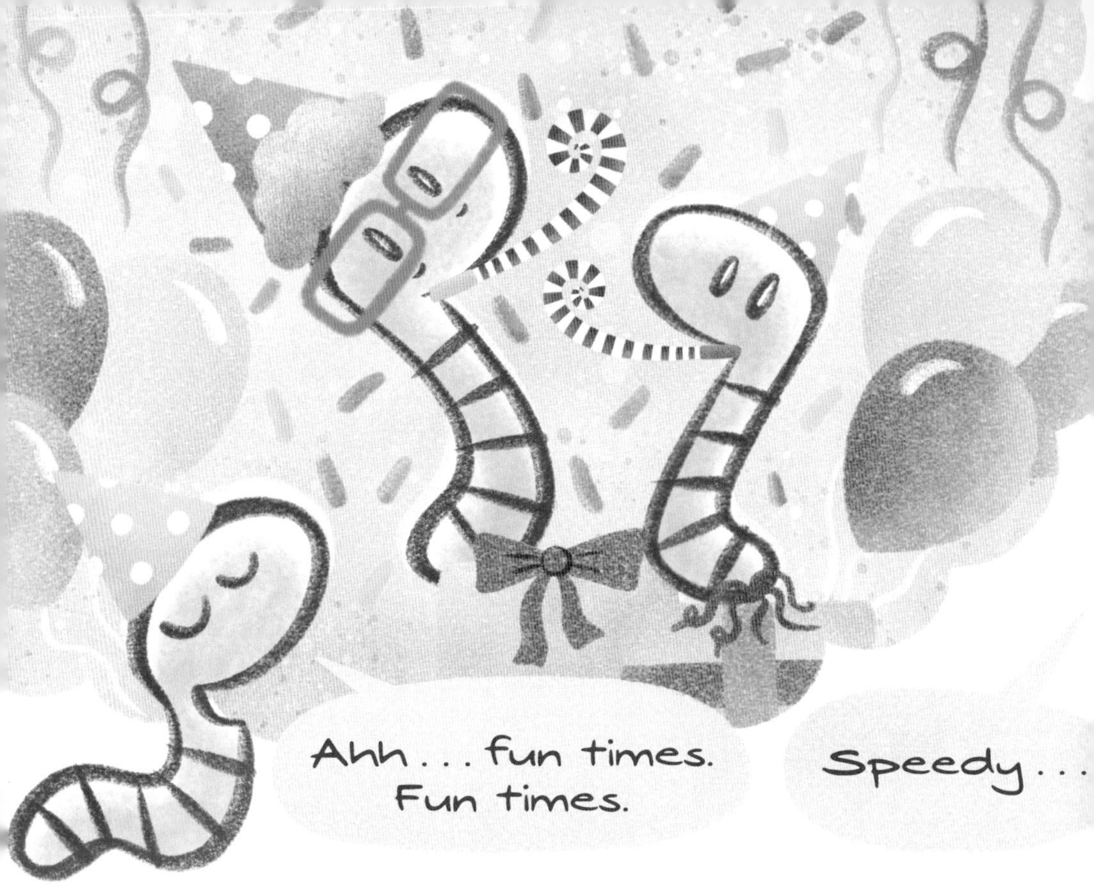
Ahh . . . fun times. Fun times.
Speedy . . .

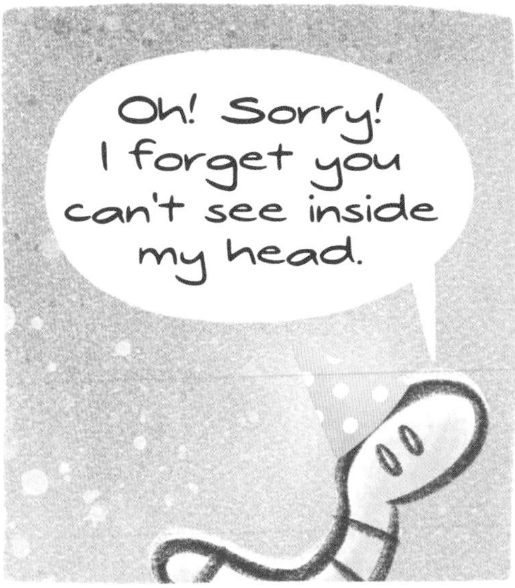
Oh! Sorry! I forget you can't see inside my head.

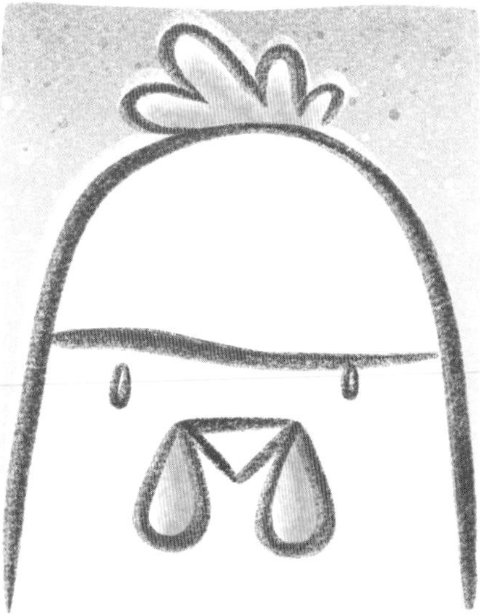

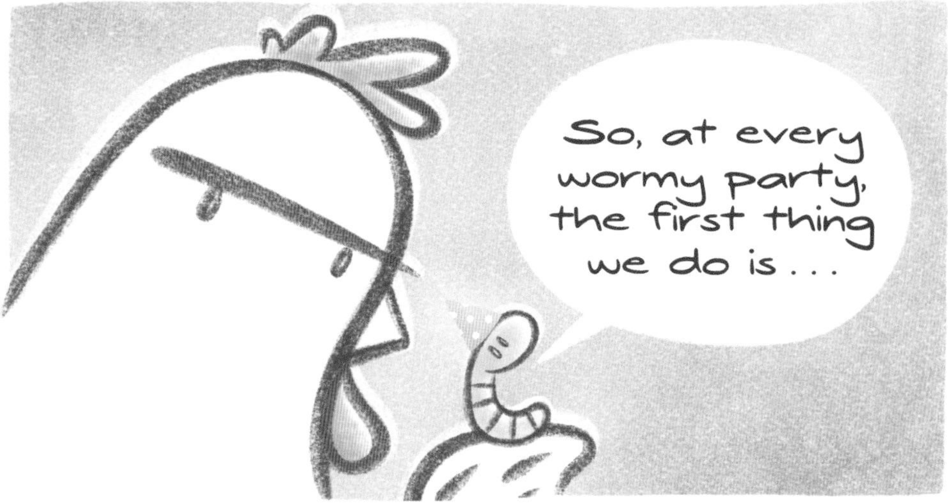
So, at every wormy party, the first thing we do is . . .

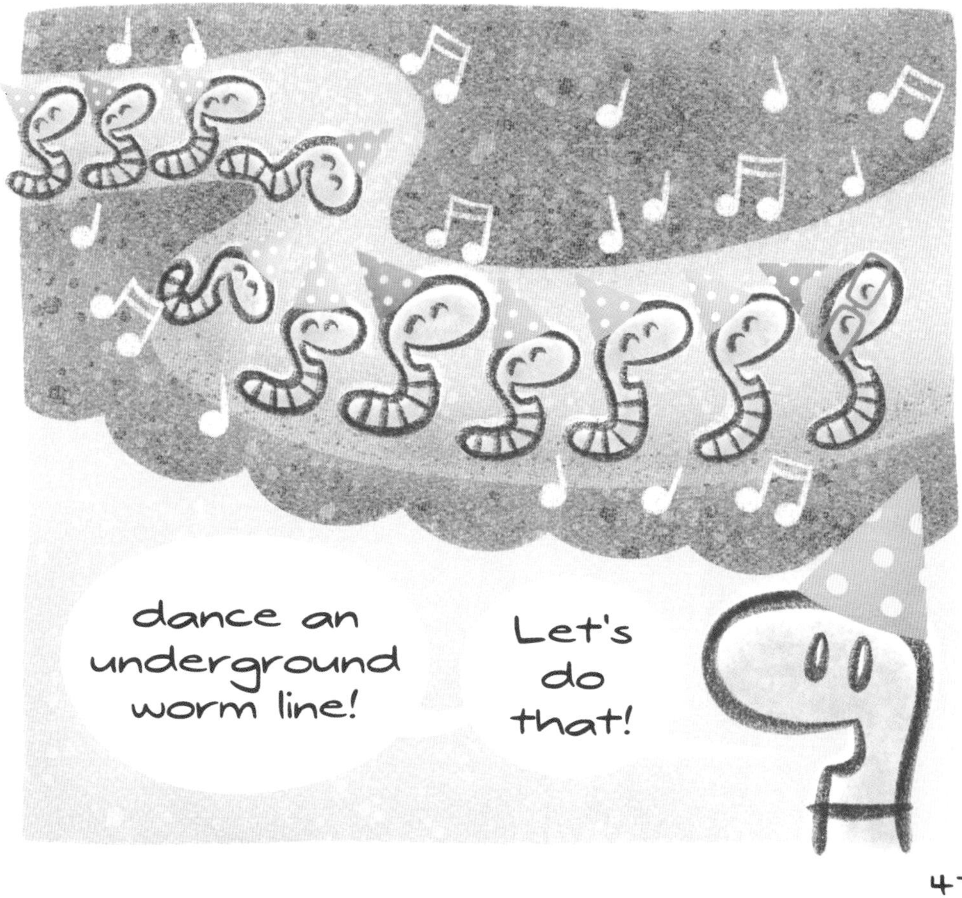
dance an underground worm line!
Let's do that!

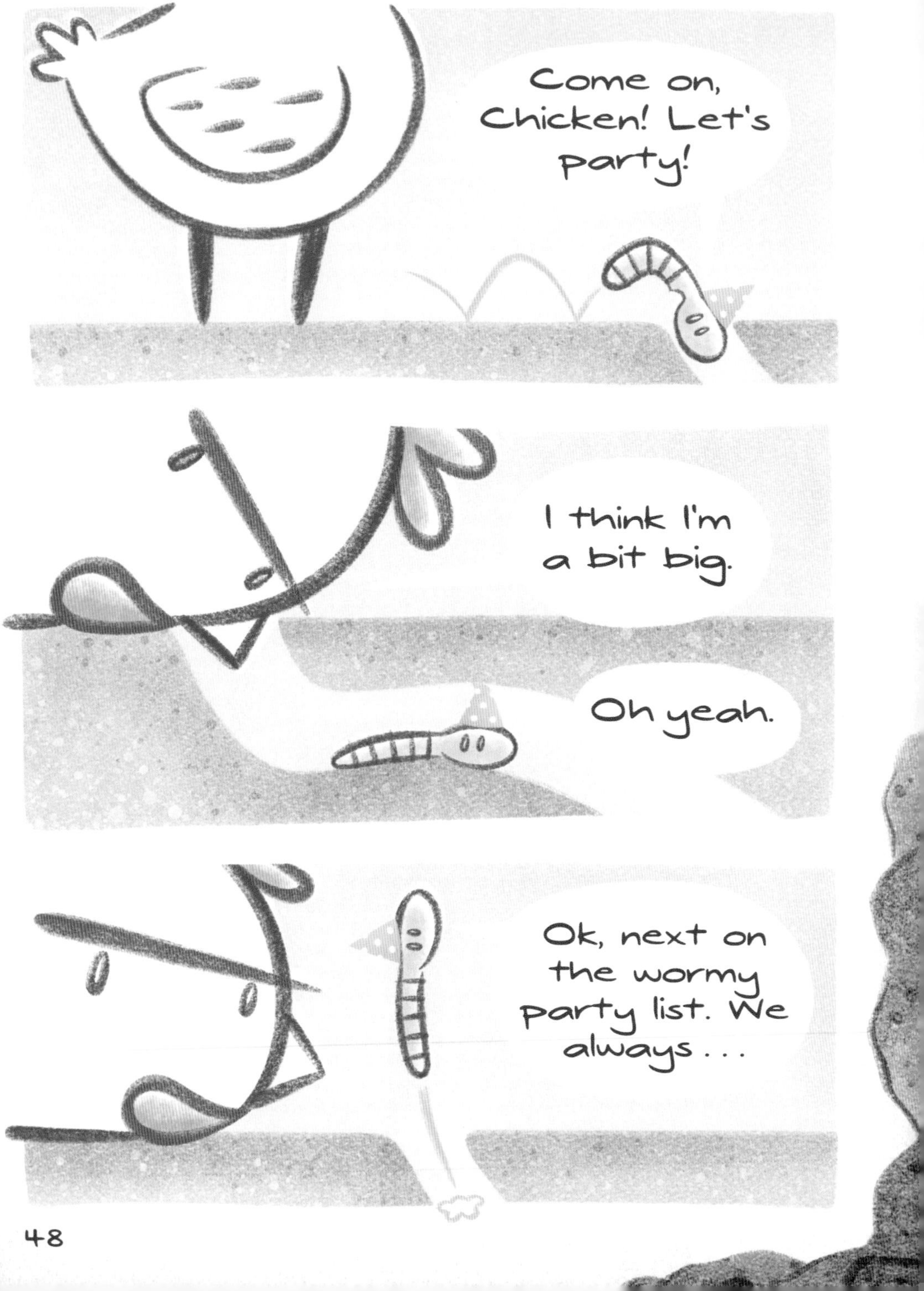
Come on, Chicken! Let's party!
I think I'm a bit big.
Oh yeah.
Ok, next on the wormy party list. We always . . .

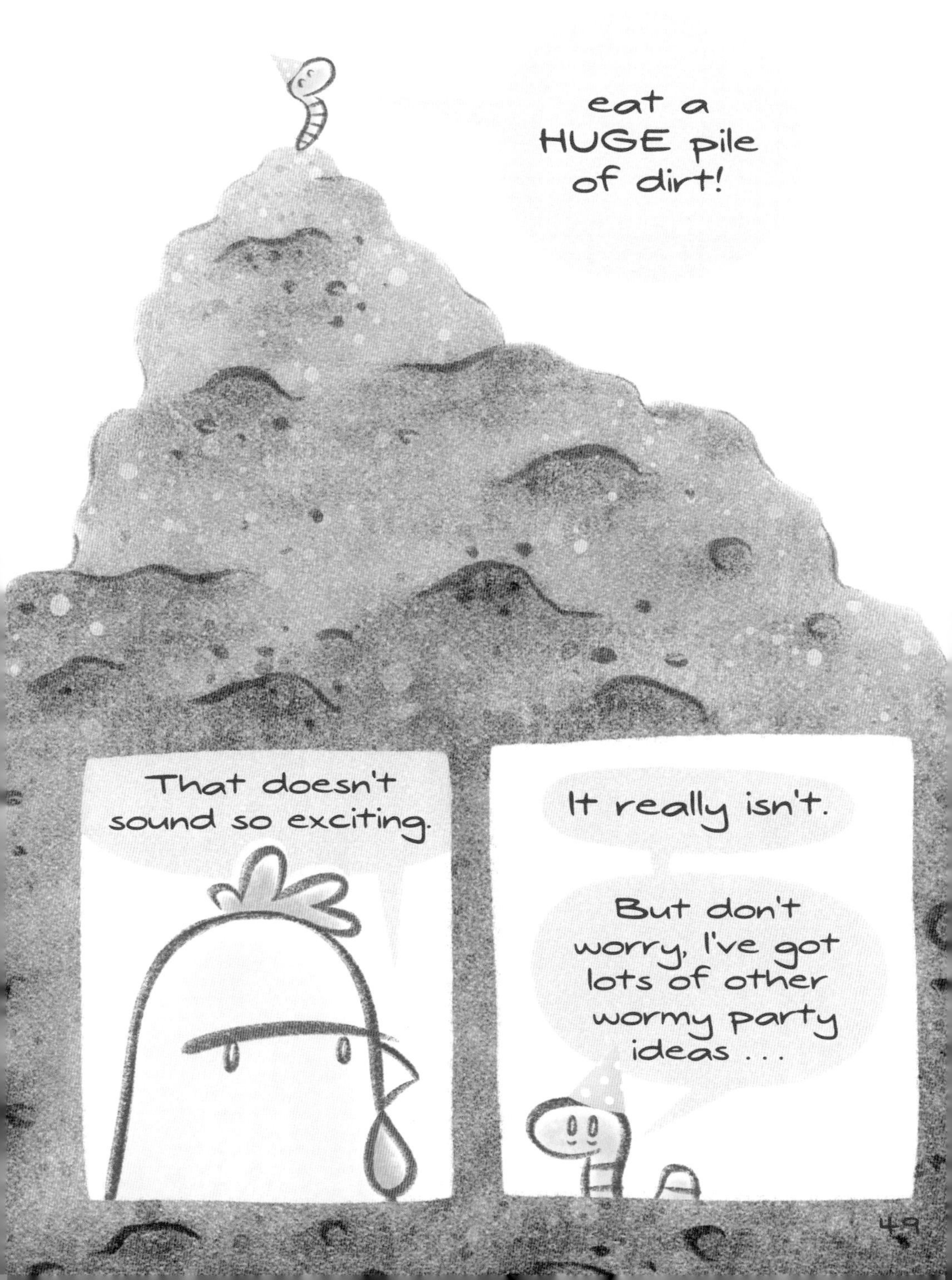

eat a HUGE pile of dirt!
That doesn't sound so exciting.
It really isn't.
But don't worry, I've got lots of other wormy party ideas . . .

Wormy PARTY Palooza!

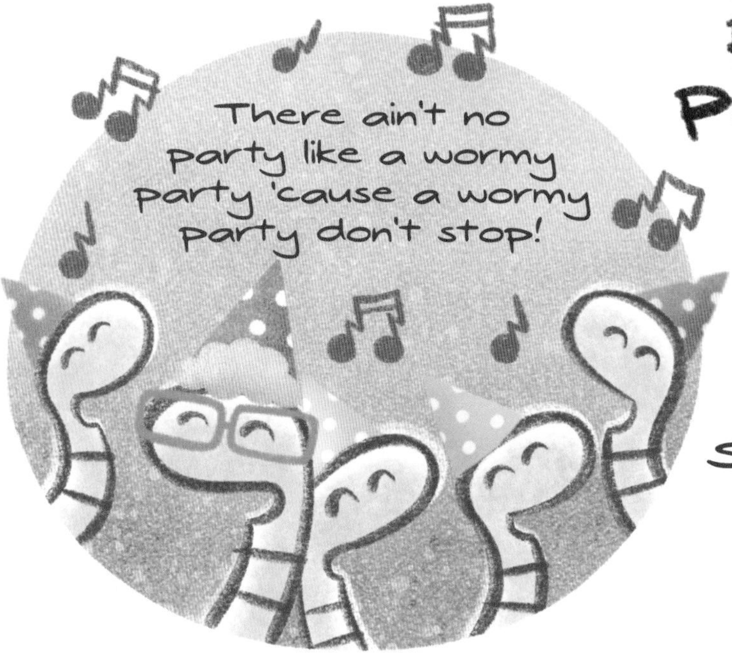
There ain't no party like a wormy party 'cause a wormy party don't stop!

Sing worm songs

Open presents

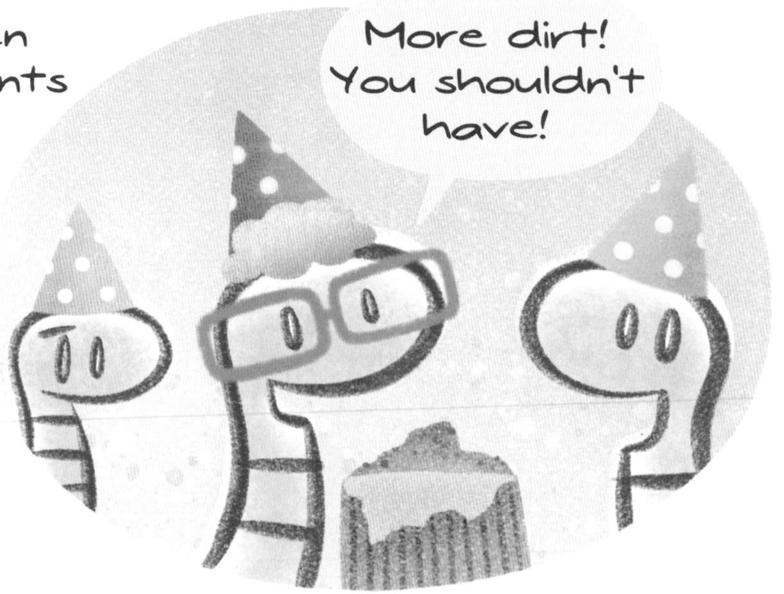
More dirt! You shouldn't have!

Worm dance circle

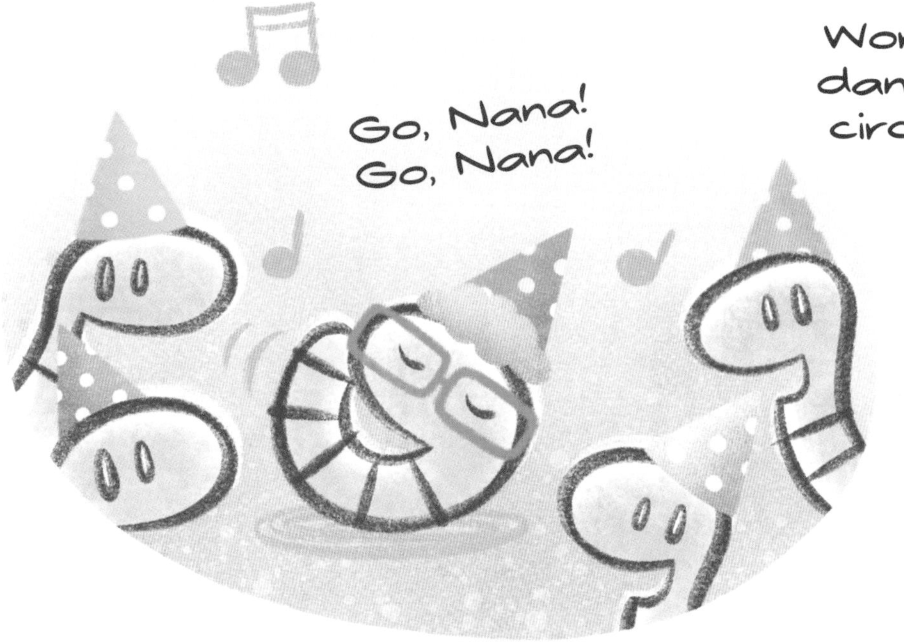
Go, Nana! Go, Nana!

Stay up all night watching worm documentaries

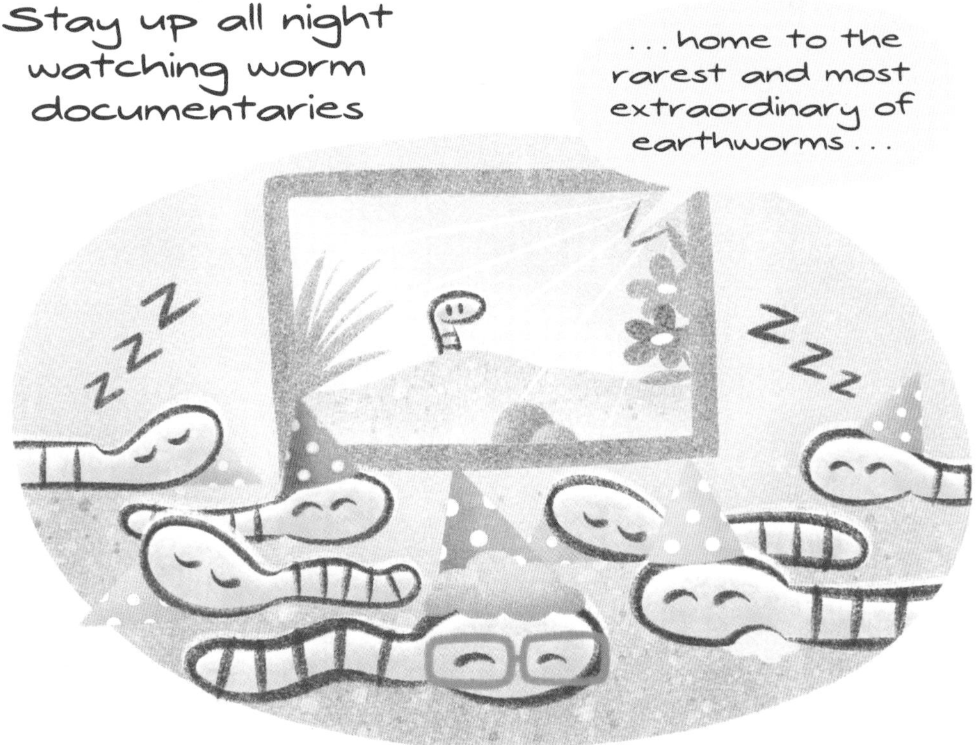
. . . home to the rarest and most extraordinary of earthworms . . .

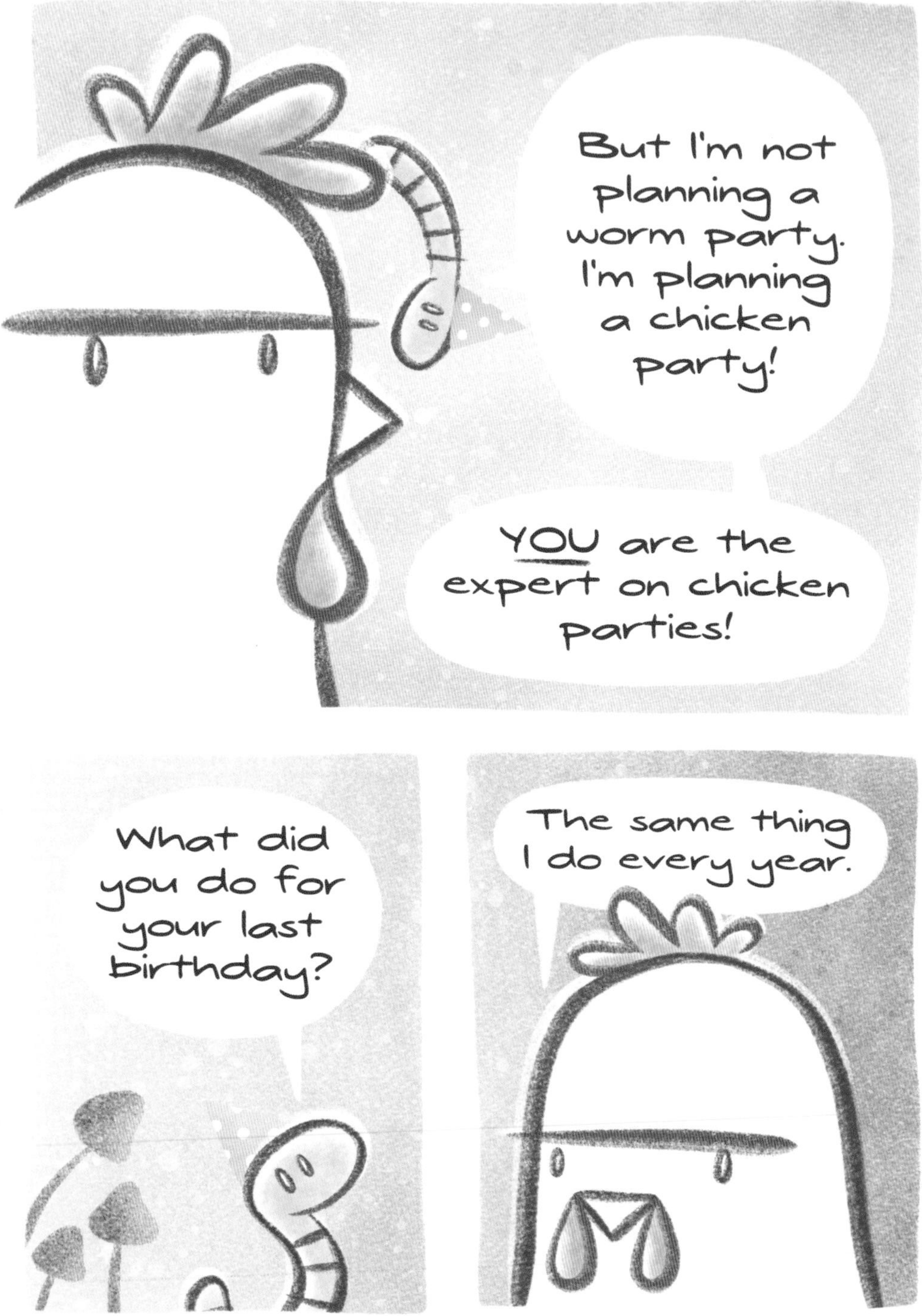
But I'm not planning a worm party. I'm planning a chicken party!
YOU are the expert on chicken parties!
What did you do for your last birthday?
The same thing I do every year.

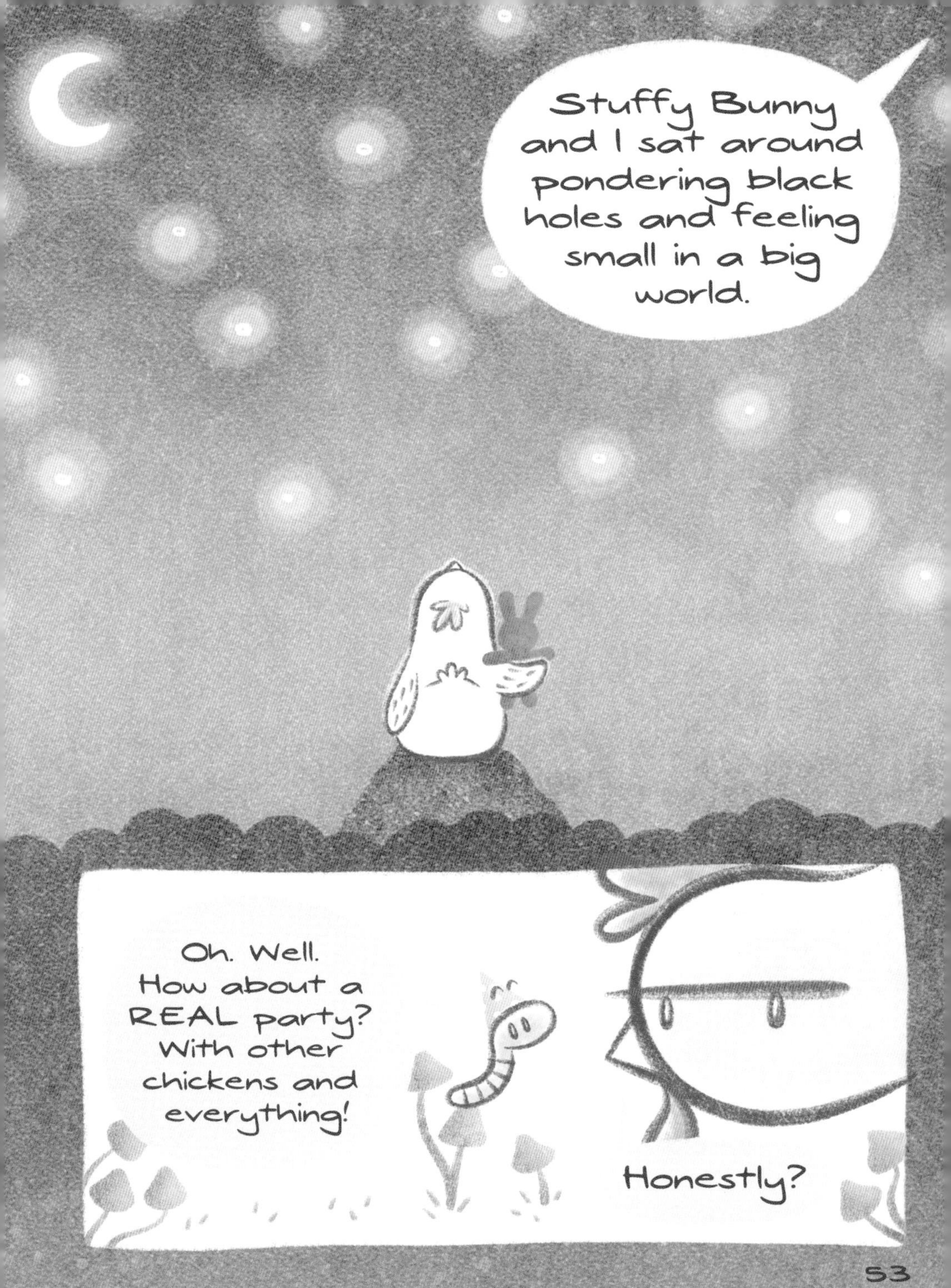
Stuffy Bunny and I sat around pondering black holes and feeling small in a big world.
Oh. Well. How about a REAL party? With other chickens and everything!
Honestly?

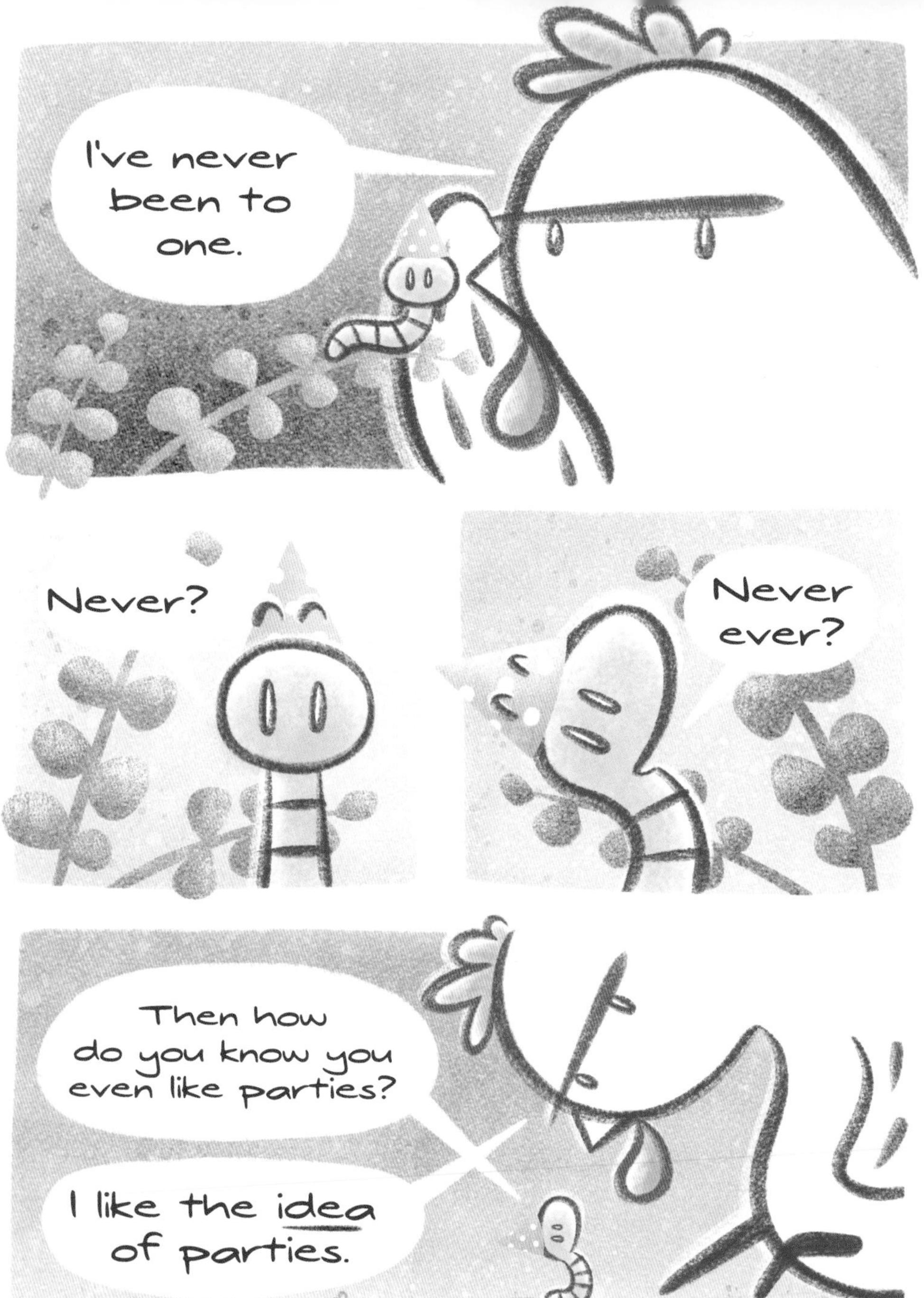
I've never been to one.
Never?
Never ever?
Then how do you know you even like parties?
I like the idea of parties.

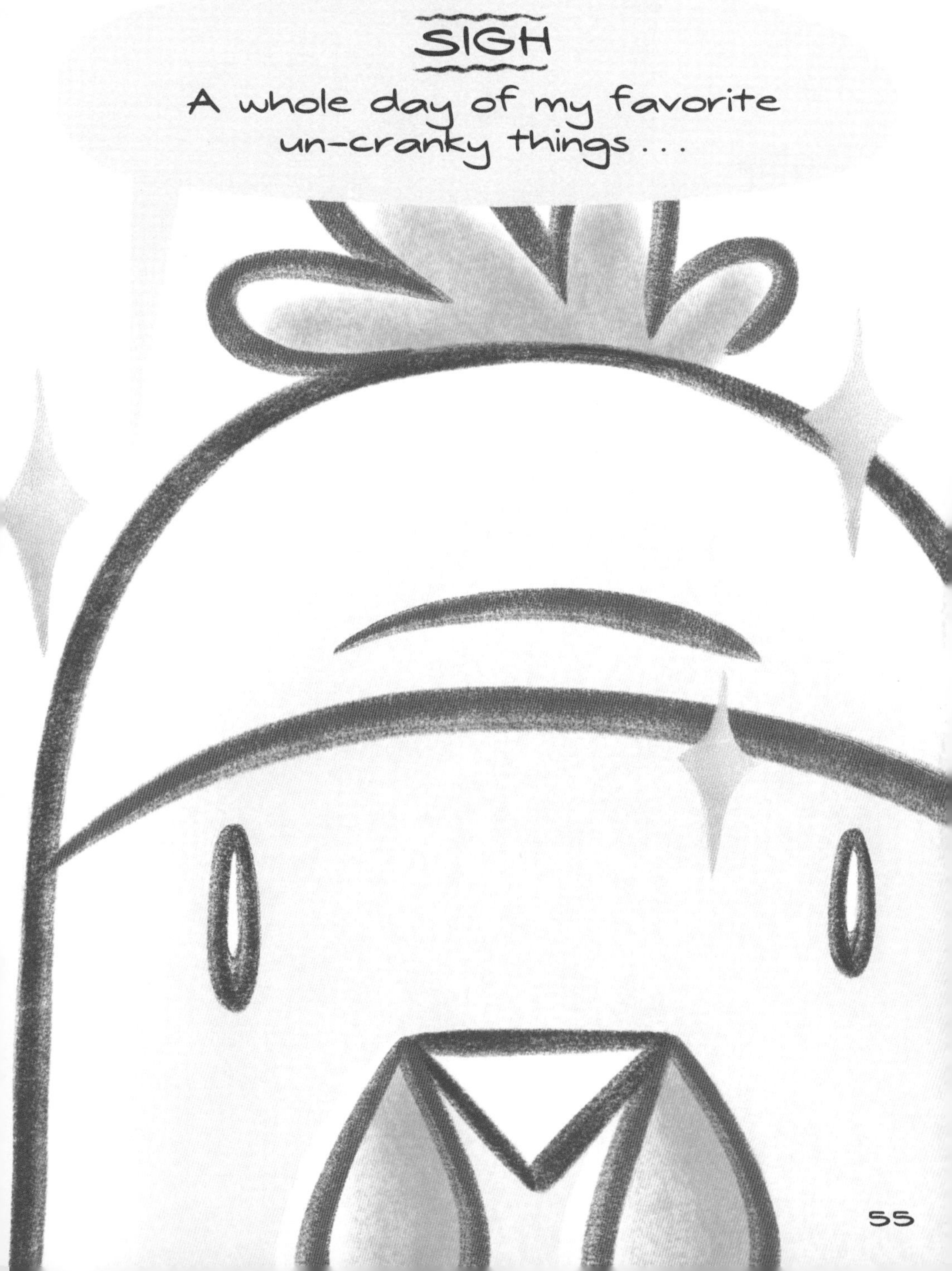
SIGH
A whole day of my favorite un-cranky things . . .

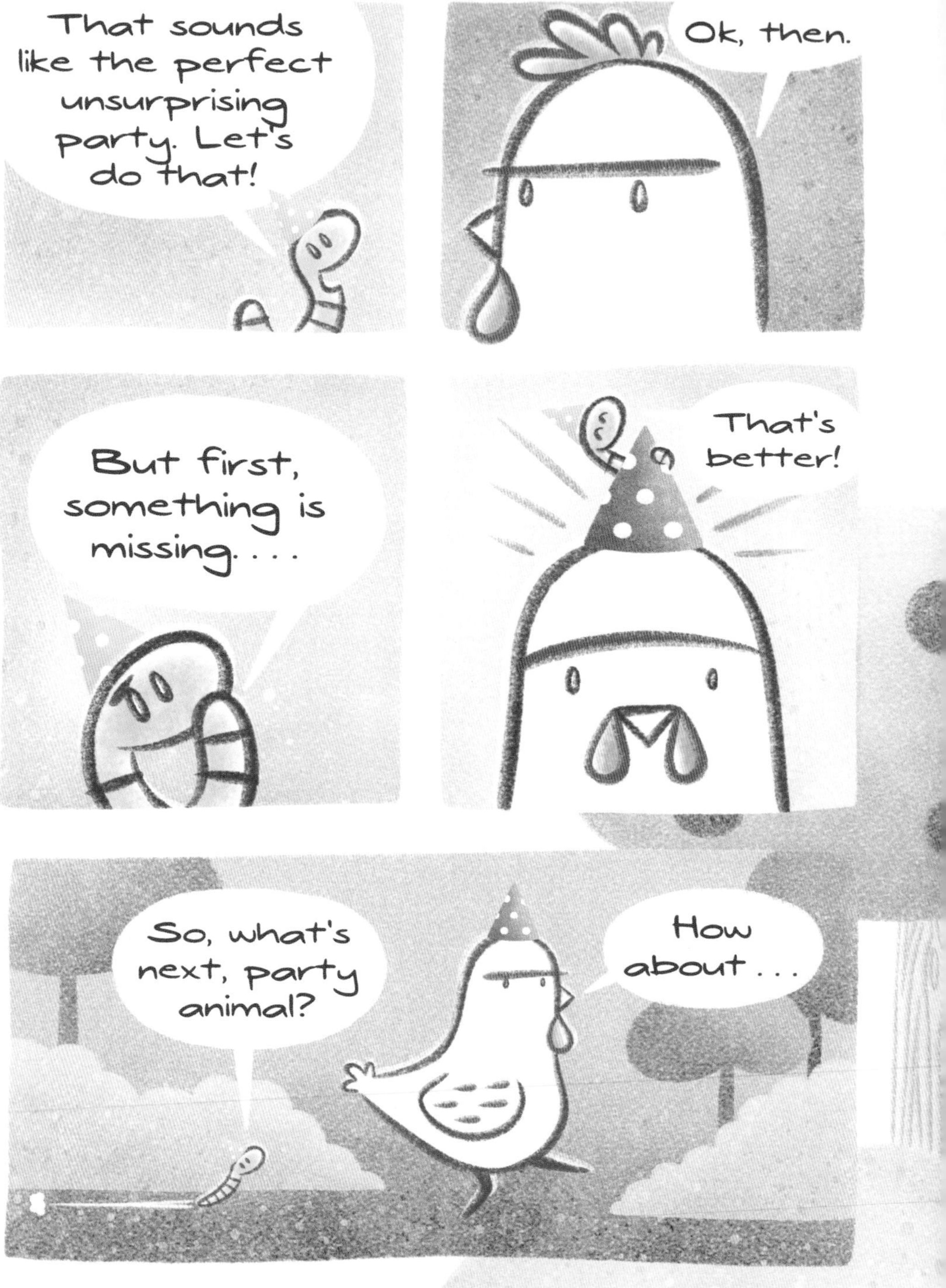
That sounds like the perfect unsurprising party. Let's do that!
Ok, then.
But first, something is missing. . . .
That's better!
So, what's next, party animal?
How about . . .

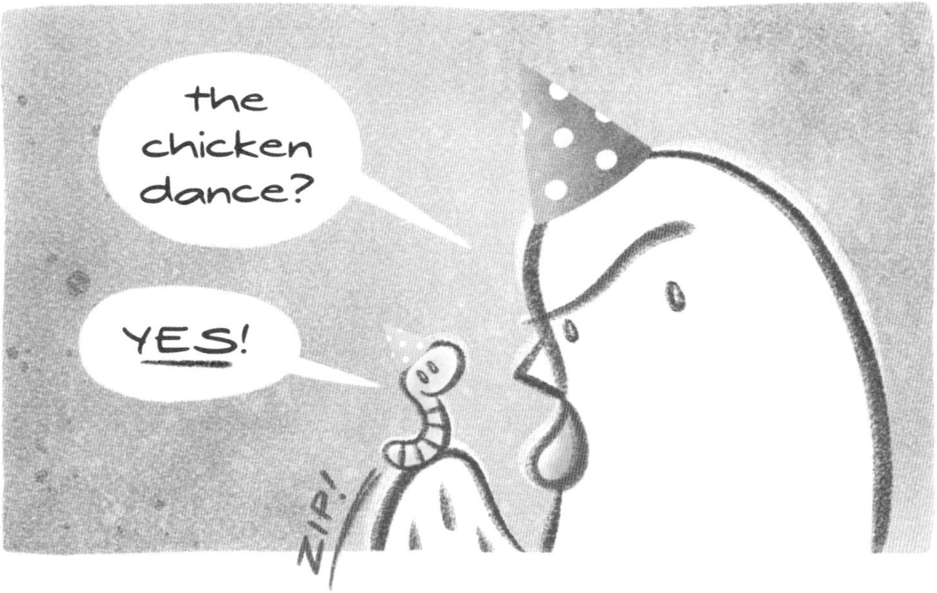
the chicken dance?
YES!
ZIP!

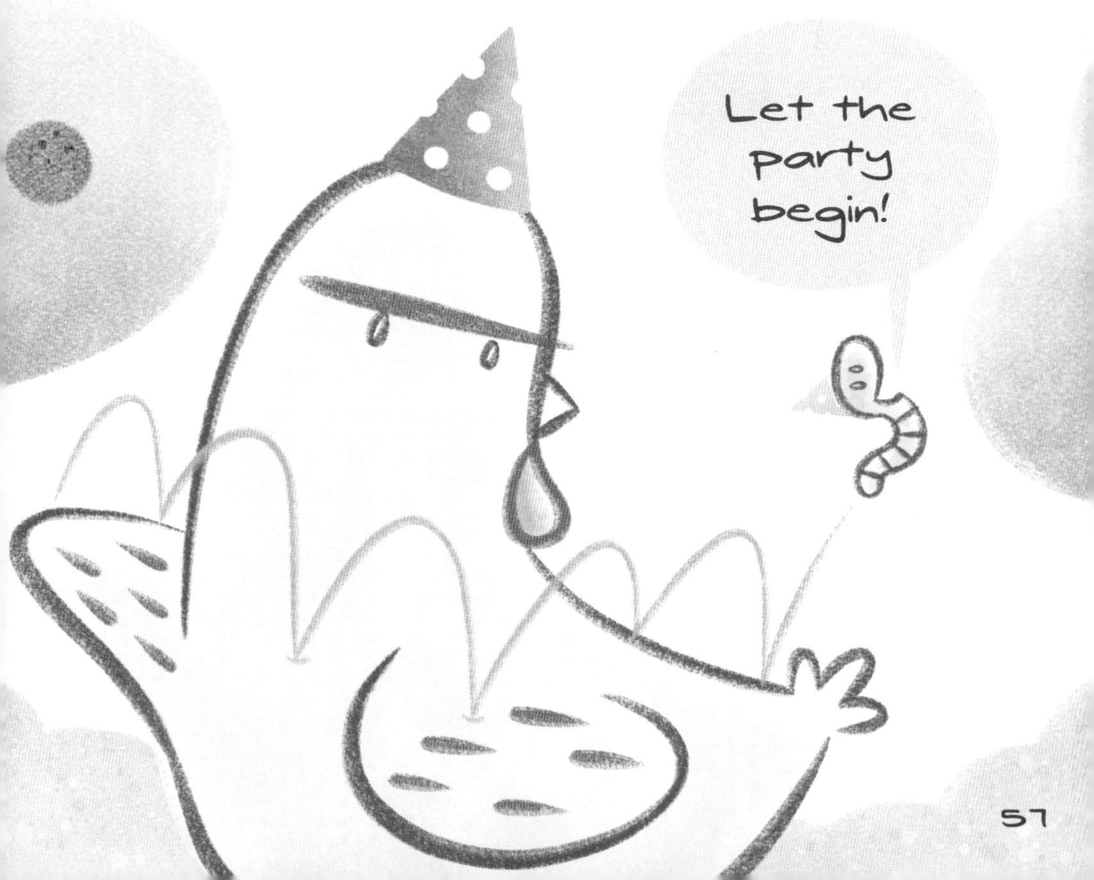
Let the party begin!

CHICKEN'S UNSURPRISING PARTY!

The REAL chicken dance

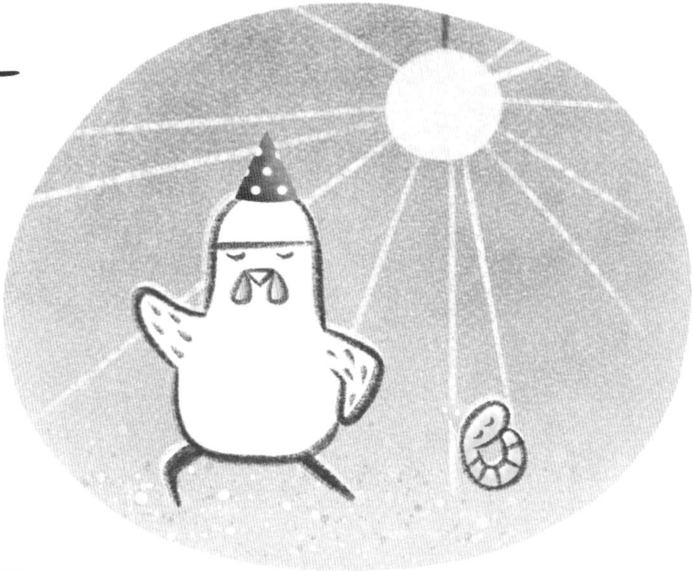

Pin the tail on the chicken

Make wishes

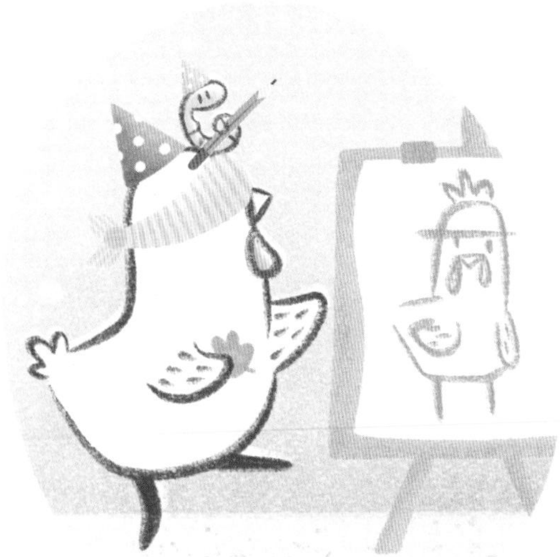

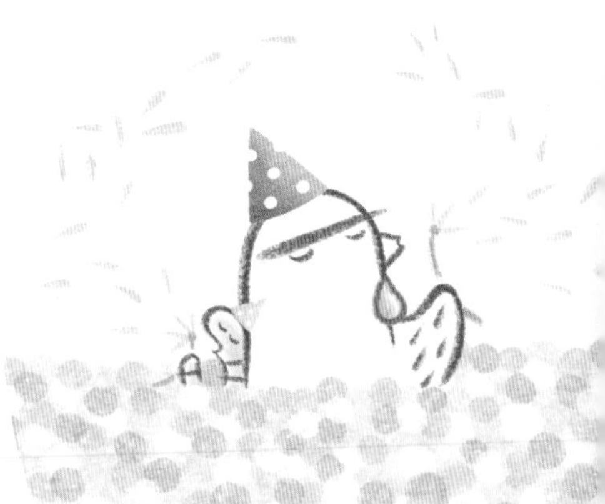

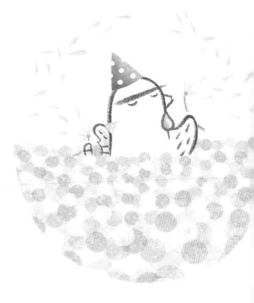

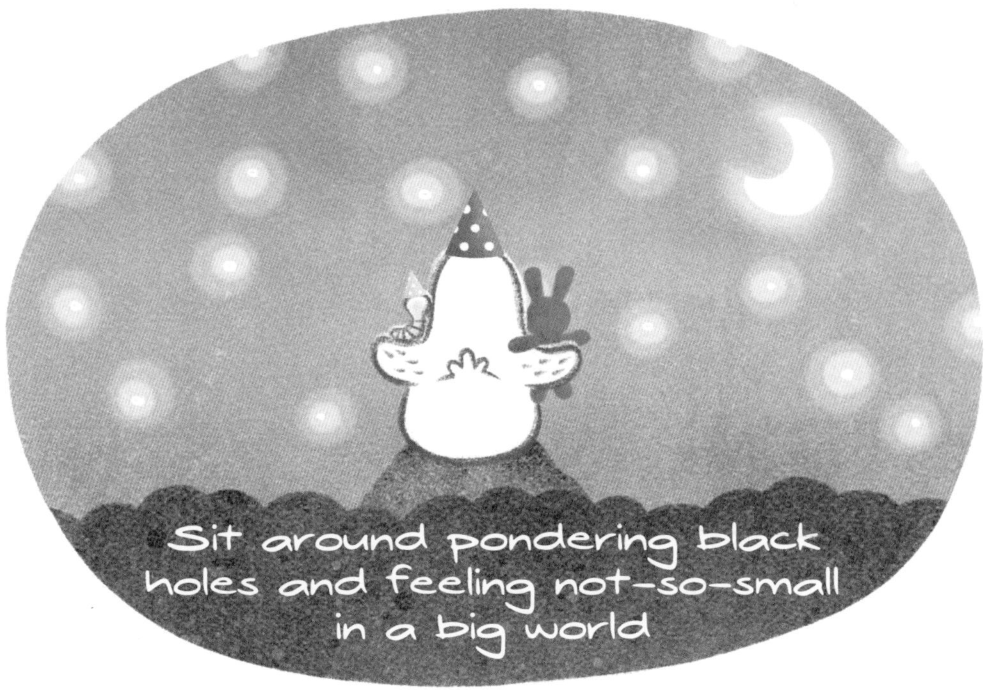
Sit around pondering black holes and feeling not-so-small in a big world

Stay up all night watching chicken documentaries

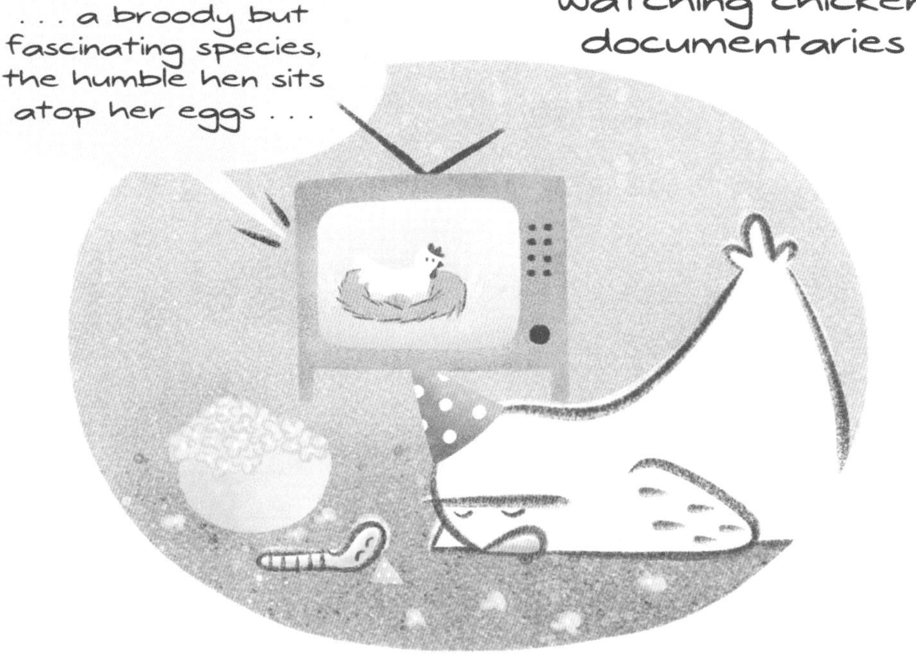
. . . a broody but fascinating species, the humble hen sits atop her eggs . . .

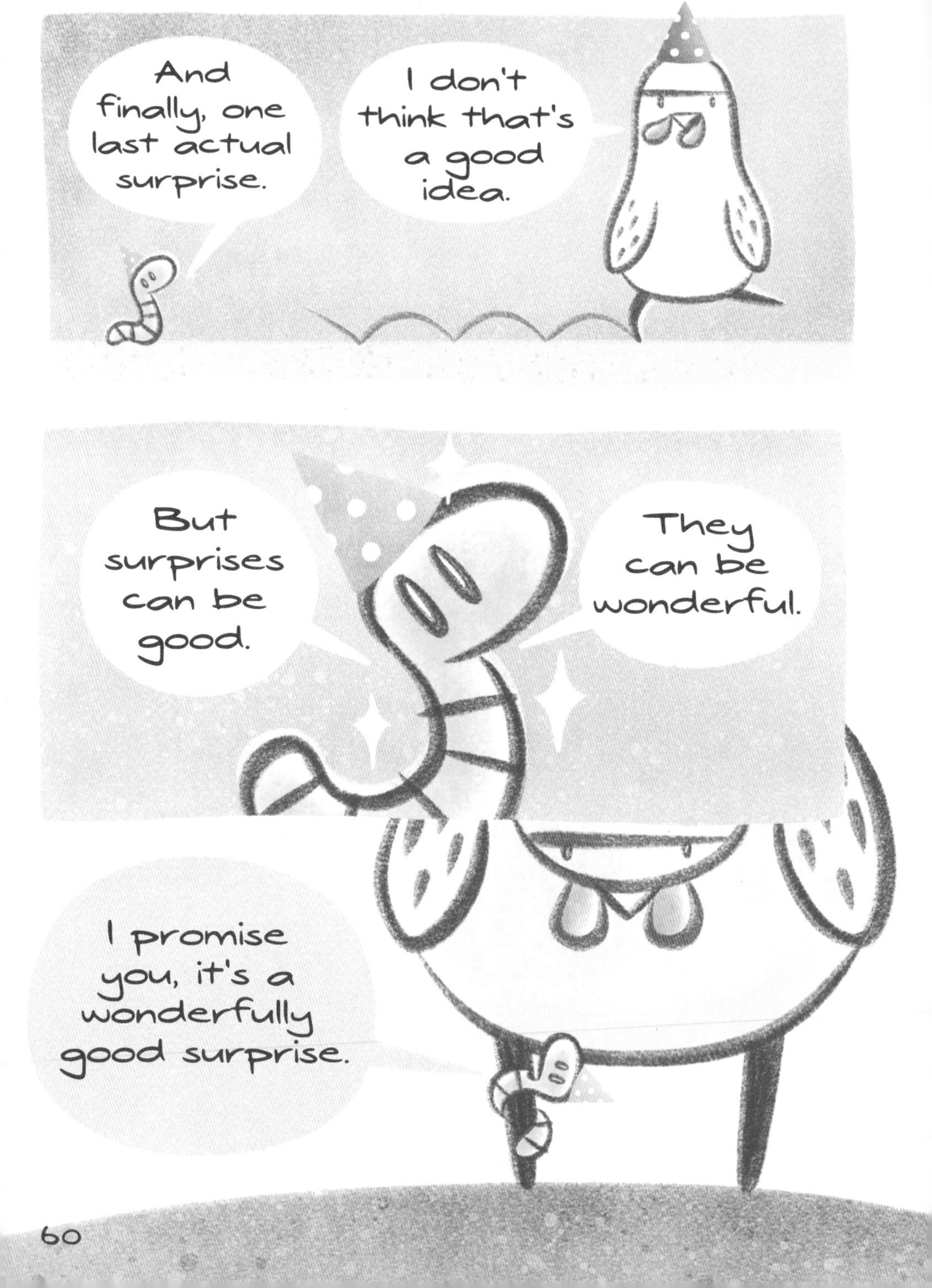
And finally, one last actual surprise.
I don't think that's a good idea.
But surprises can be good.
They can be wonderful.
I promise you, it's a wonderfully good surprise.

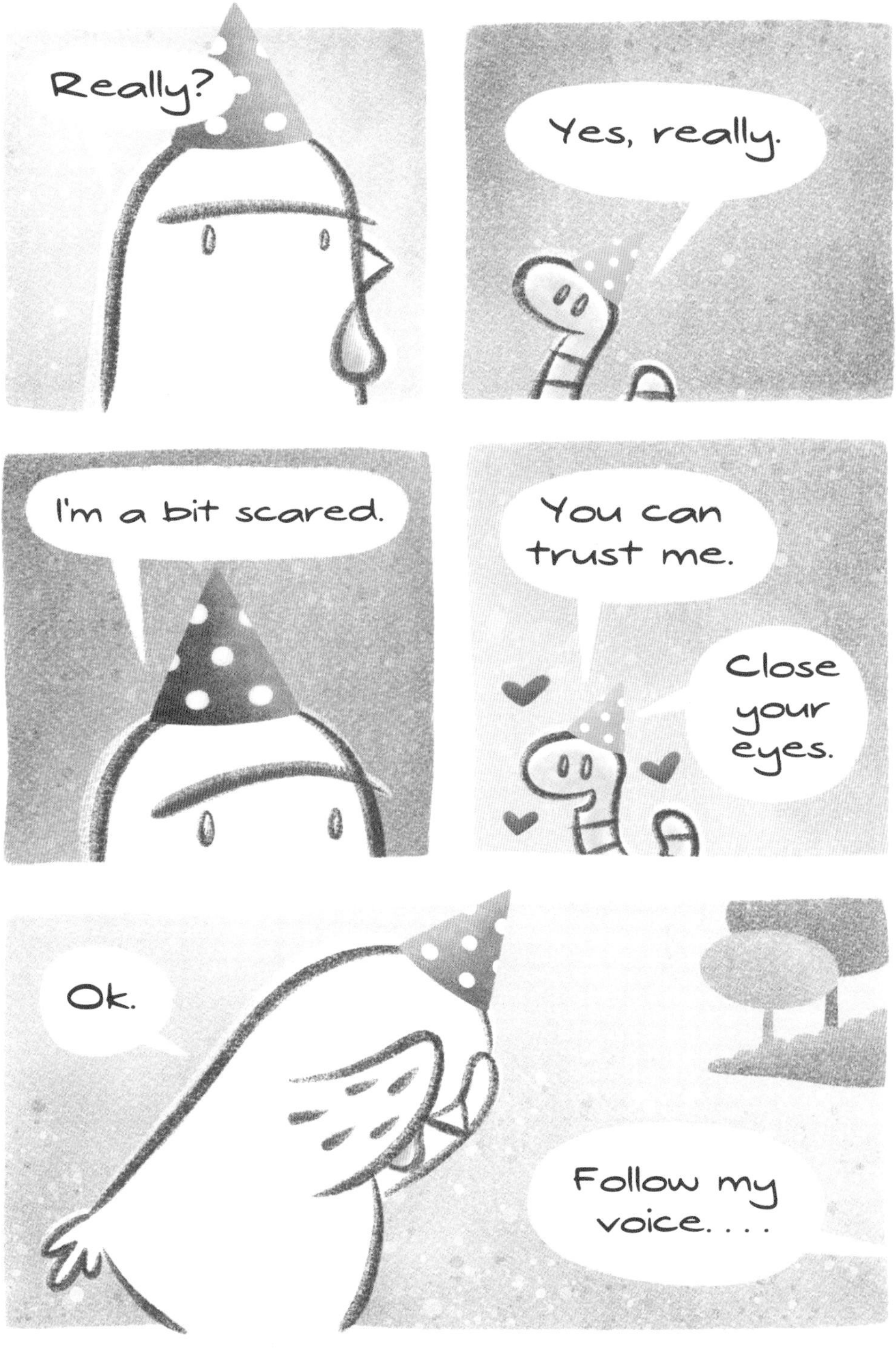

Really?
Yes, really.
I'm a bit scared.
You can trust me.
Close your eyes.
Ok.
Follow my voice. . . .

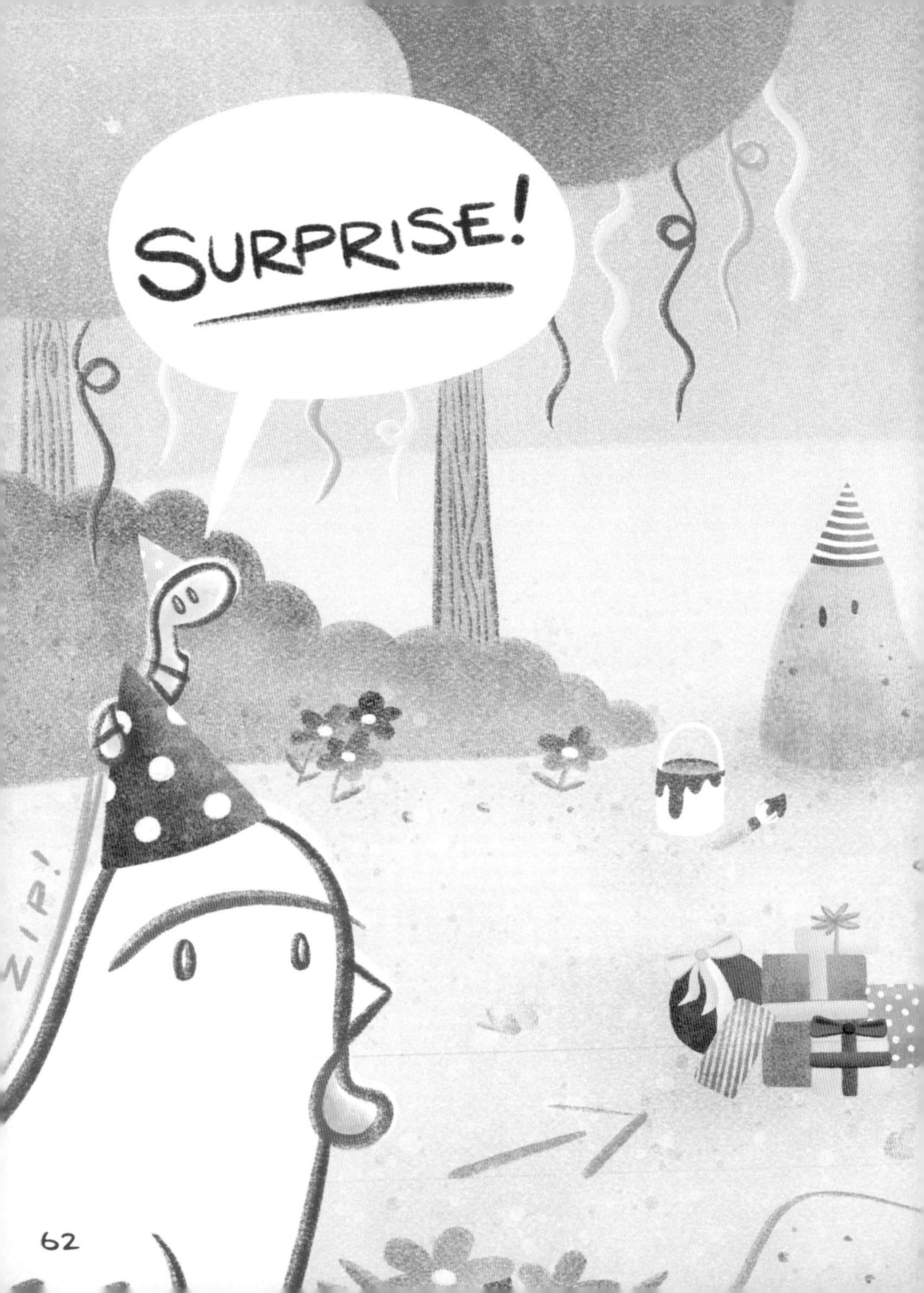
SURPRISE!
ZIP!

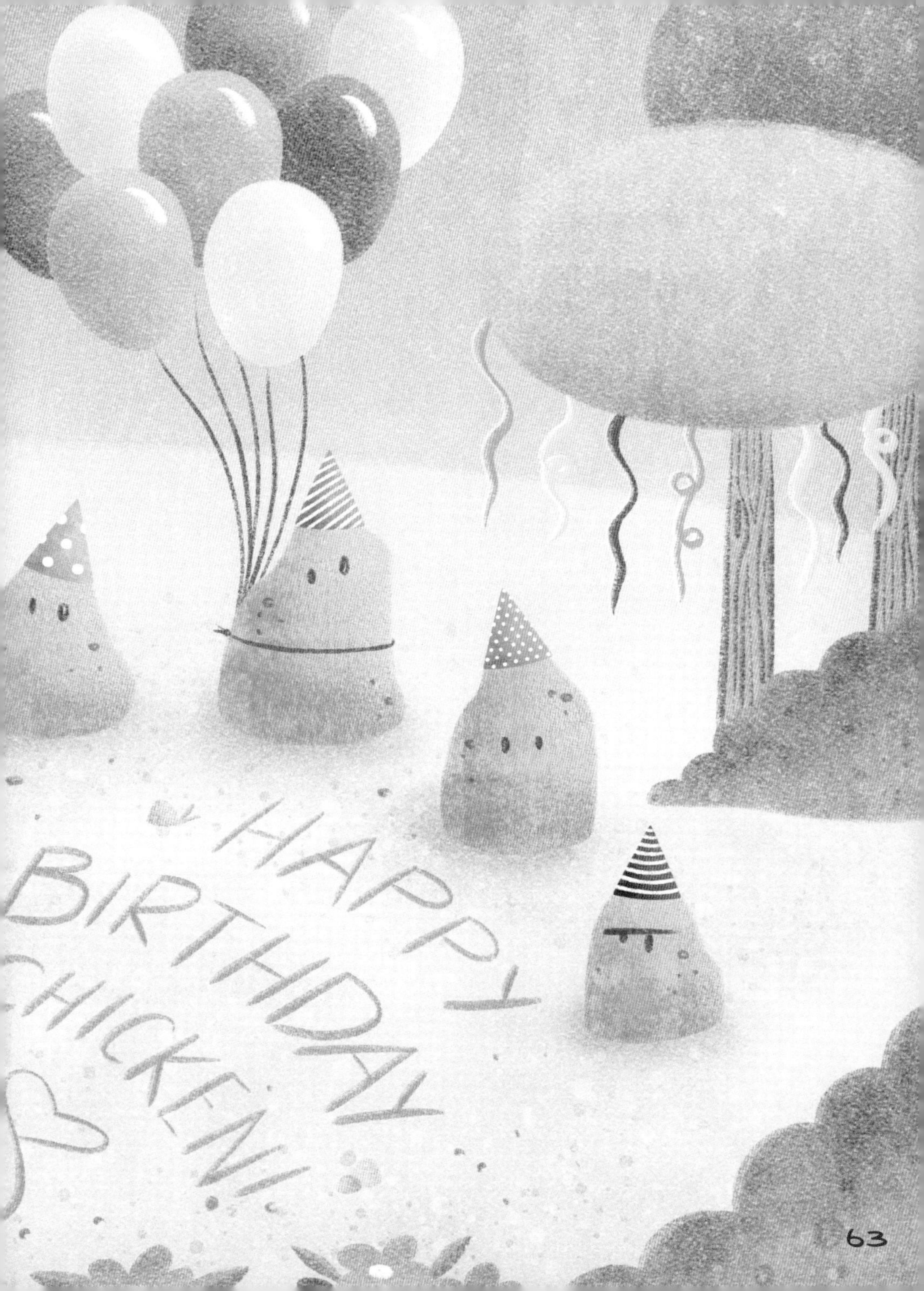
HAPPY
BIRTHDAY
CHICKEN!

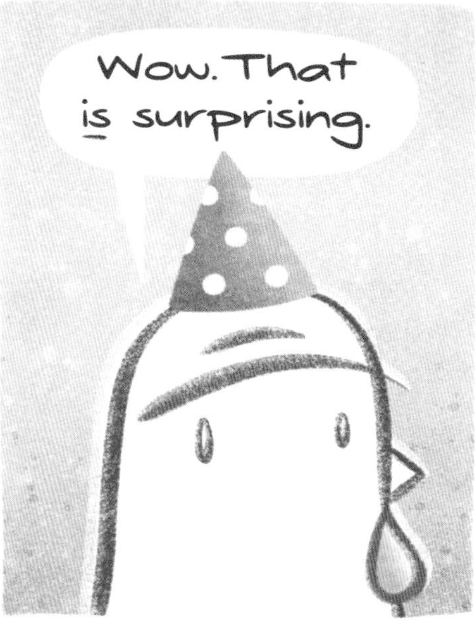
Wow. That is surprising.

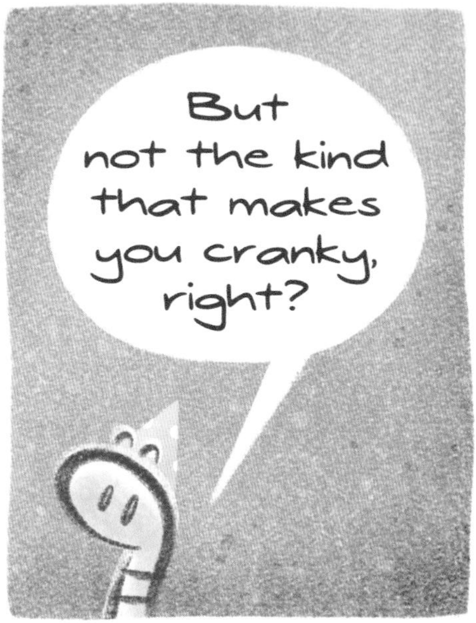
But not the kind that makes you cranky, right?

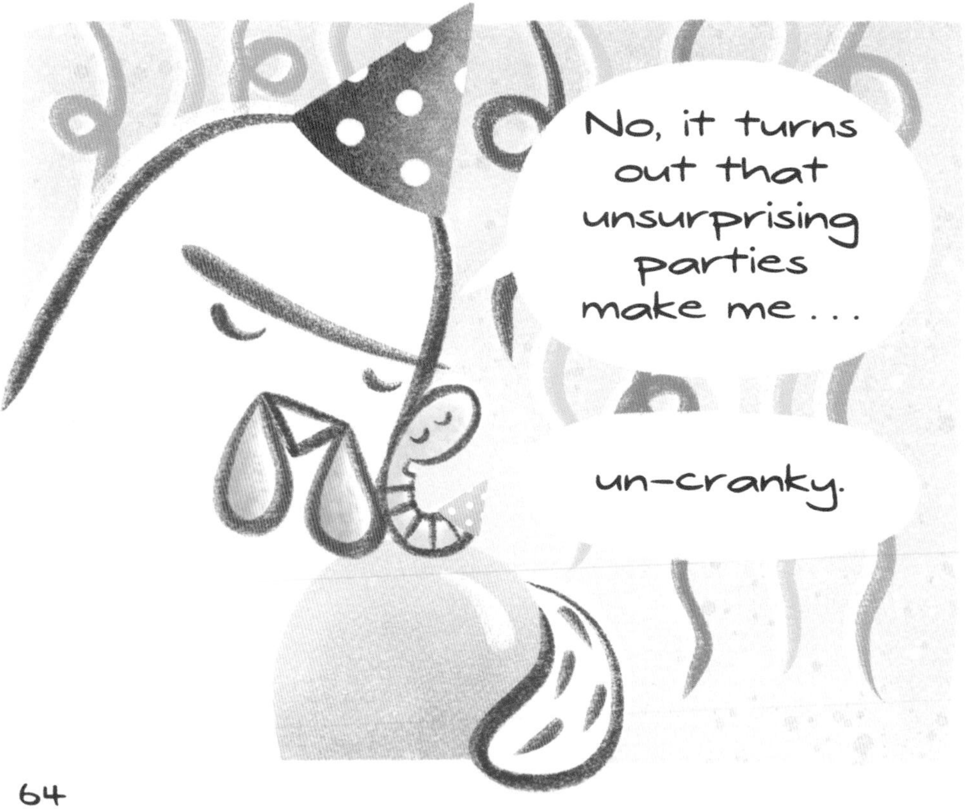
No, it turns out that unsurprising parties make me . . .
un-cranky.

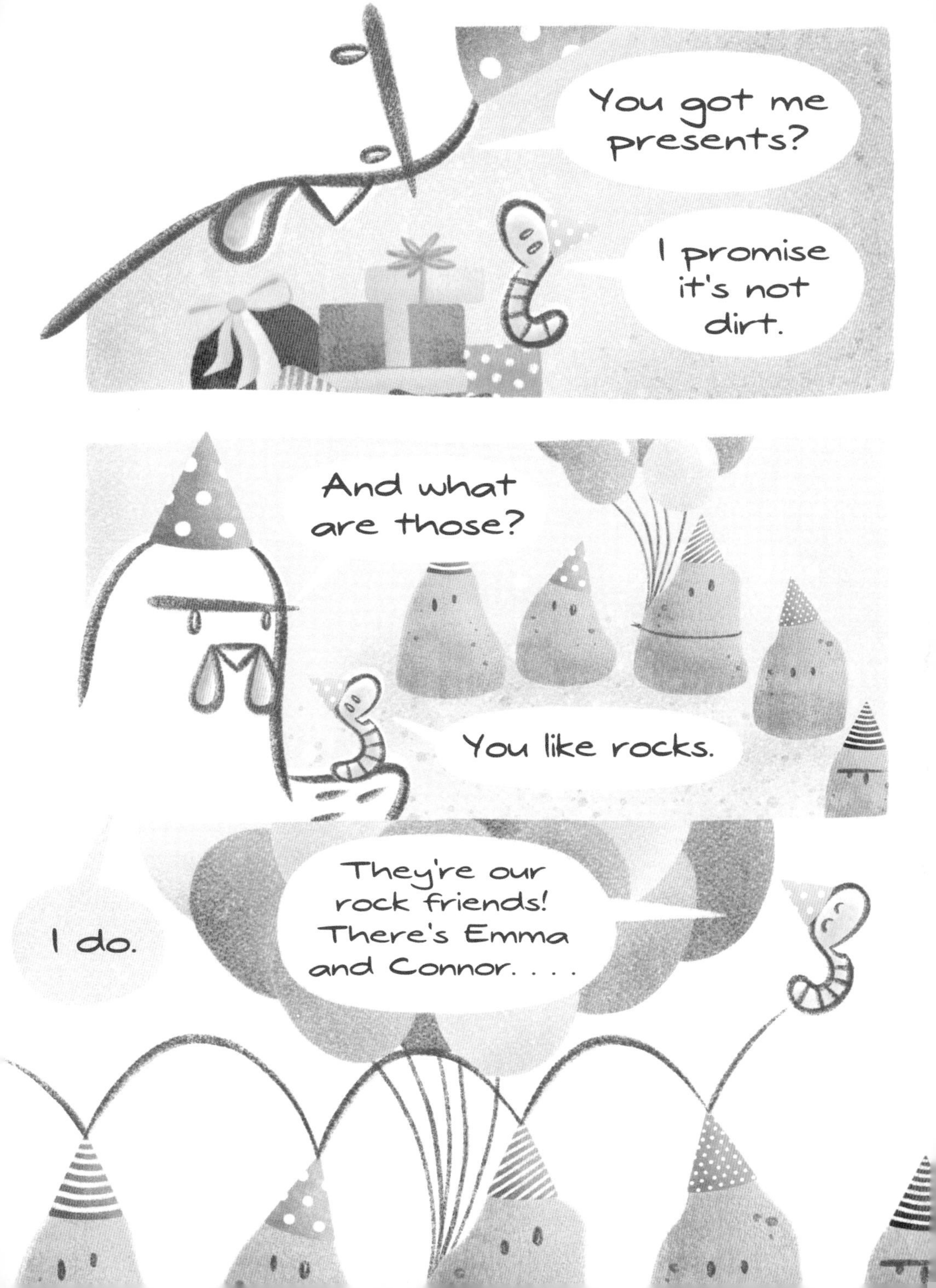
You got me presents?
I promise it's not dirt.
And what are those?
You like rocks.
I do.
They're our rock friends! There's Emma and Connor. . . .

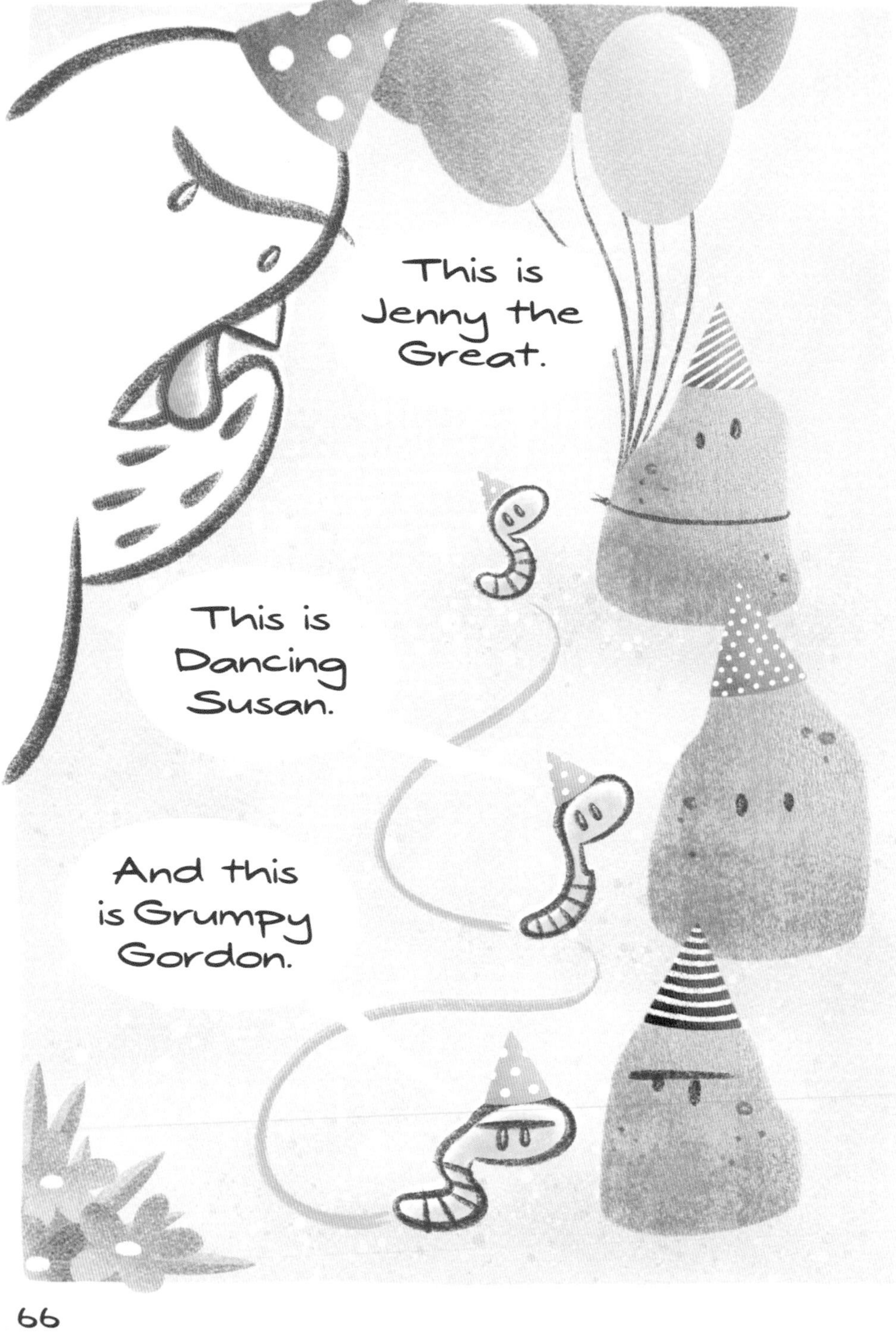
This is
Jenny the
Great.
This is
Dancing
Susan.
And this
is Grumpy
Gordon.

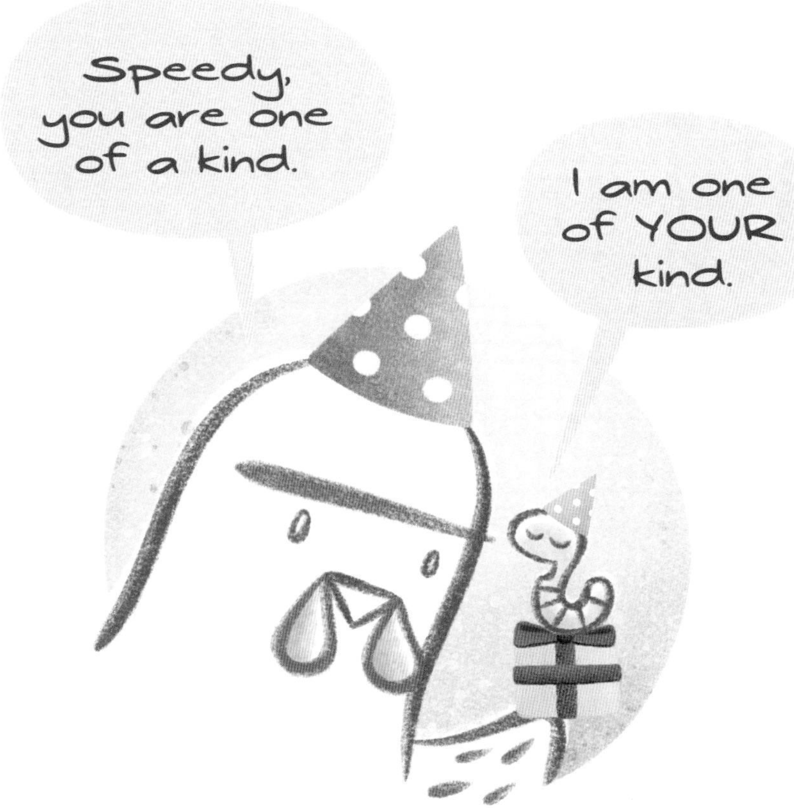
Speedy, you are one of a kind.
I am one of YOUR kind.

STUFF
and
NONSENSE

68

Speedy's Favorite Movies

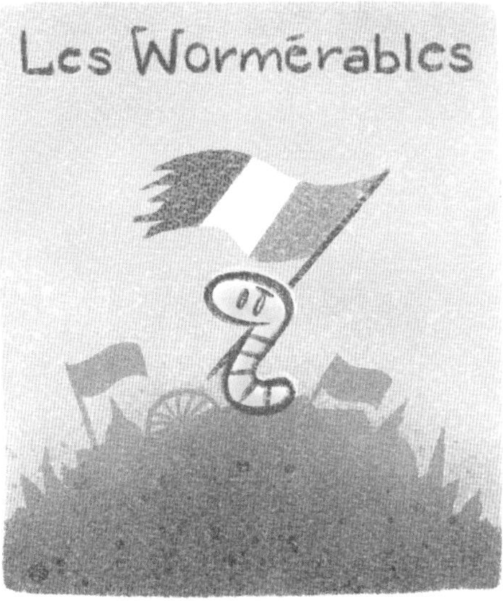
Les Wormérables

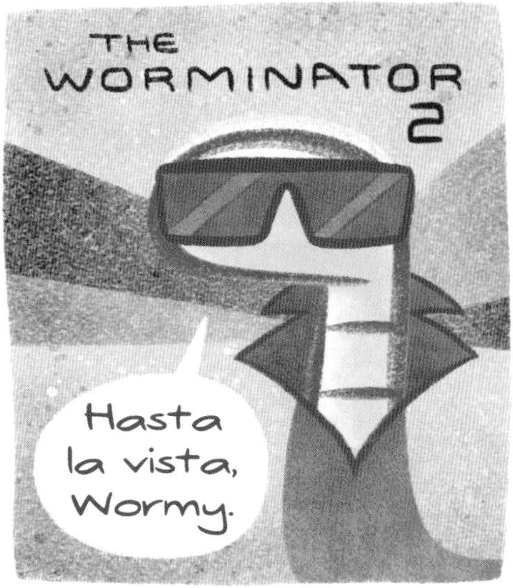
THE WORMINATOR 2
Hasta la vista, Wormy.

Chicken's Favorite Movies

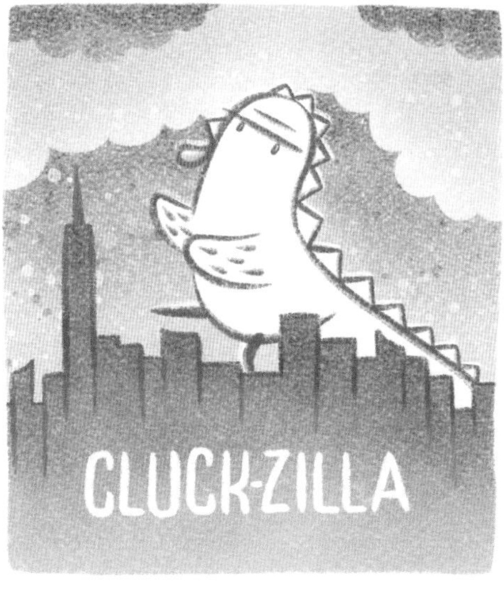
CLUCK-ZILLA

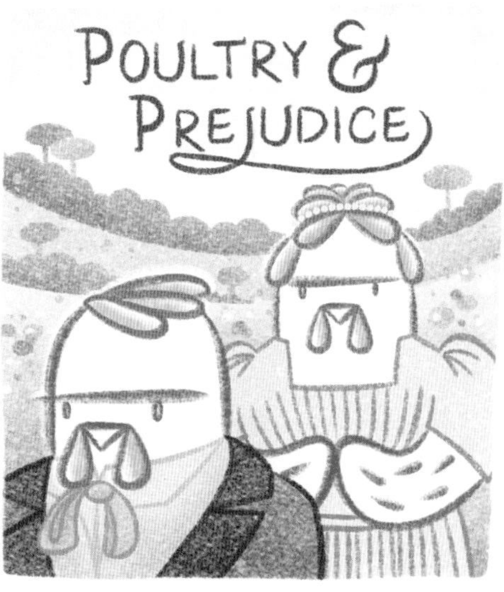
POULTRY & PREJUDICE

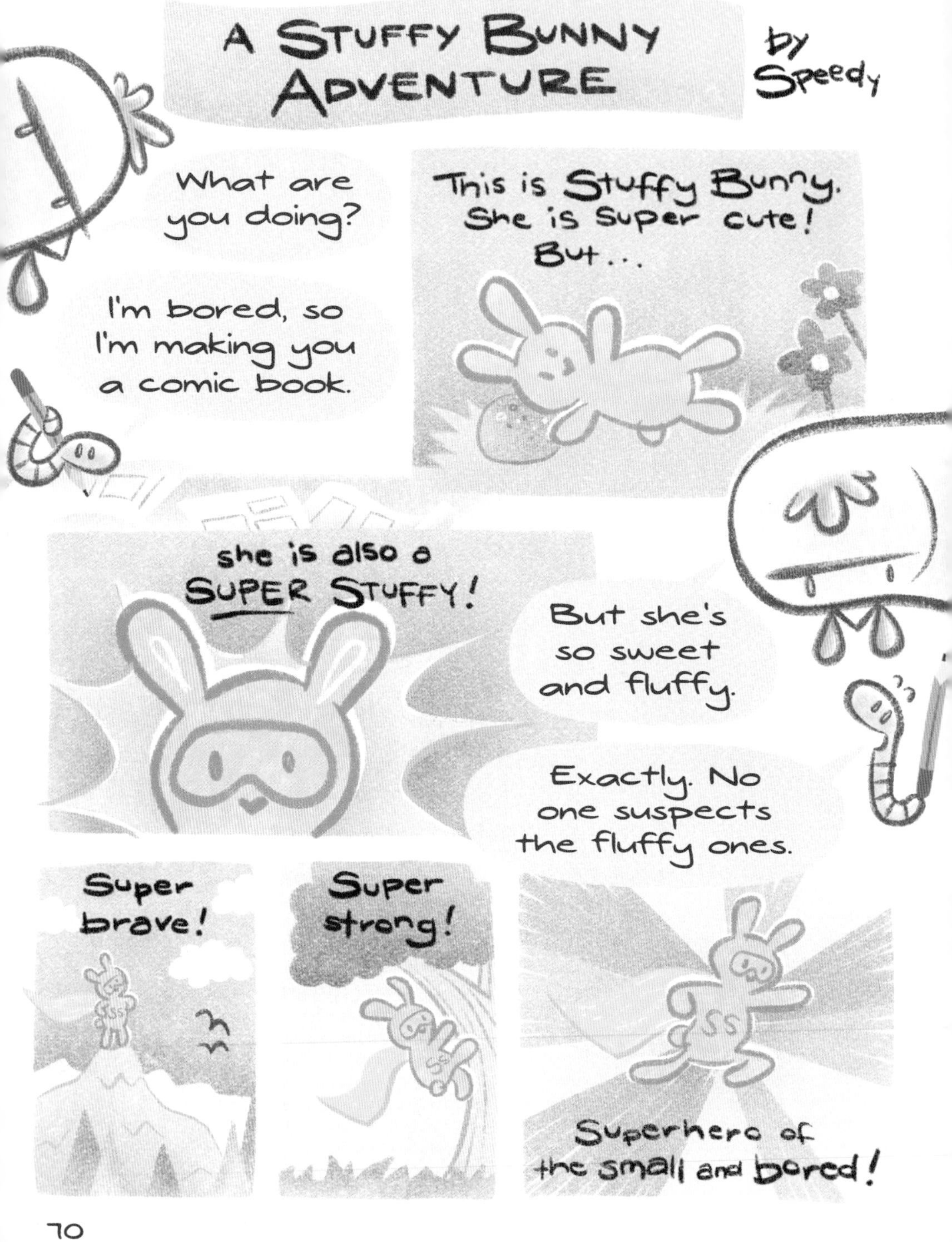
A STUFFY BUNNY ADVENTURE
by Speedy
What are you doing?
I'm bored, so I'm making you a comic book.
This is Stuffy Bunny. She is Super cute! But . . .
she is also a SUPER STUFFY!
But she's so sweet and fluffy.
Exactly. No one suspects the fluffy ones.
Super brave!
Super strong!
Superhero of the small and bored!

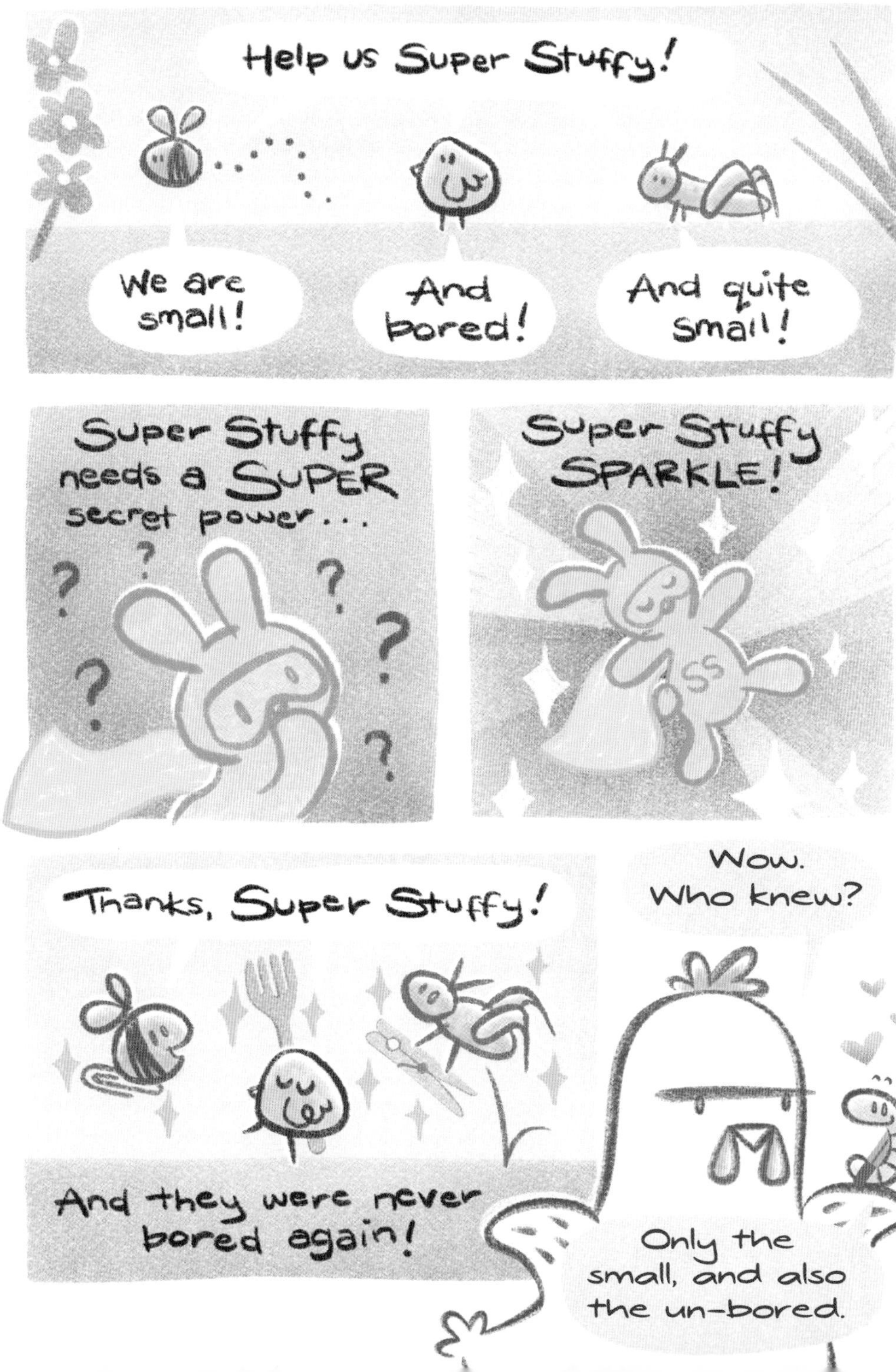
Help us Super Stuffy!
We are small!
And bored!
And quite small!
Super Stuffy needs a SUPER secret power...
Super Stuffy SPARKLE!
SS
Thanks, Super Stuffy!
And they were never bored again!
Wow. Who knew?
Only the small, and also the un-bored.

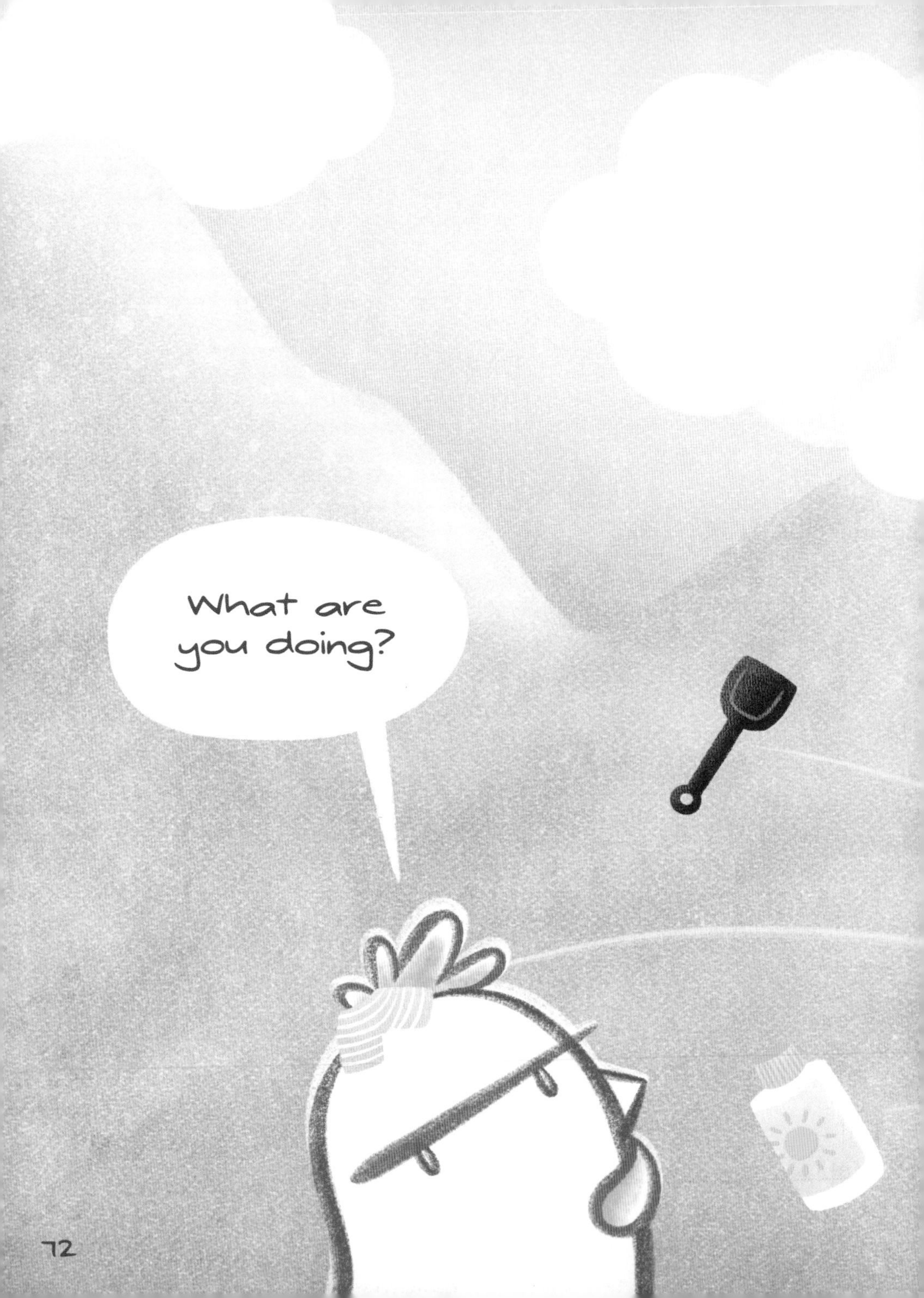
What are you doing?

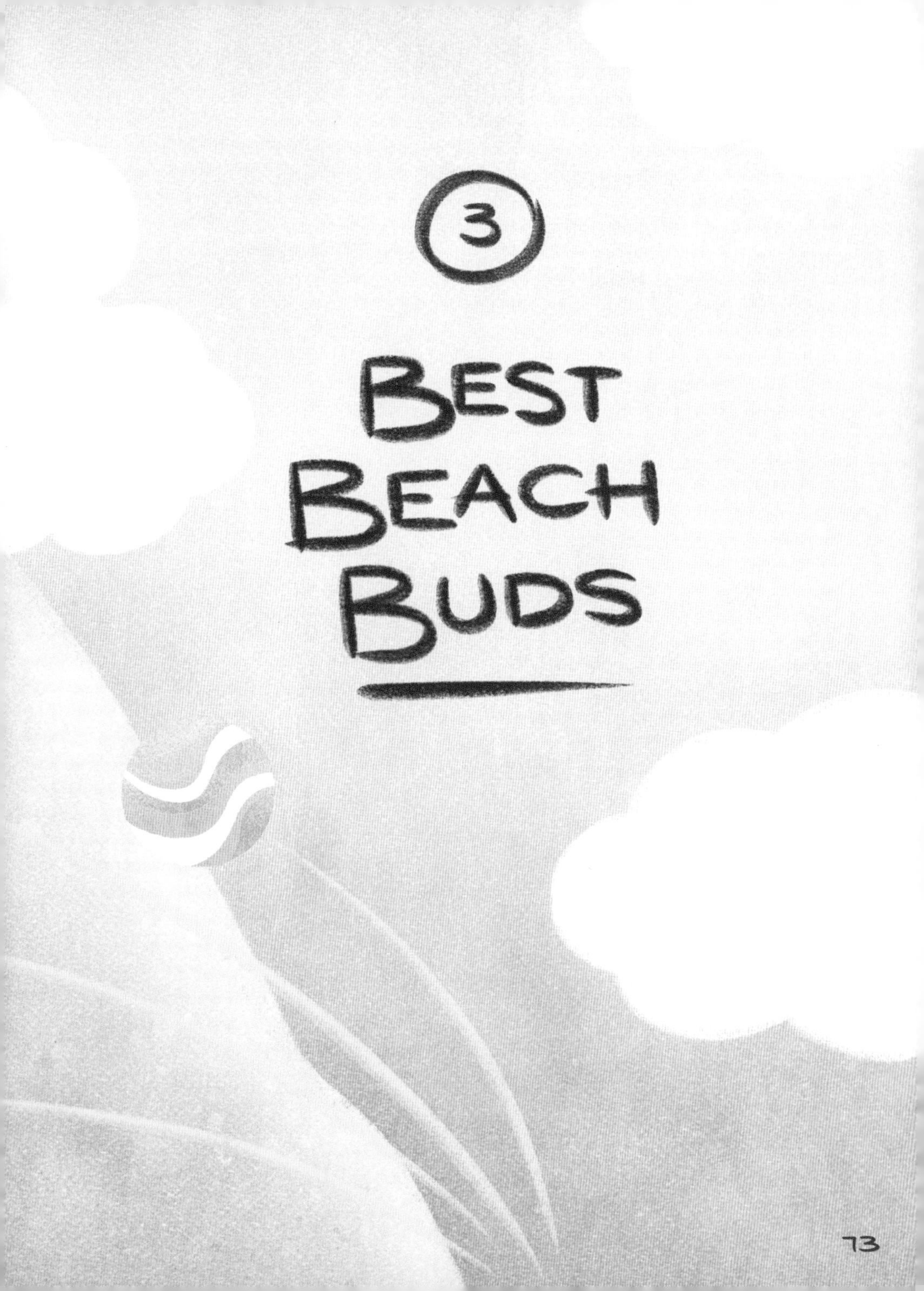

3

Best Beach Buds

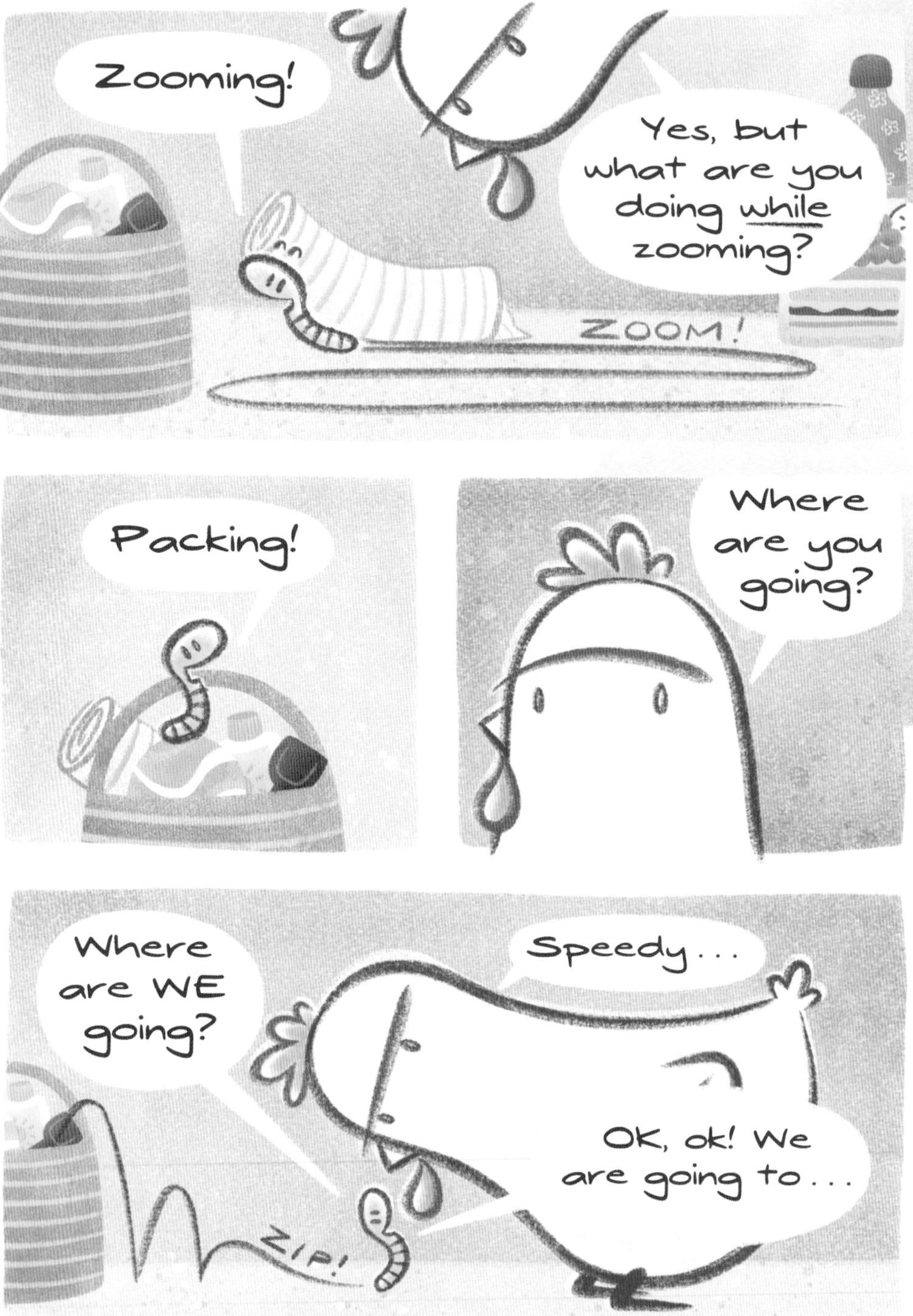
Zooming!
Yes, but what are you doing while zooming?
ZOOM!
Packing!
Where are you going?
Where are WE going?
Speedy . . .
OK, ok! We are going to . . .
ZIP!

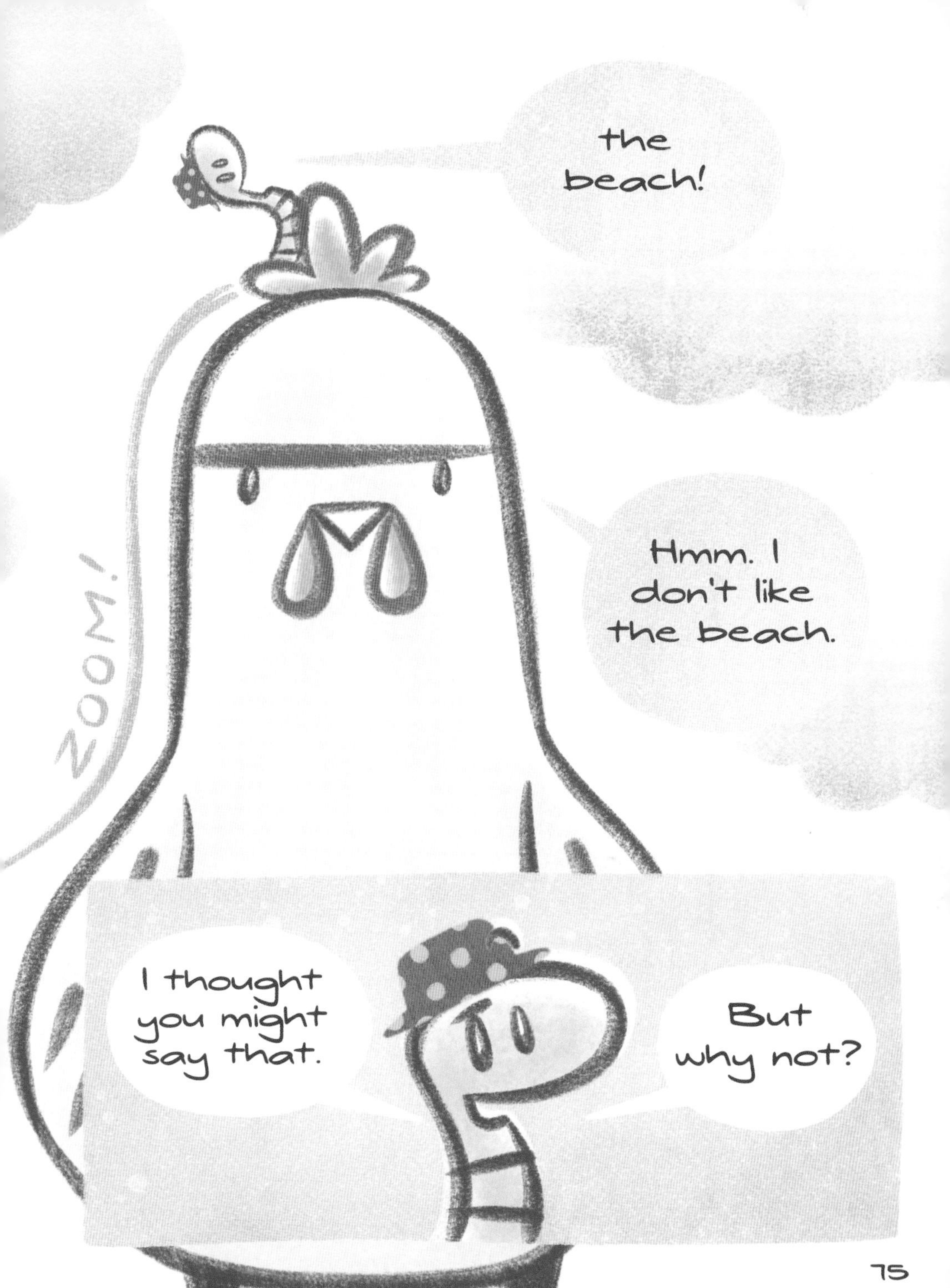
the beach!
ZOOM!
Hmm. I don't like the beach.
I thought you might say that.
But why not?

Why the Beach Makes Chicken Cranky

Crabs

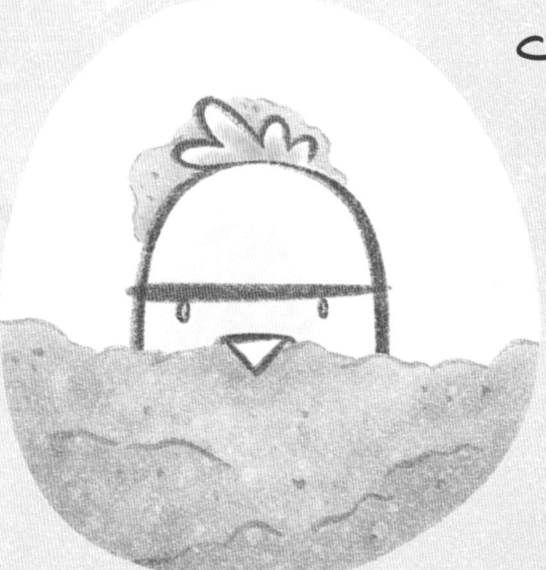

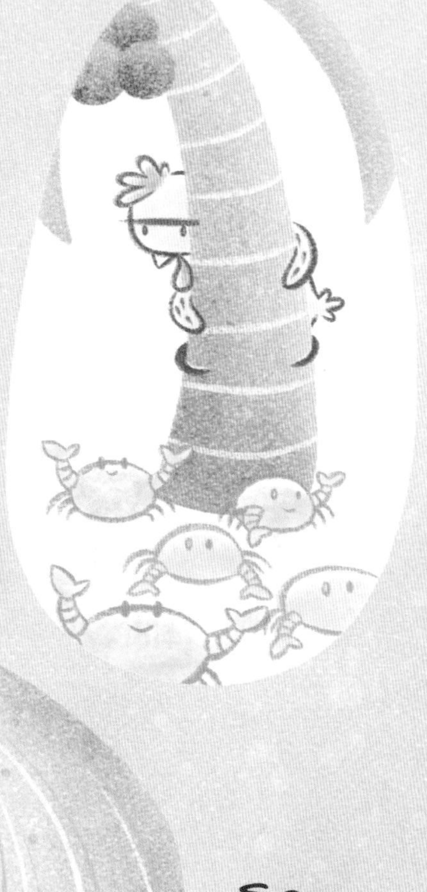

Too sandy

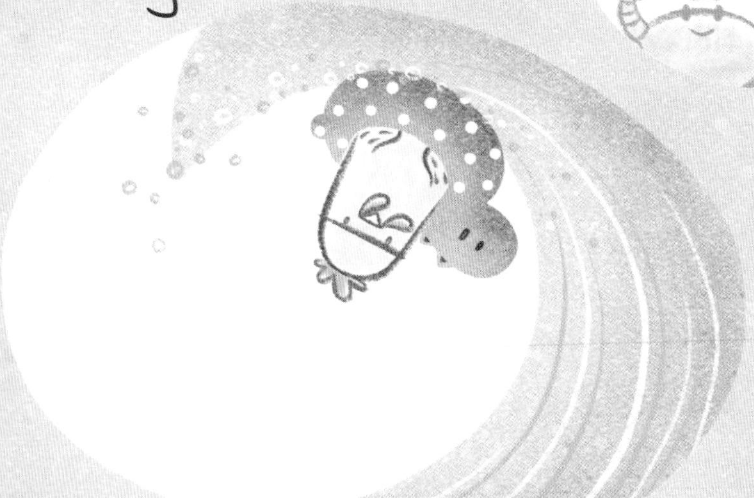

Sea too rough

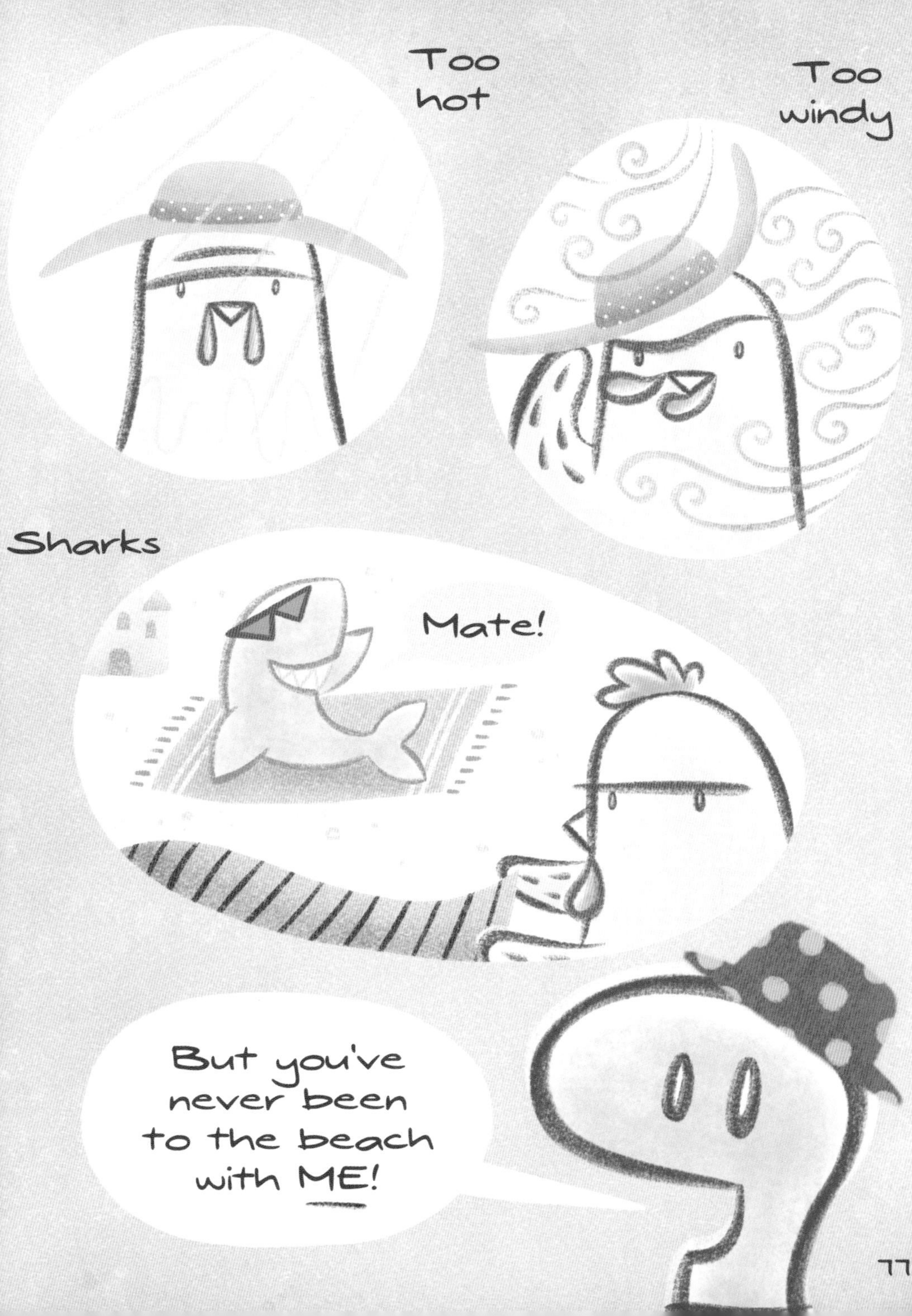
Too hot
Too windy
Sharks
Mate!
But you've never been to the beach with ME!

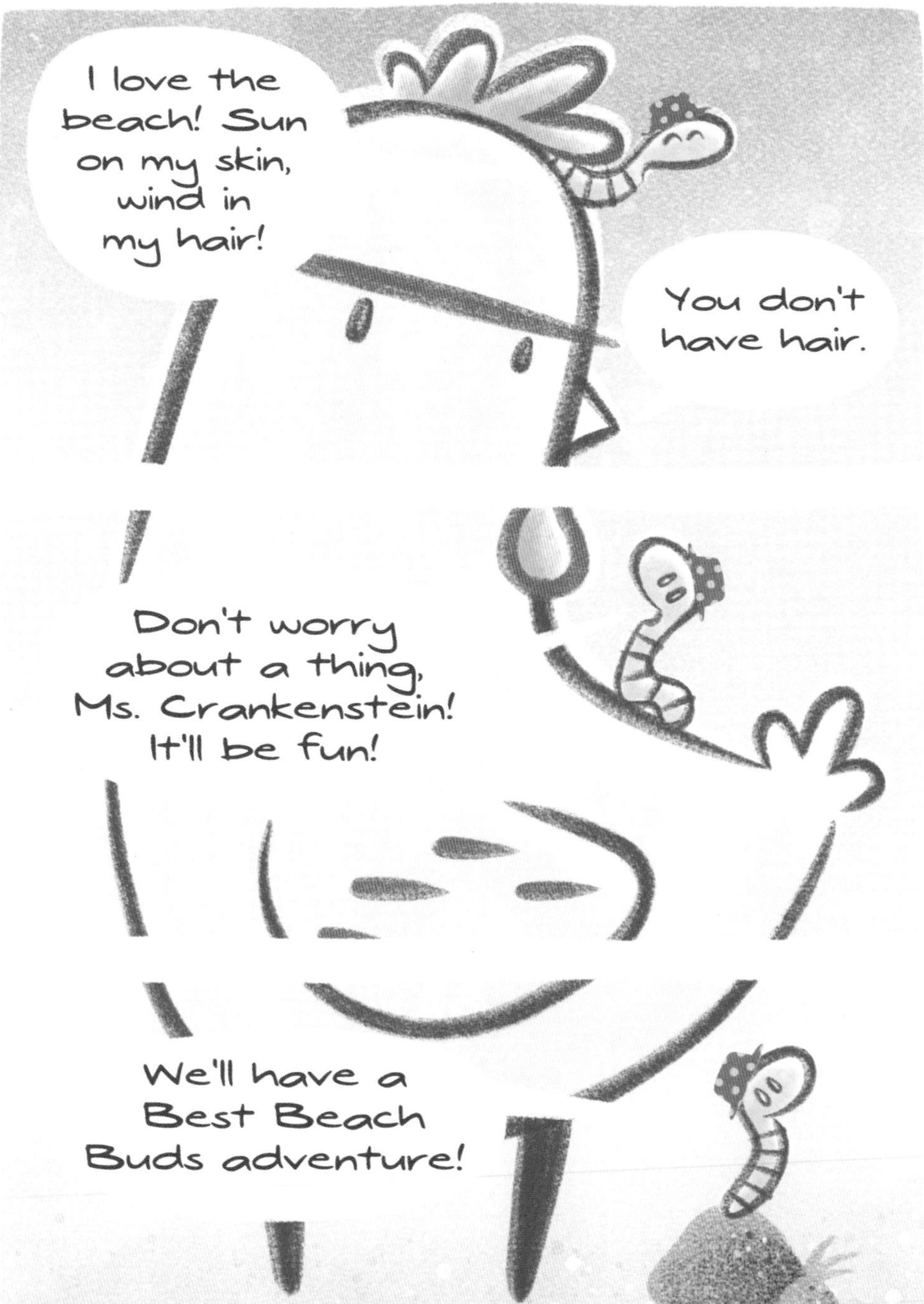
I love the beach! Sun on my skin, wind in my hair!
You don't have hair.
Don't worry about a thing, Ms. Crankenstein! It'll be fun!
We'll have a Best Beach Buds adventure!

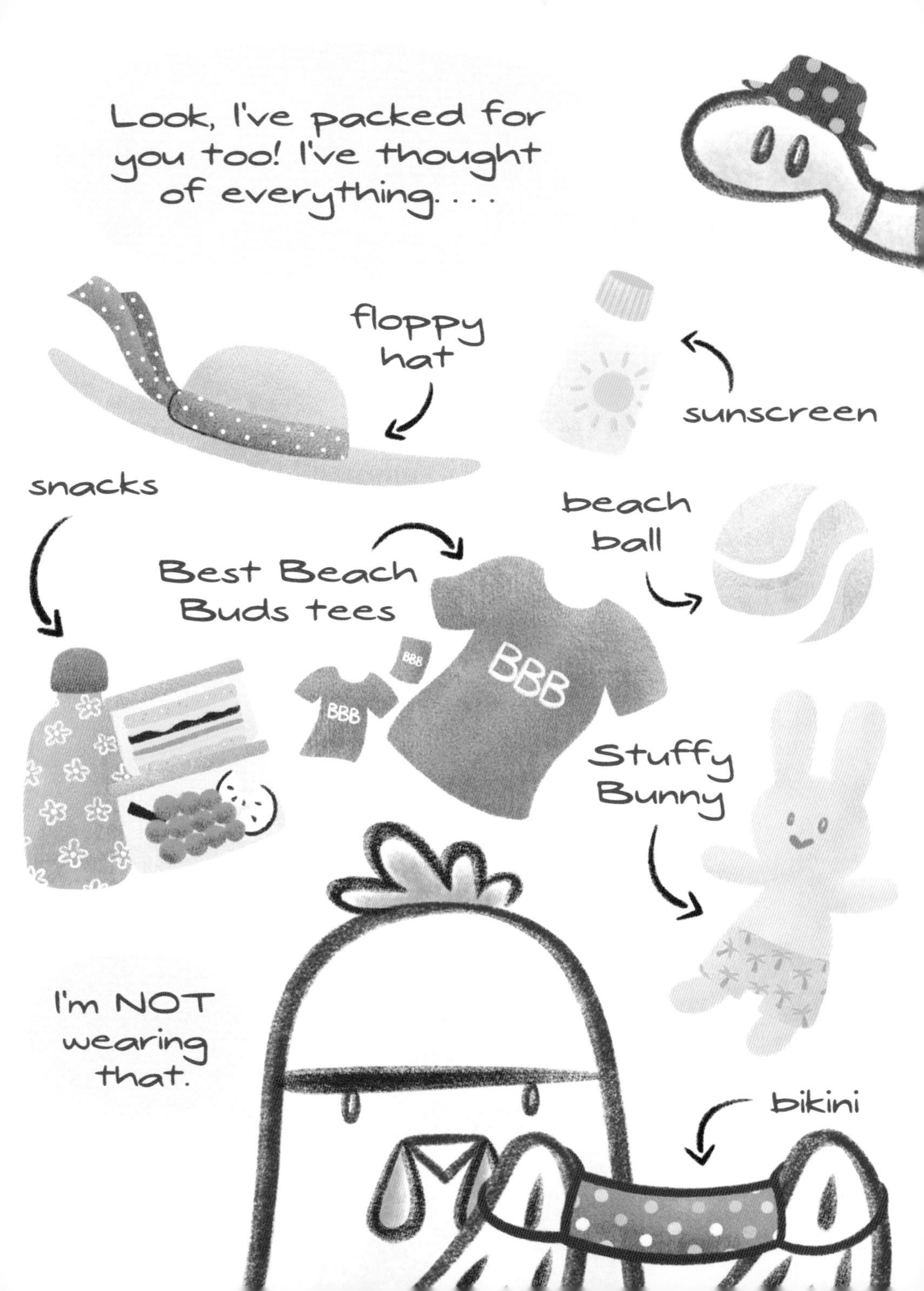
Look, I've packed for you too! I've thought of everything. . . .
floppy hat
sunscreen
snacks
beach ball
Best Beach Buds tees
BBB
BBB
BBB
Stuffy Bunny
I'm NOT wearing that.
bikini

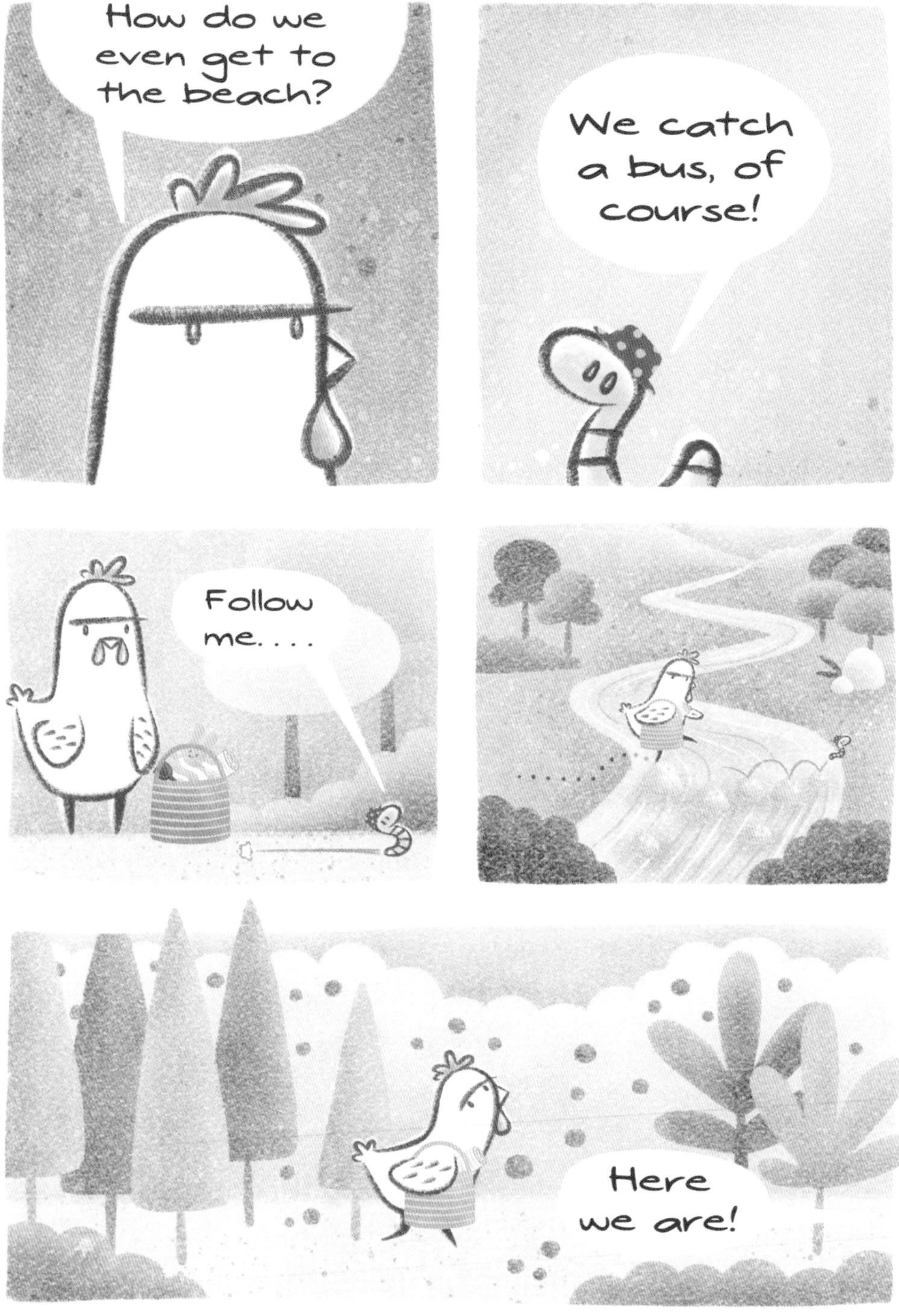
How do we even get to the beach?
We catch a bus, of course!
Follow me. . . .
Here we are!

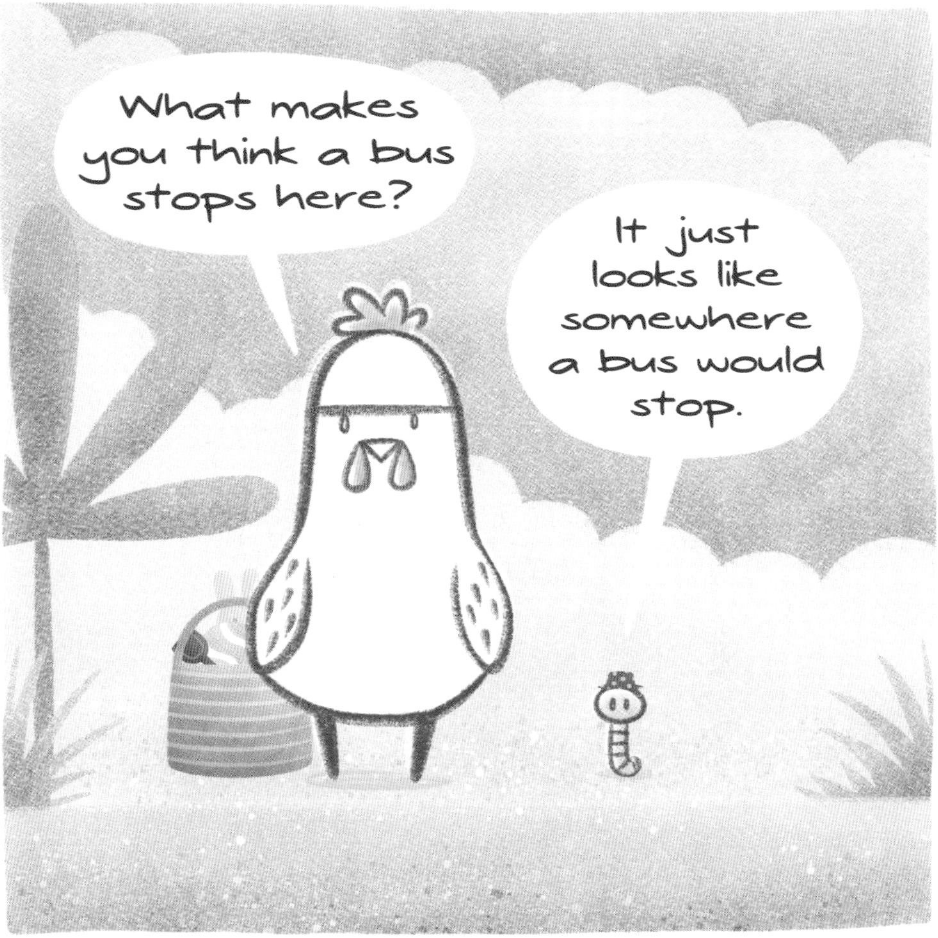
What makes you think a bus stops here?
It just looks like somewhere a bus would stop.

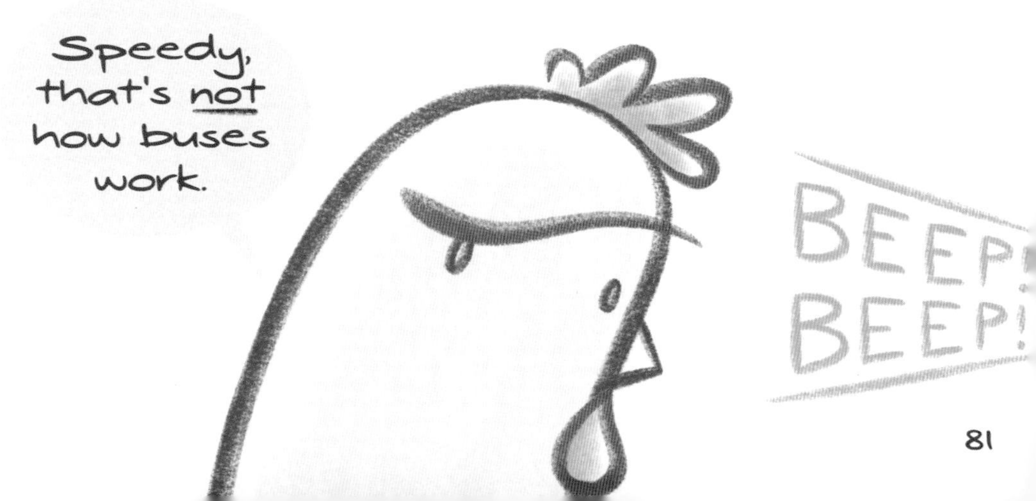
Speedy, that's not how buses work.
BEEP! BEEP!

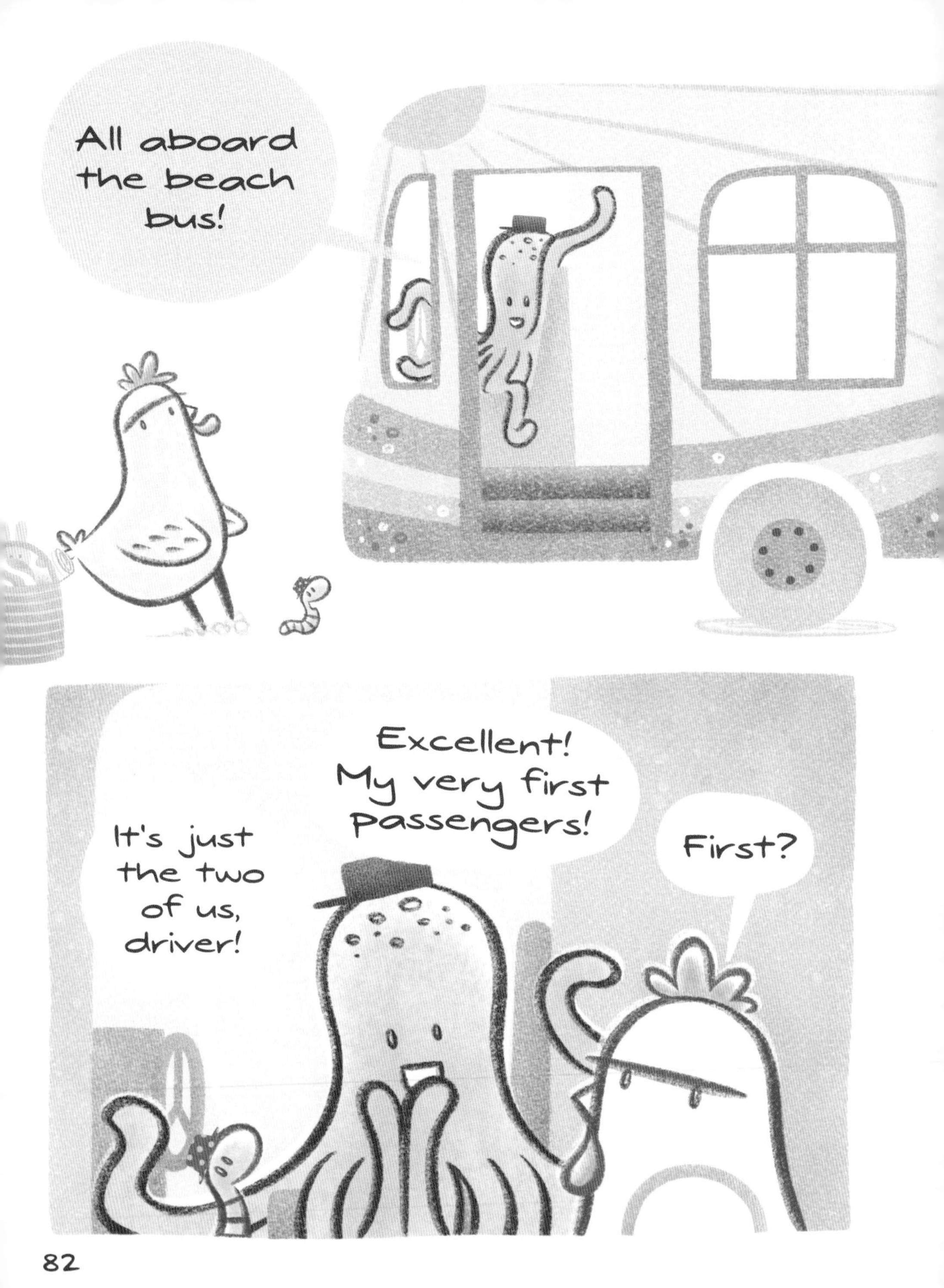
All aboard the beach bus!
Excellent! My very first passengers!
It's just the two of us, driver!
First?

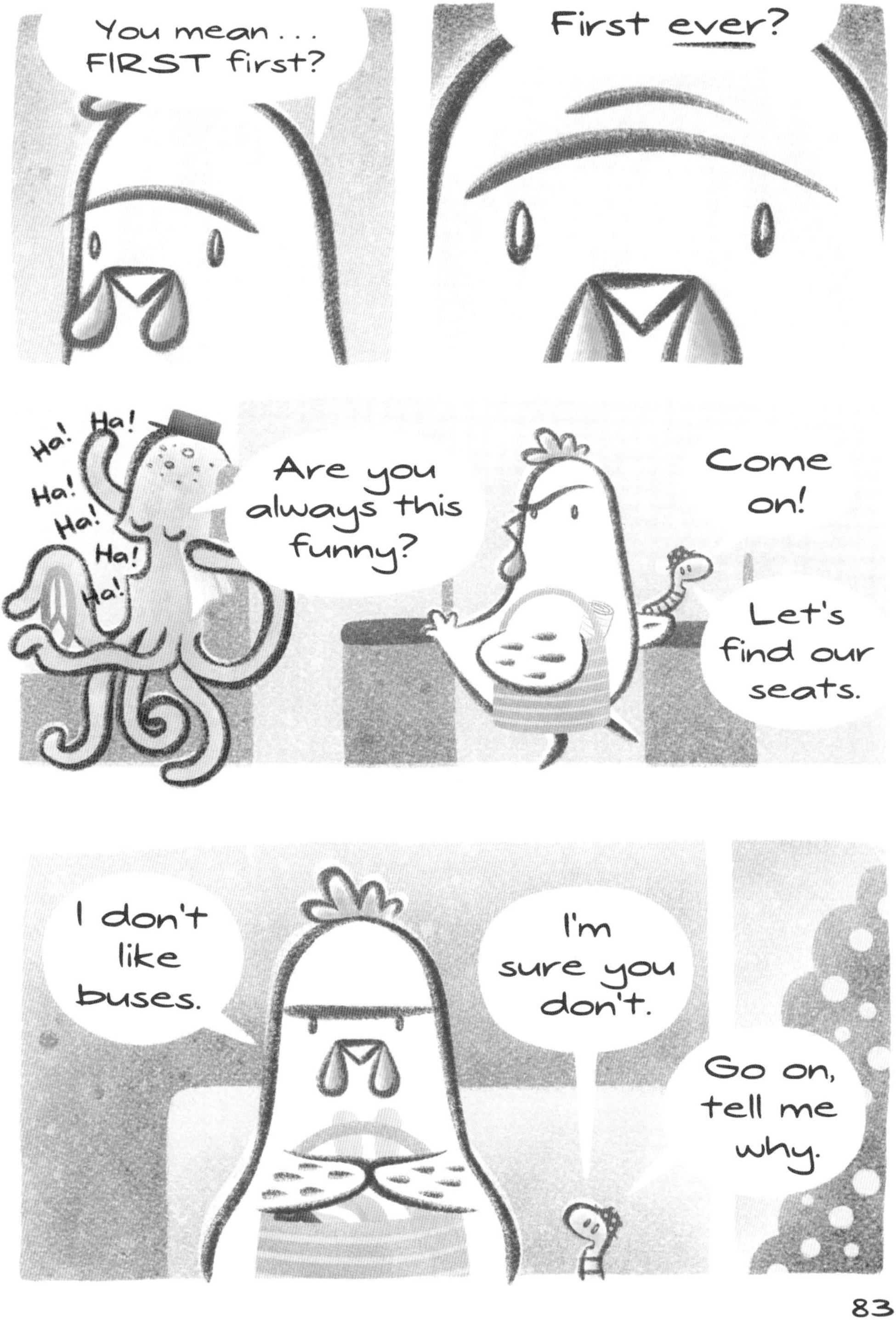

You mean . . . FIRST first?
First ever?
Ha! Ha! Ha! Ha! Ha! Ha!
Are you always this funny?
Come on!
Let's find our seats.
I don't like buses.
I'm sure you don't.
Go on, tell me why.

WHY BUSES MAKE CHICKEN CRANKY

Seats too hard

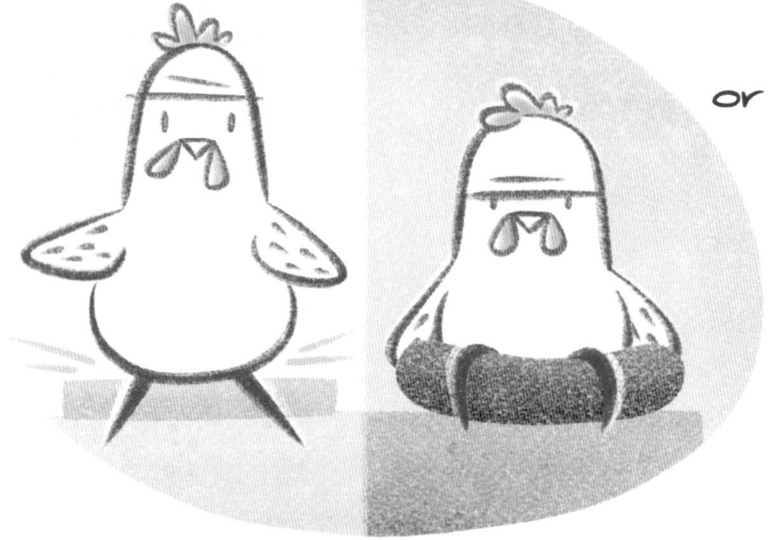

or soft

No personal space

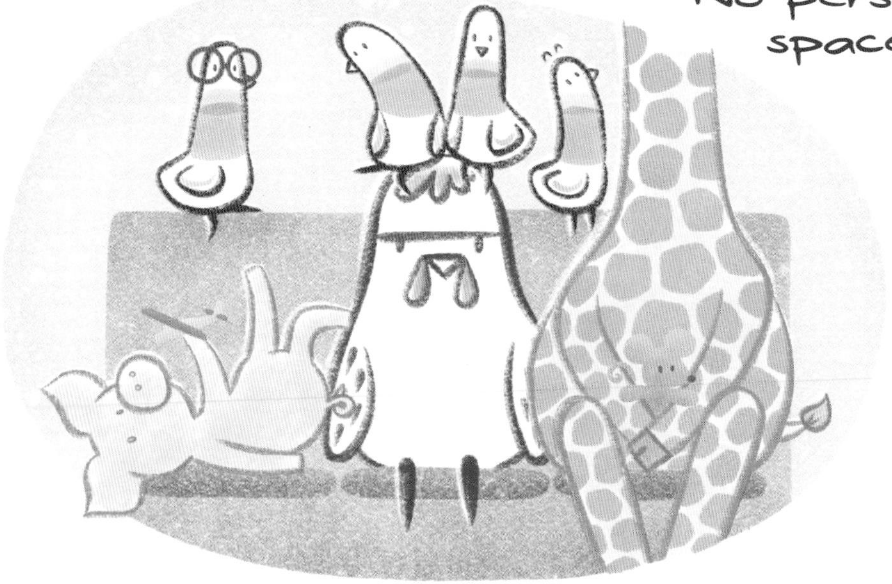

Roads too bumpy

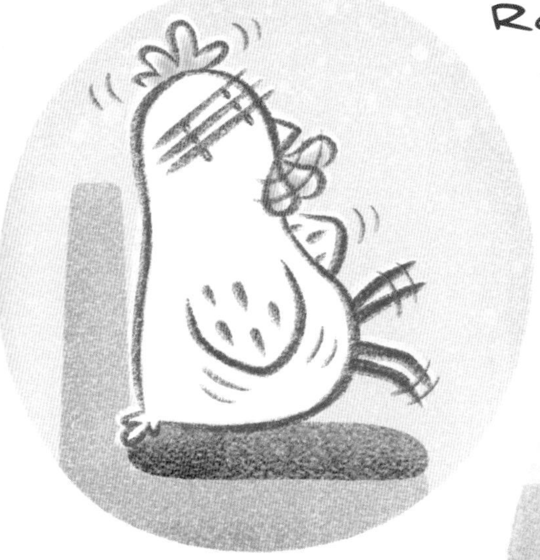

or bendy

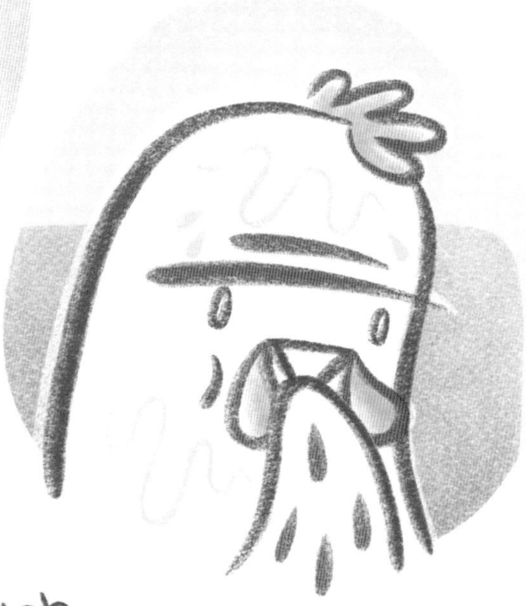

Chatty passengers

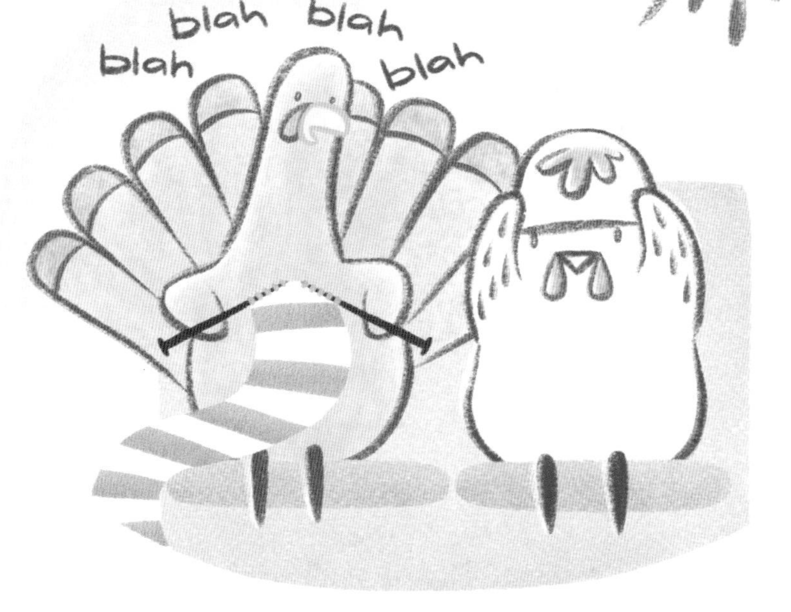
blah blah
blah
blah

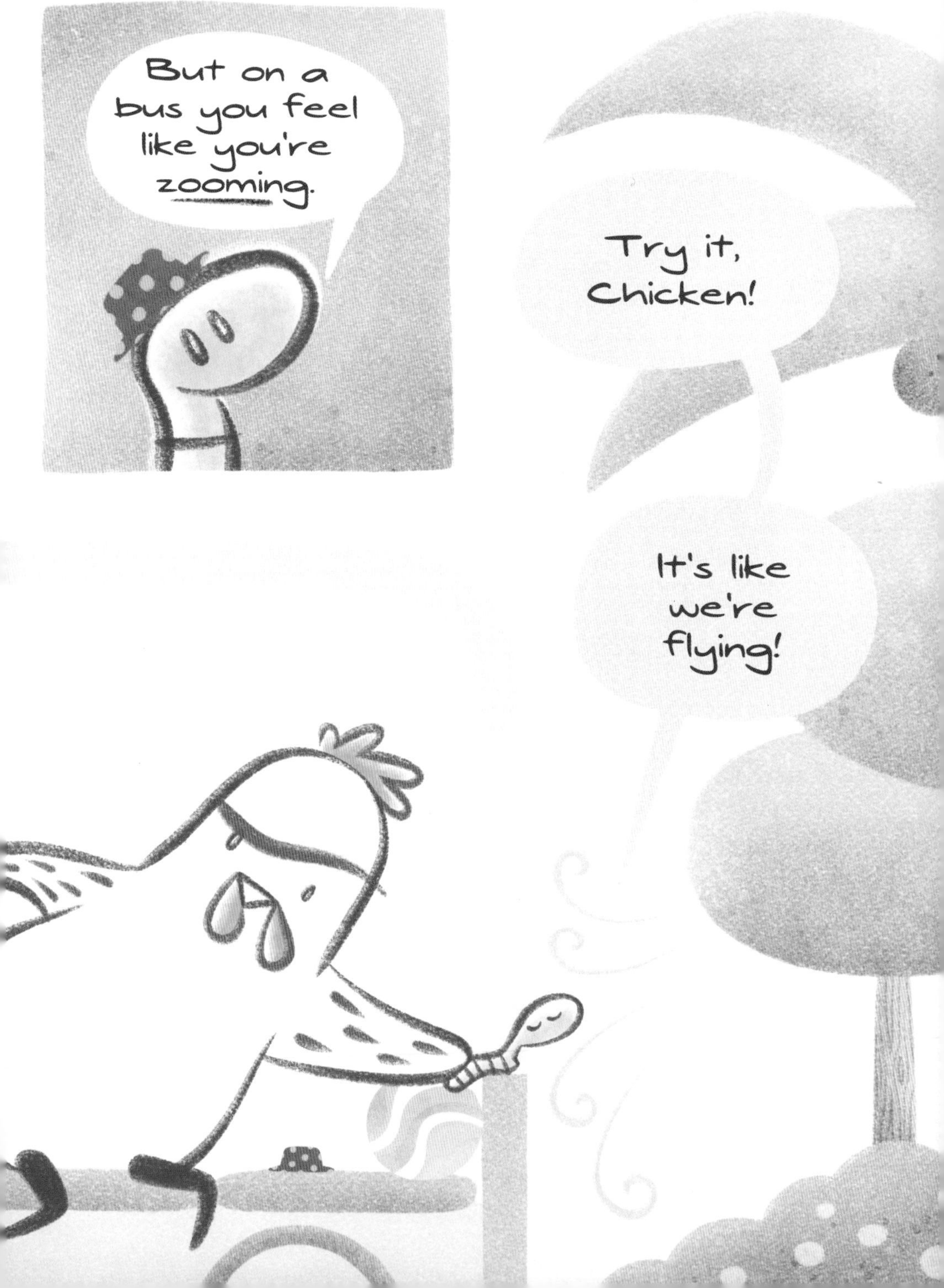

But on a bus you feel like you're zooming.
Try it, Chicken!
It's like we're flying!

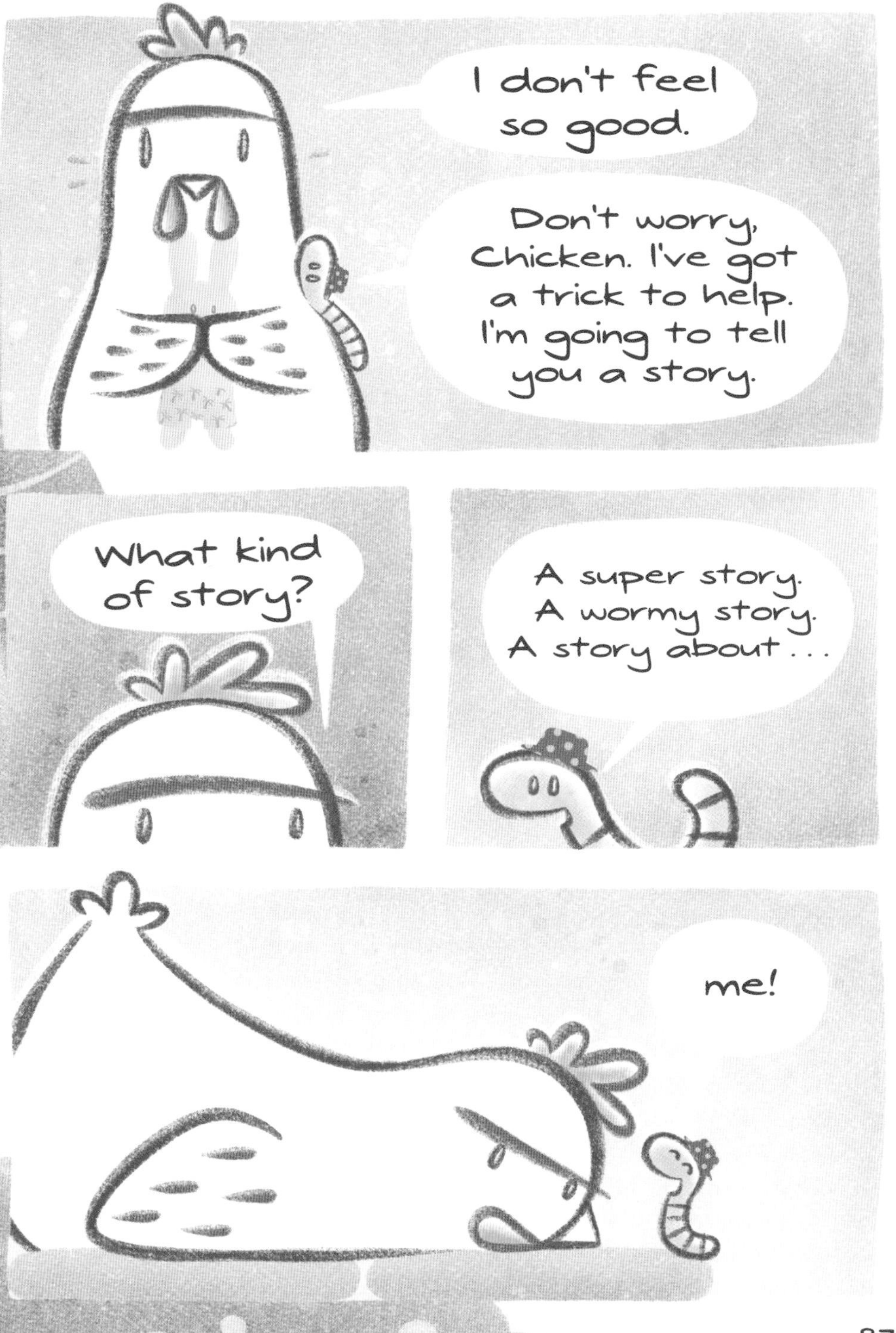

I don't feel so good.
Don't worry, Chicken. I've got a trick to help. I'm going to tell you a story.
What kind of story?
A super story. A wormy story. A story about . . .
me!

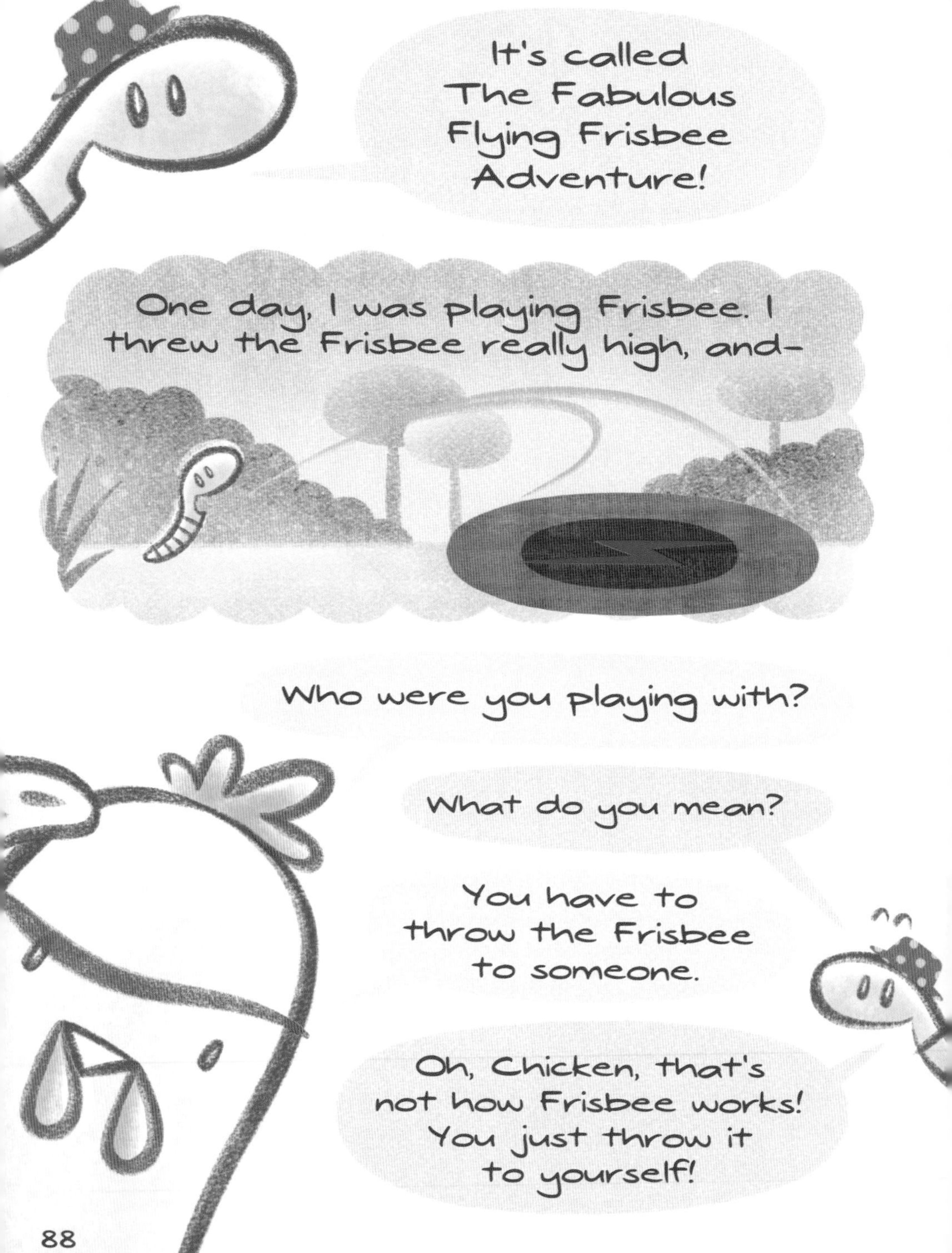
It's called The Fabulous Flying Frisbee Adventure!
One day, I was playing Frisbee. I threw the Frisbee really high, and–
Who were you playing with?
What do you mean?
You have to throw the Frisbee to someone.
Oh, Chicken, that's not how Frisbee works! You just throw it to yourself!

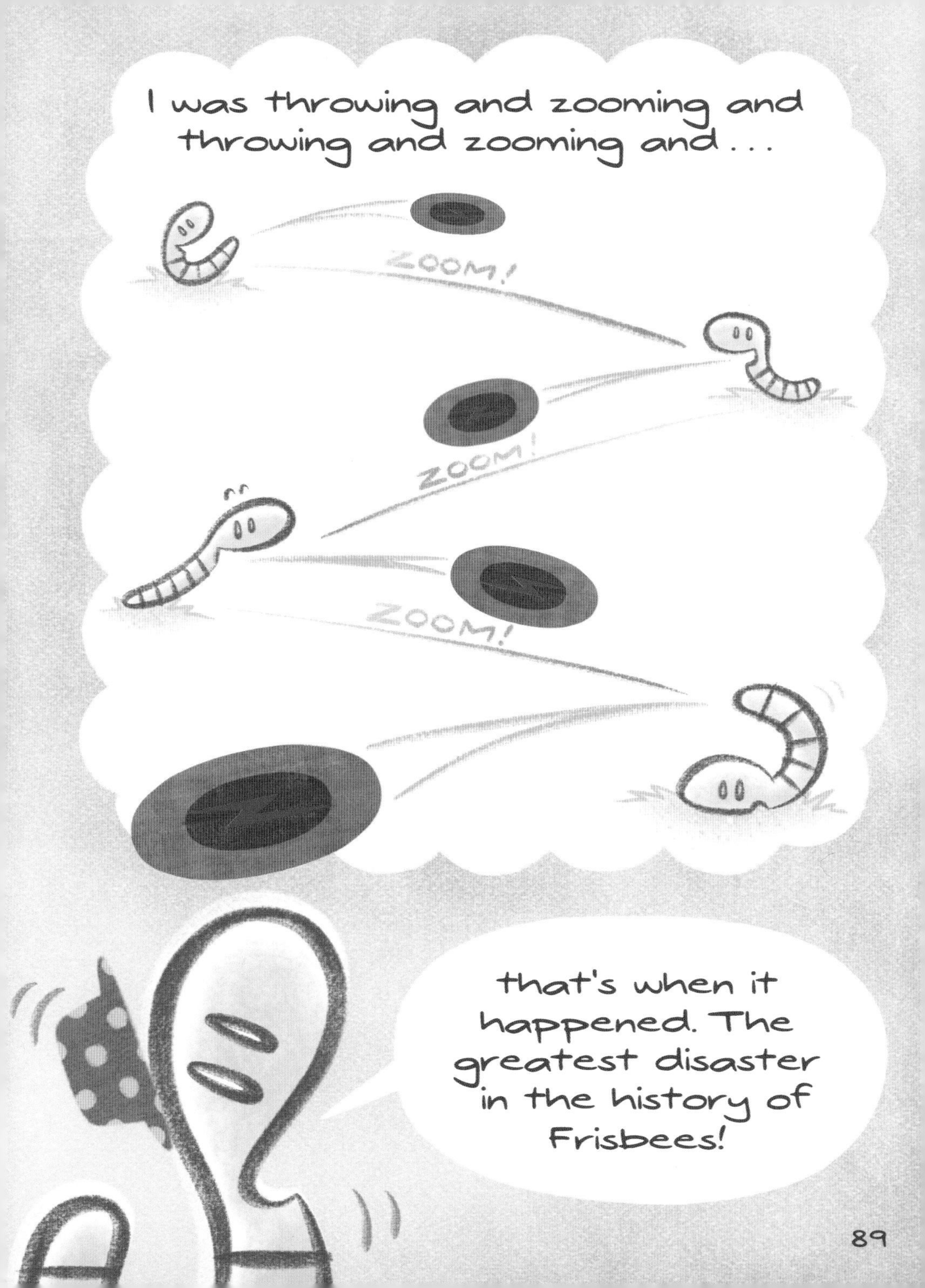
I was throwing and zooming and throwing and zooming and . . .
ZOOM!
ZOOM!
ZOOM!
that's when it happened. The greatest disaster in the history of Frisbees!

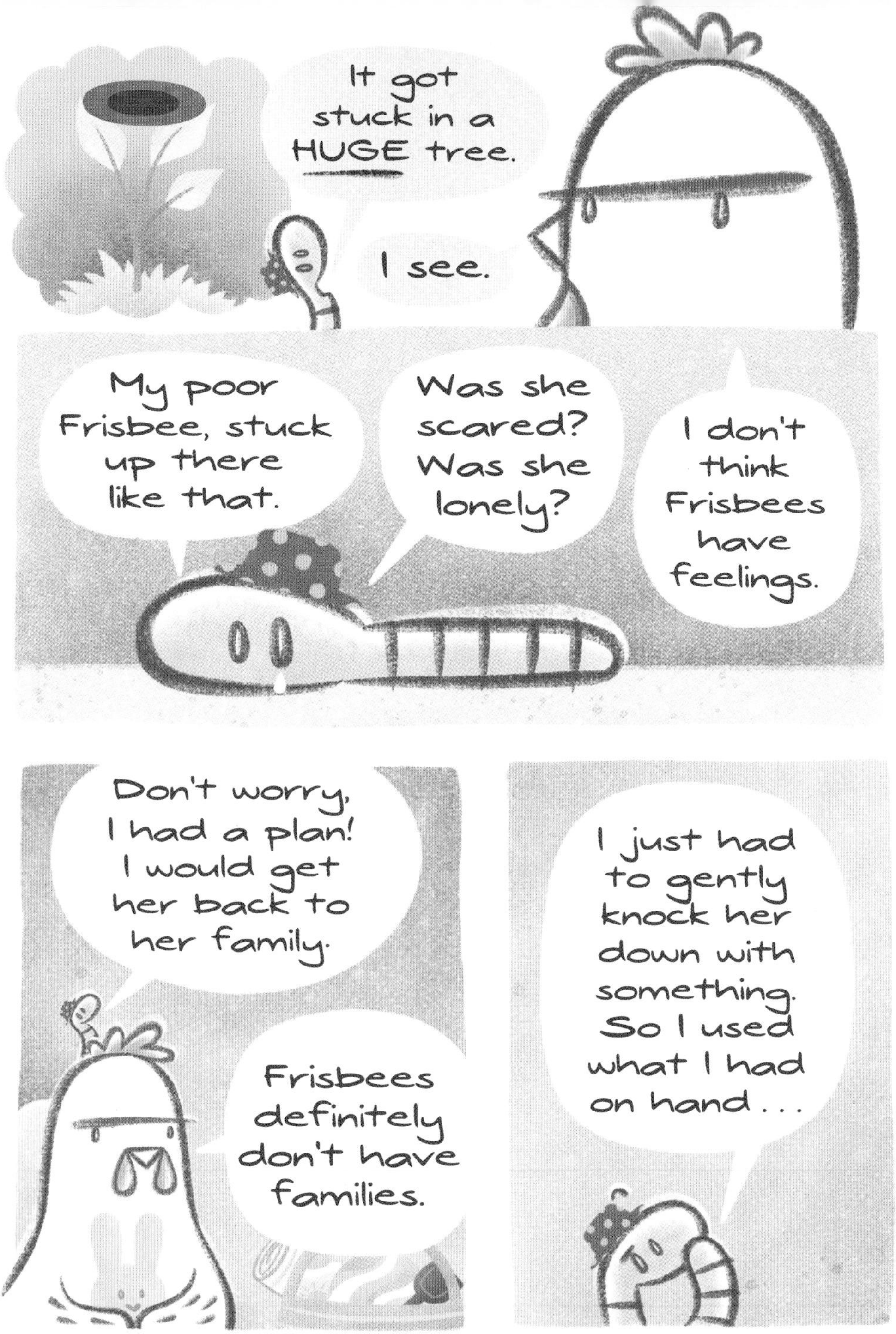
It got stuck in a HUGE tree.
I see.
My poor Frisbee, stuck up there like that.
Was she scared? Was she lonely?
I don't think Frisbees have feelings.
Don't worry, I had a plan! I would get her back to her family.
Frisbees definitely don't have families.
I just had to gently knock her down with something. So I used what I had on hand . . .

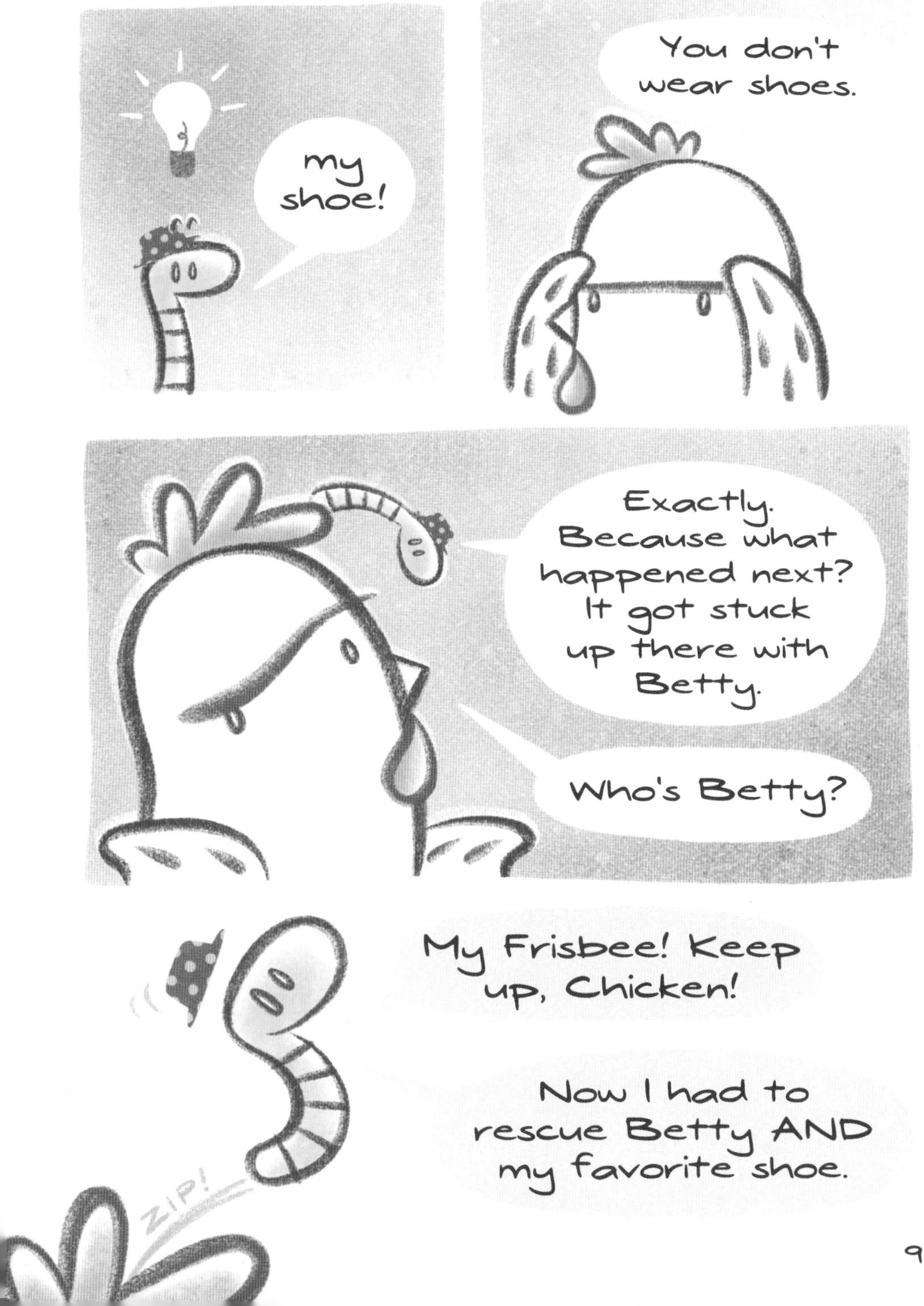
my shoe!
You don't wear shoes.
Exactly. Because what happened next? It got stuck up there with Betty.
Who's Betty?
My Frisbee! Keep up, Chicken!
Now I had to rescue Betty AND my favorite shoe.
ZIP!

So I started throwing everything I could find.

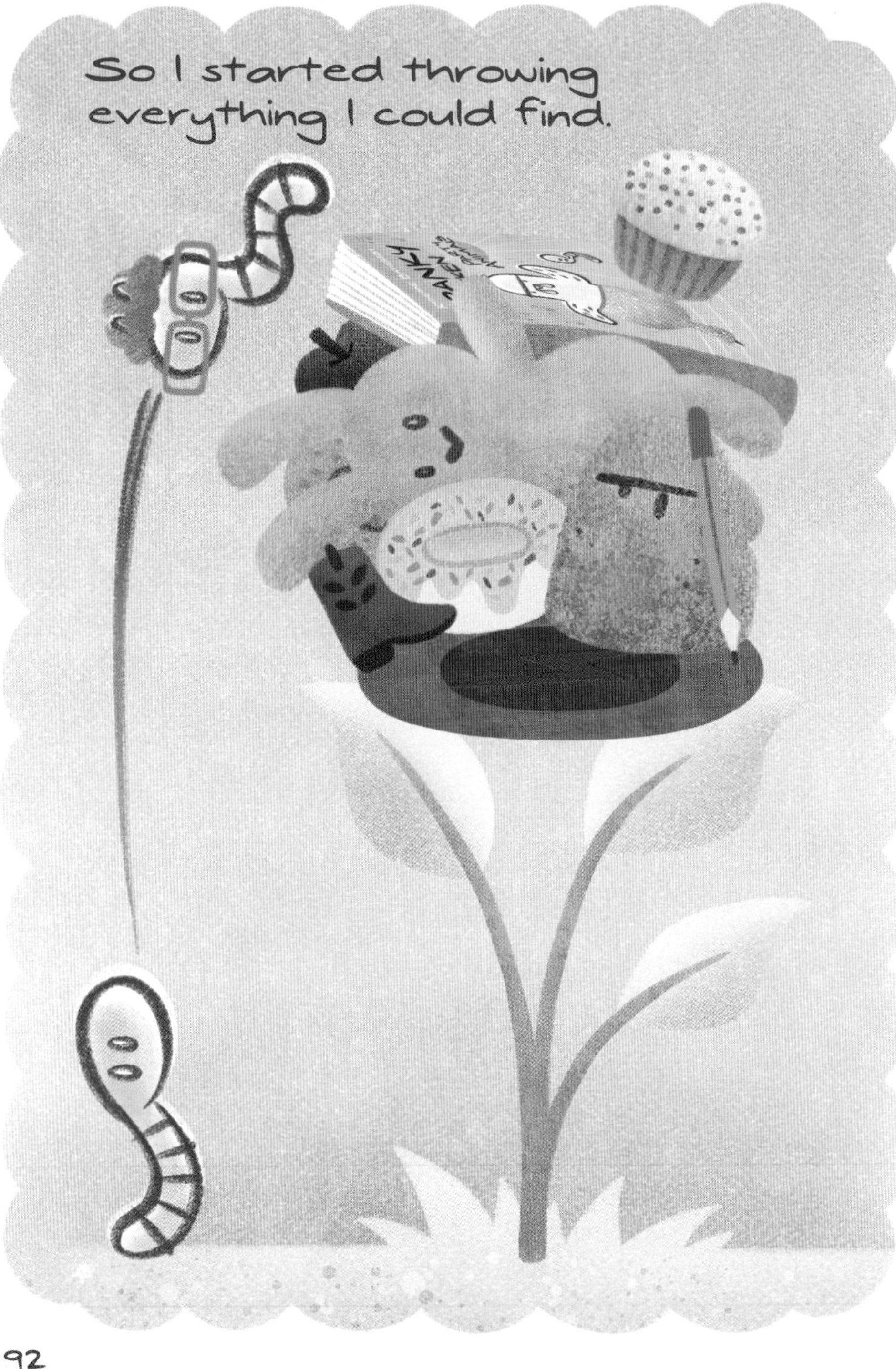

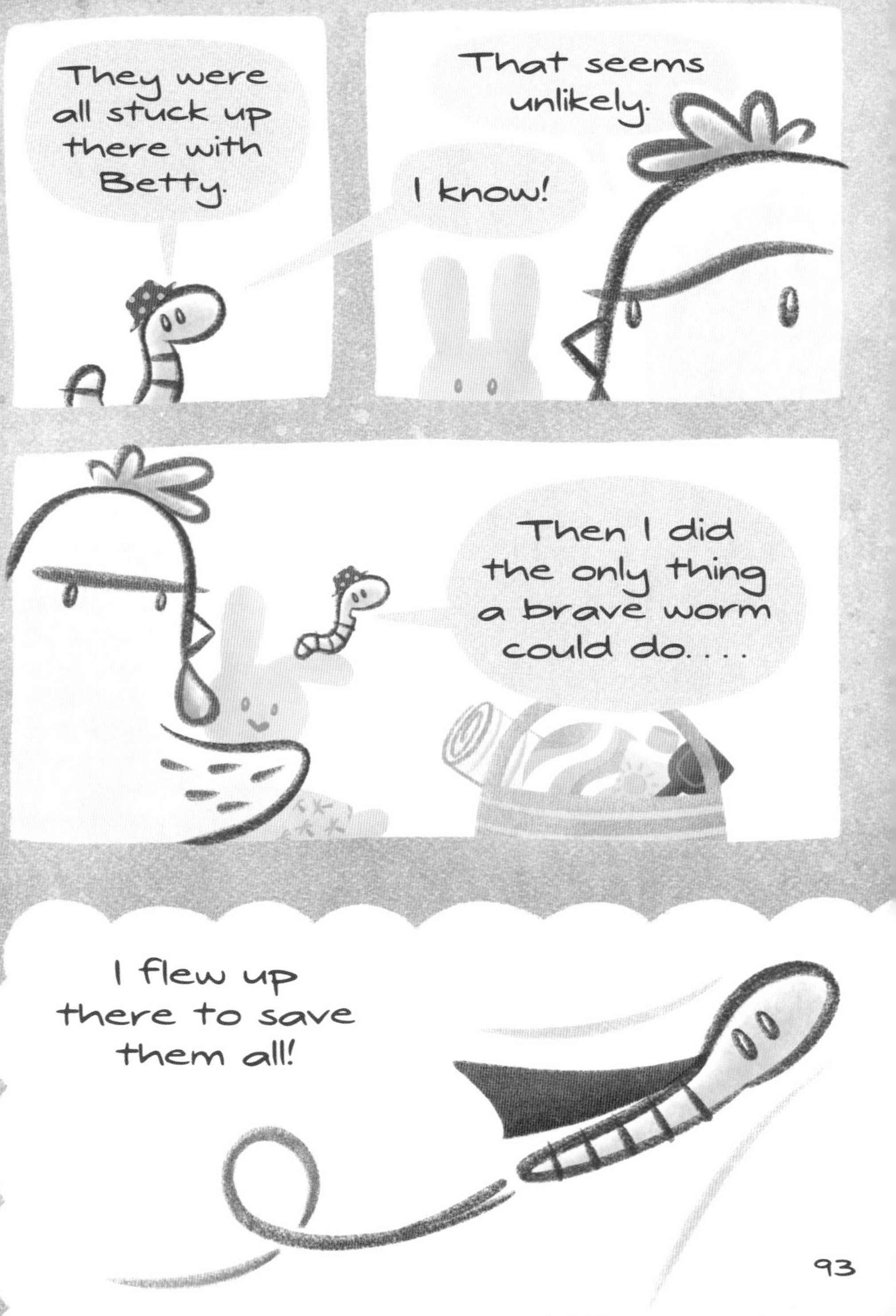
They were all stuck up there with Betty.
That seems unlikely.
I know!
Then I did the only thing a brave worm could do. . . .
I flew up there to save them all!

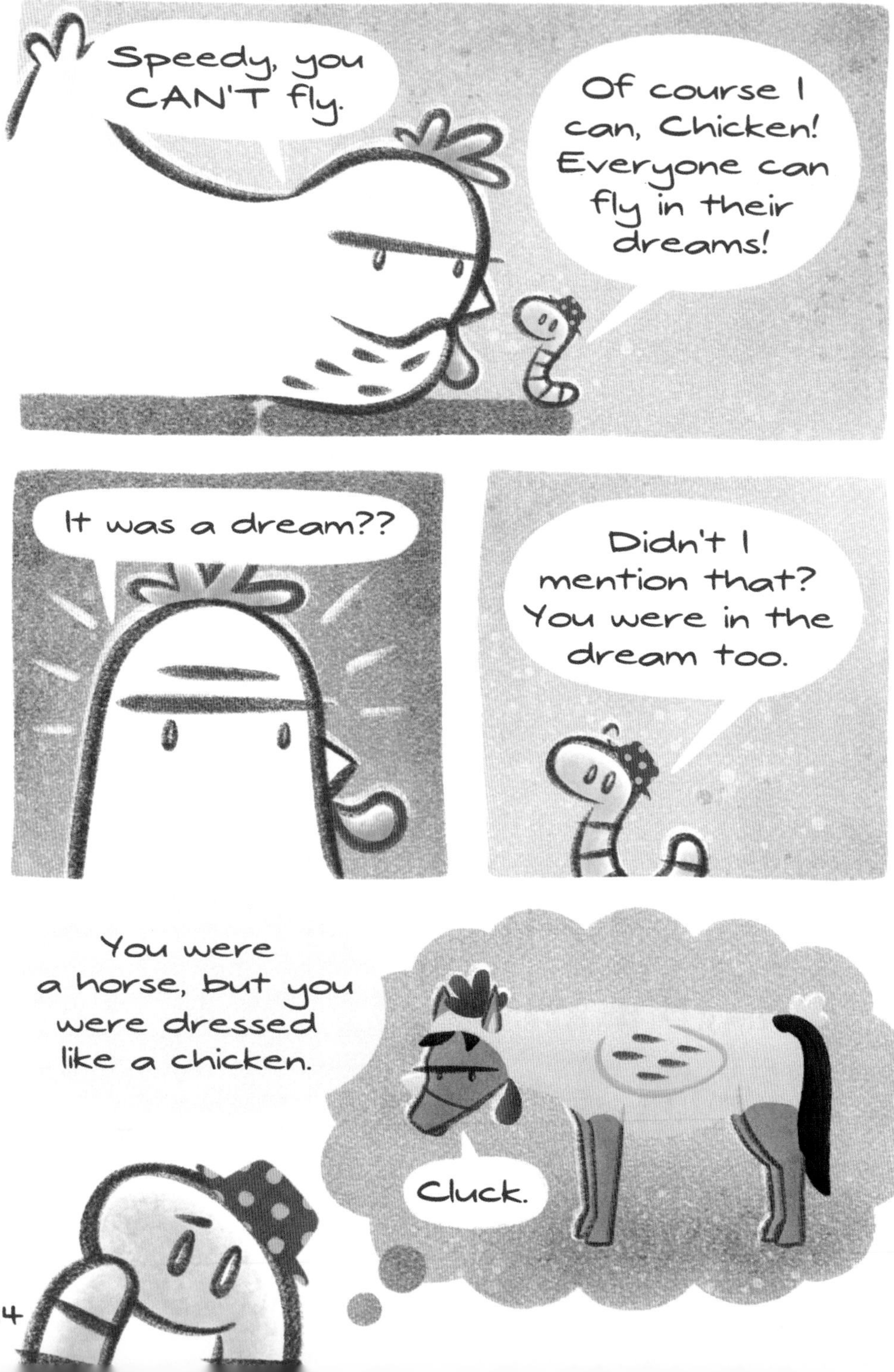
Speedy, you CAN'T fly.
Of course I can, Chicken! Everyone can fly in their dreams!
It was a dream??
Didn't I mention that? You were in the dream too.
You were a horse, but you were dressed like a chicken.
Cluck.

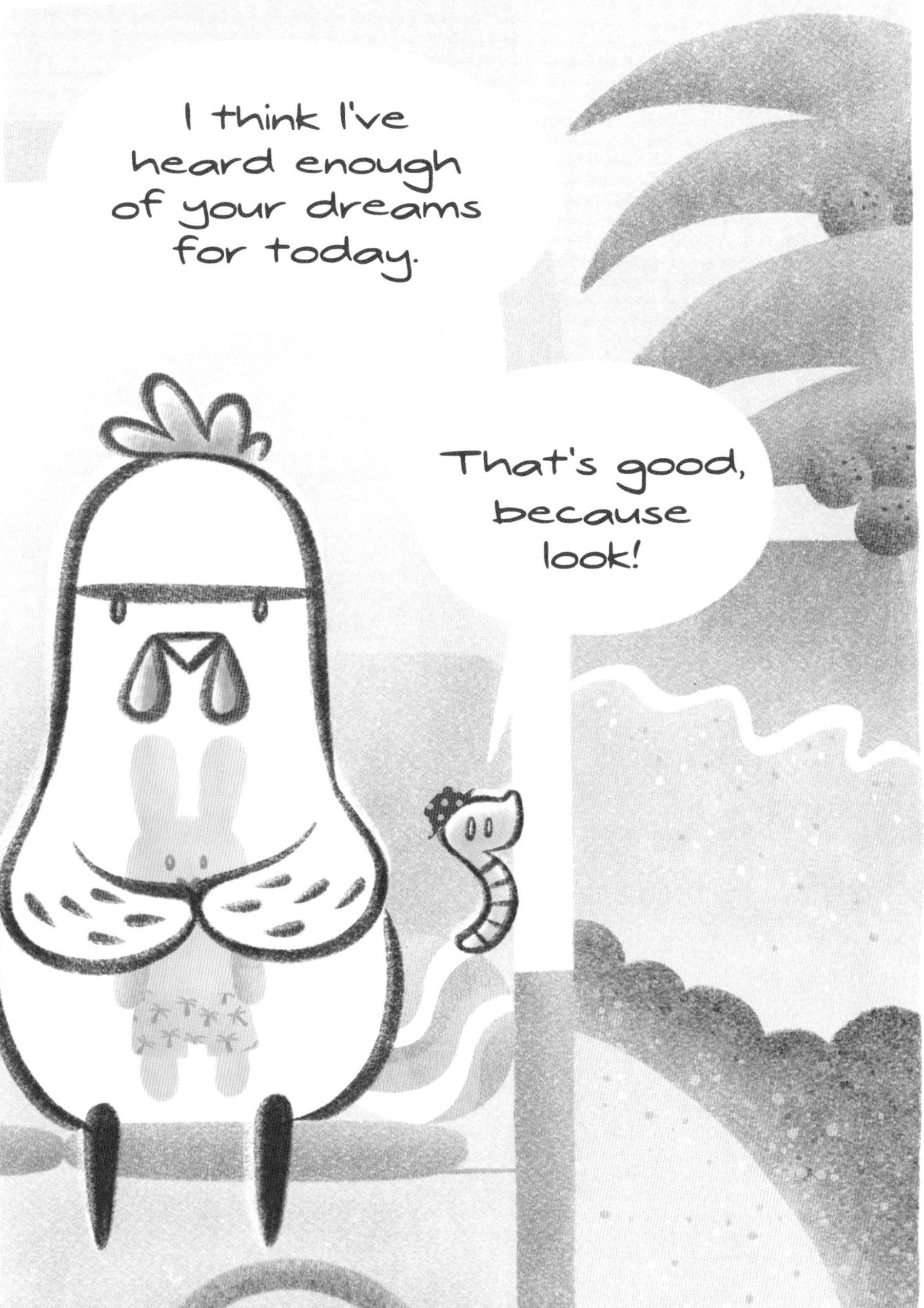
I think I've heard enough of your dreams for today.
That's good, because look!

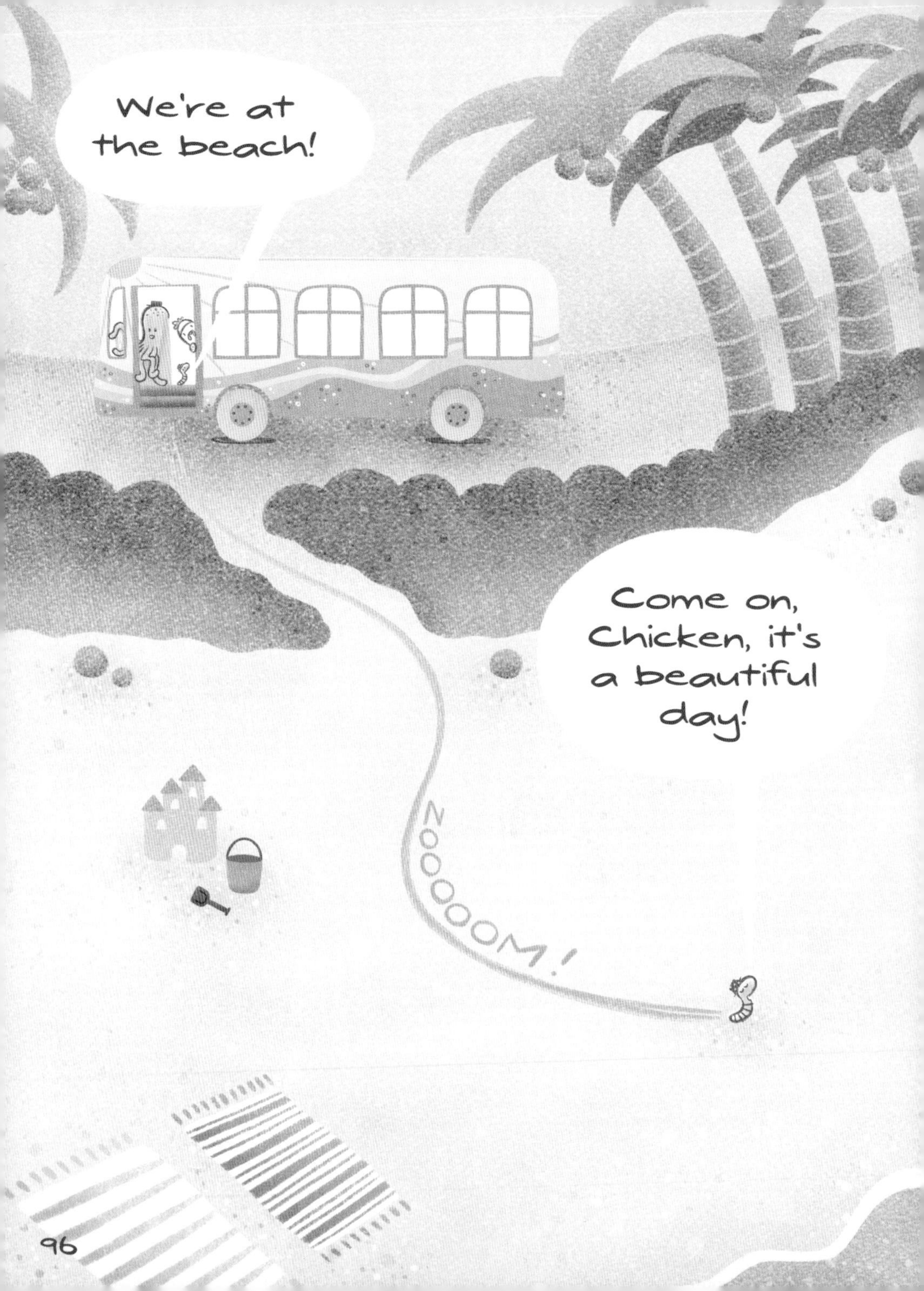
We're at the beach!
Come on, Chicken, it's a beautiful day!
NOOOOOM!

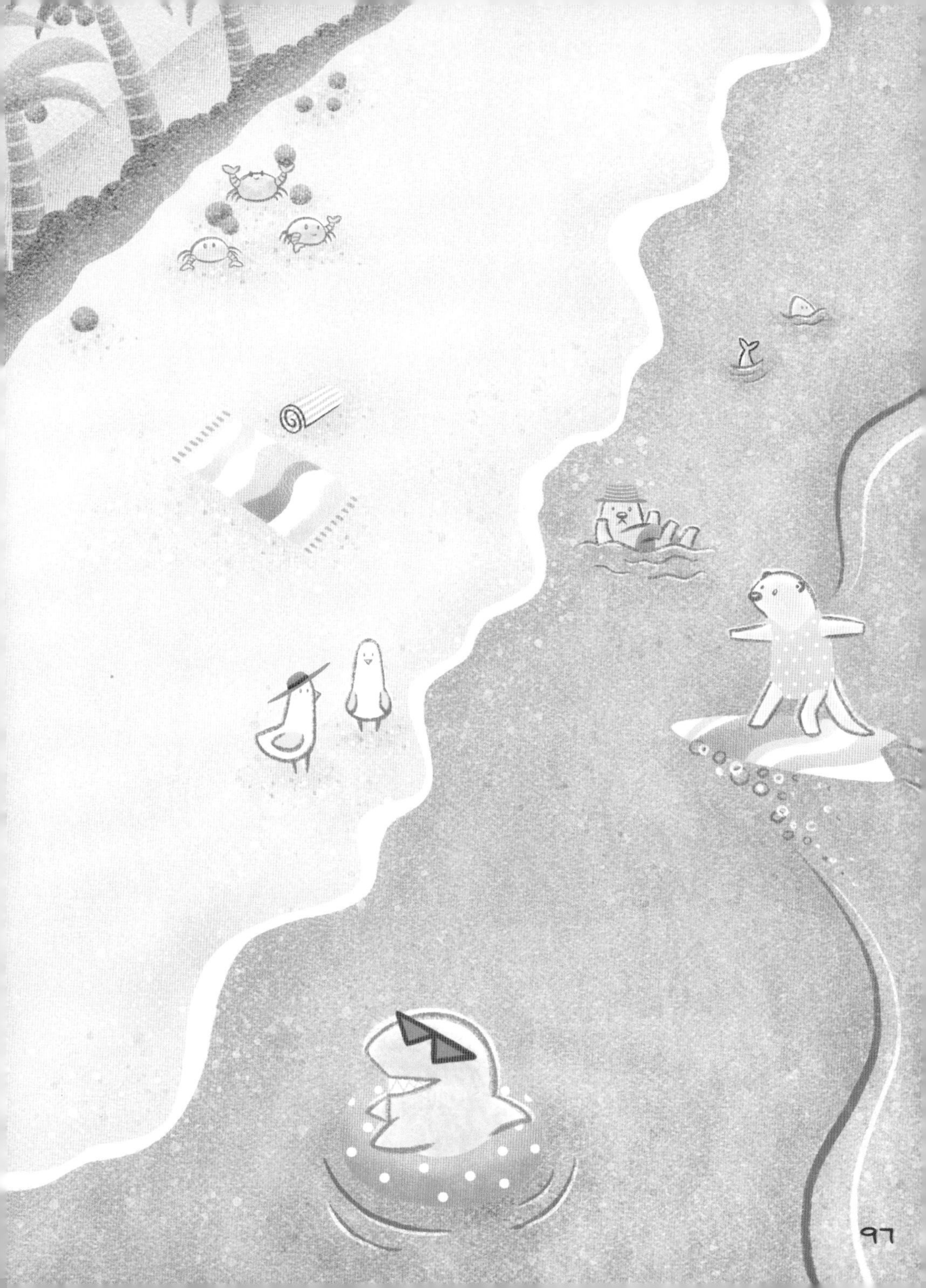

HOW TO HAVE A BEST BEACH BUDS ADVENTURE

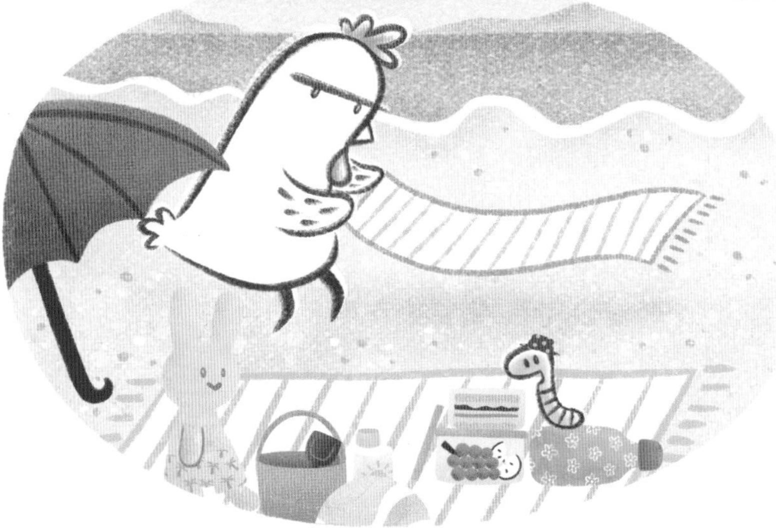

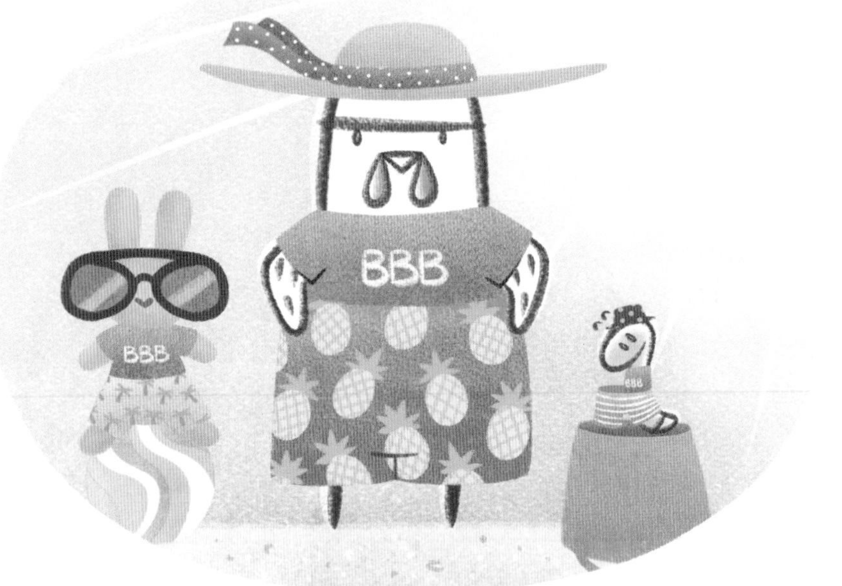
BBB
BBB
BBB

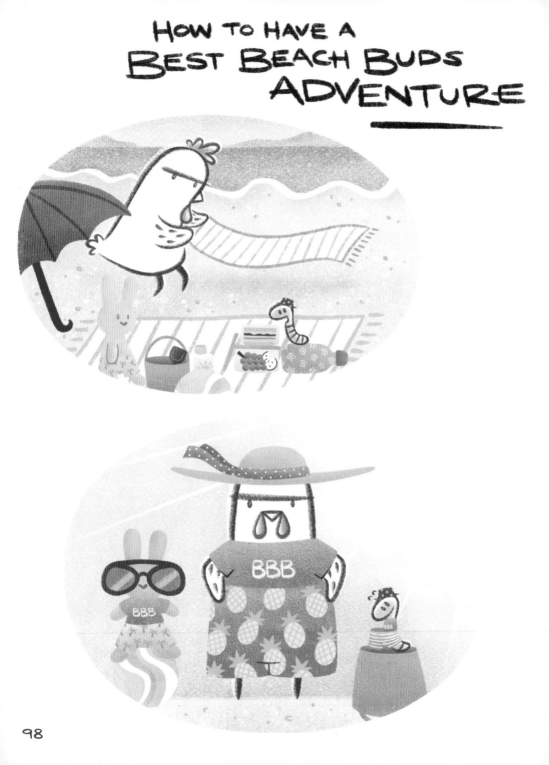

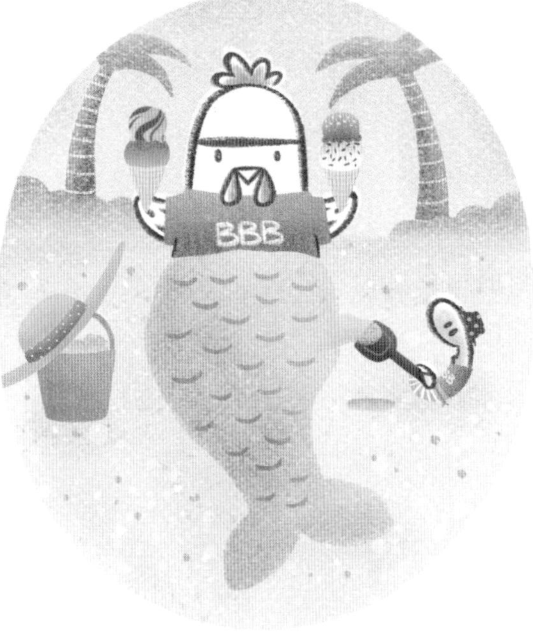
BBB
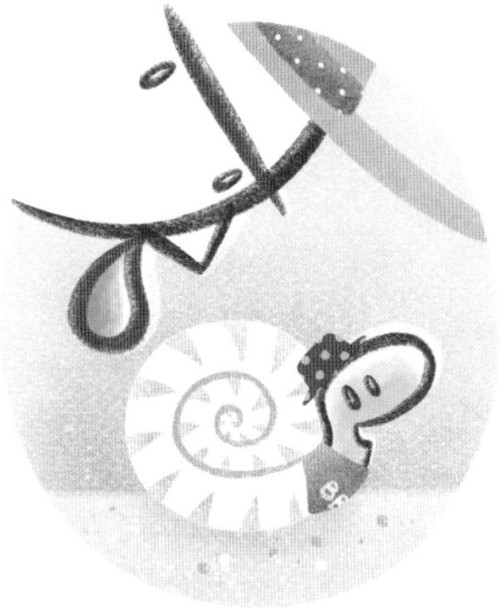
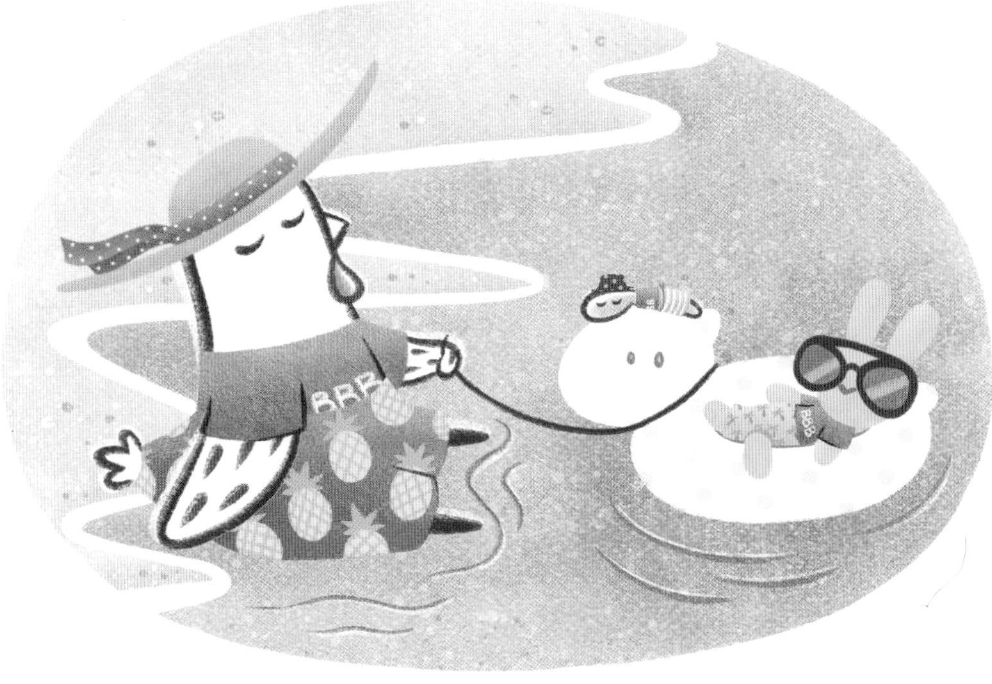
BBB
BBB

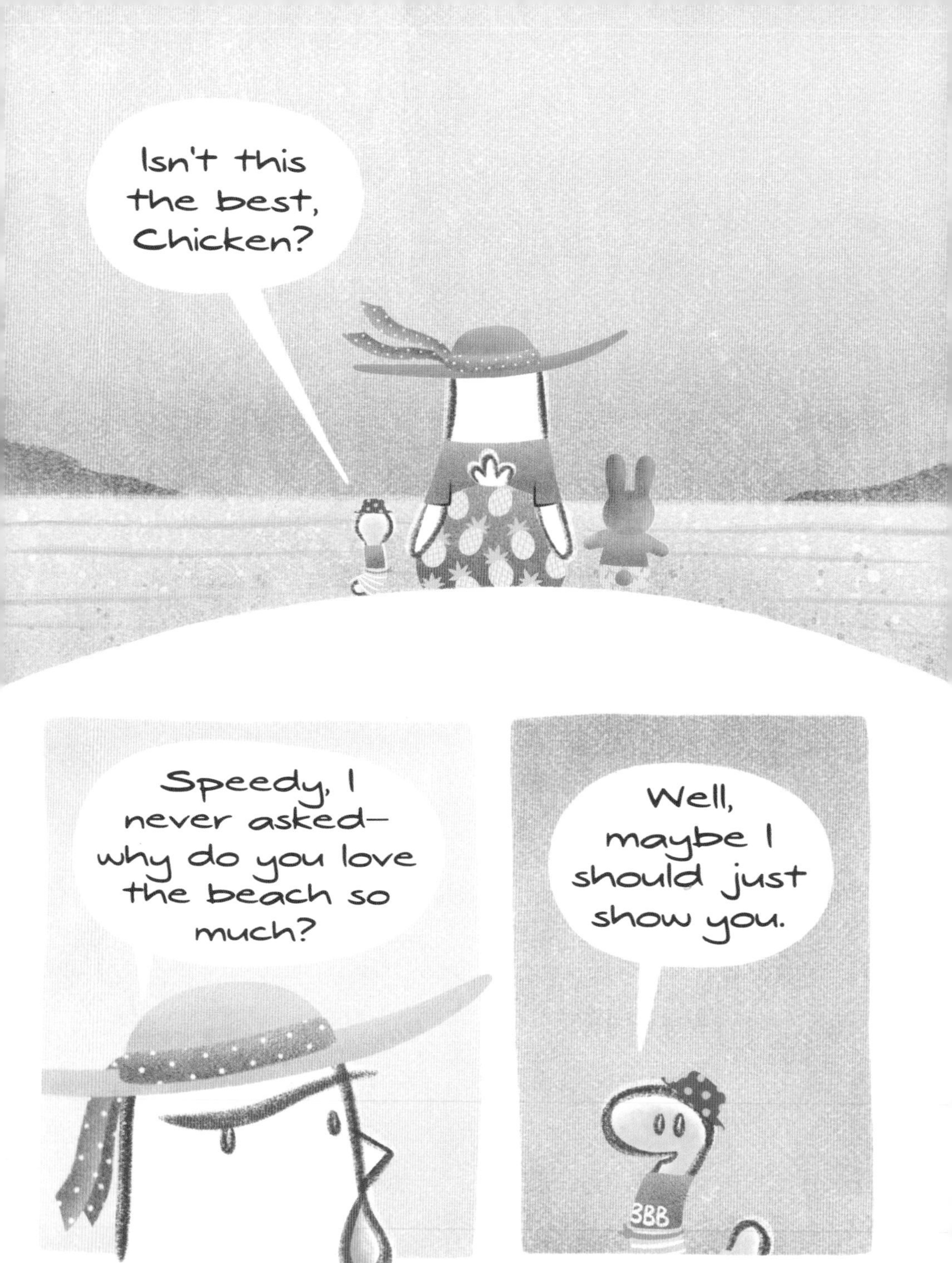
Isn't this the best, Chicken?
Speedy, I never asked— why do you love the beach so much?
Well, maybe I should just show you.
3BB

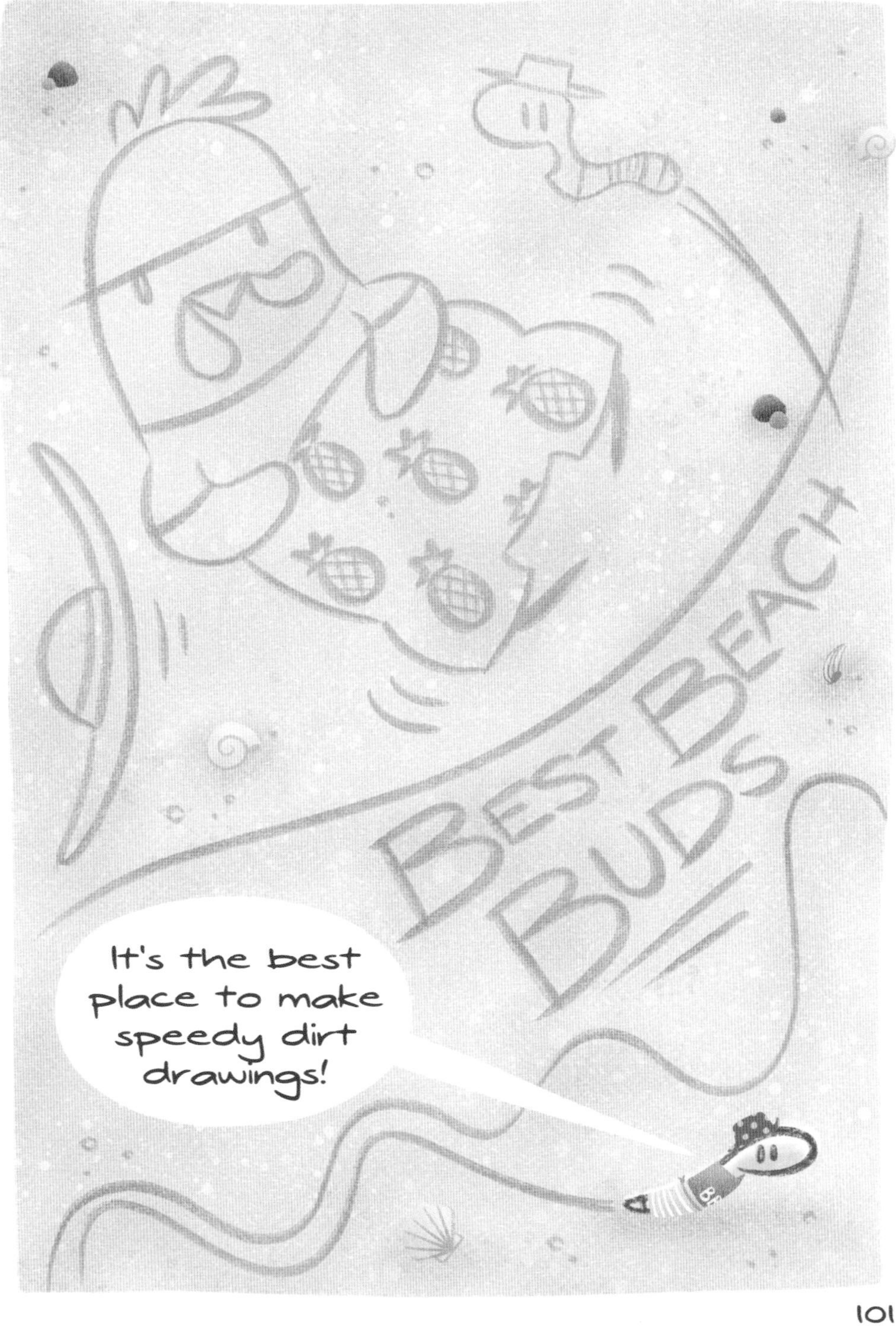
BEST BEACH BUDS
It's the best place to make speedy dirt drawings!

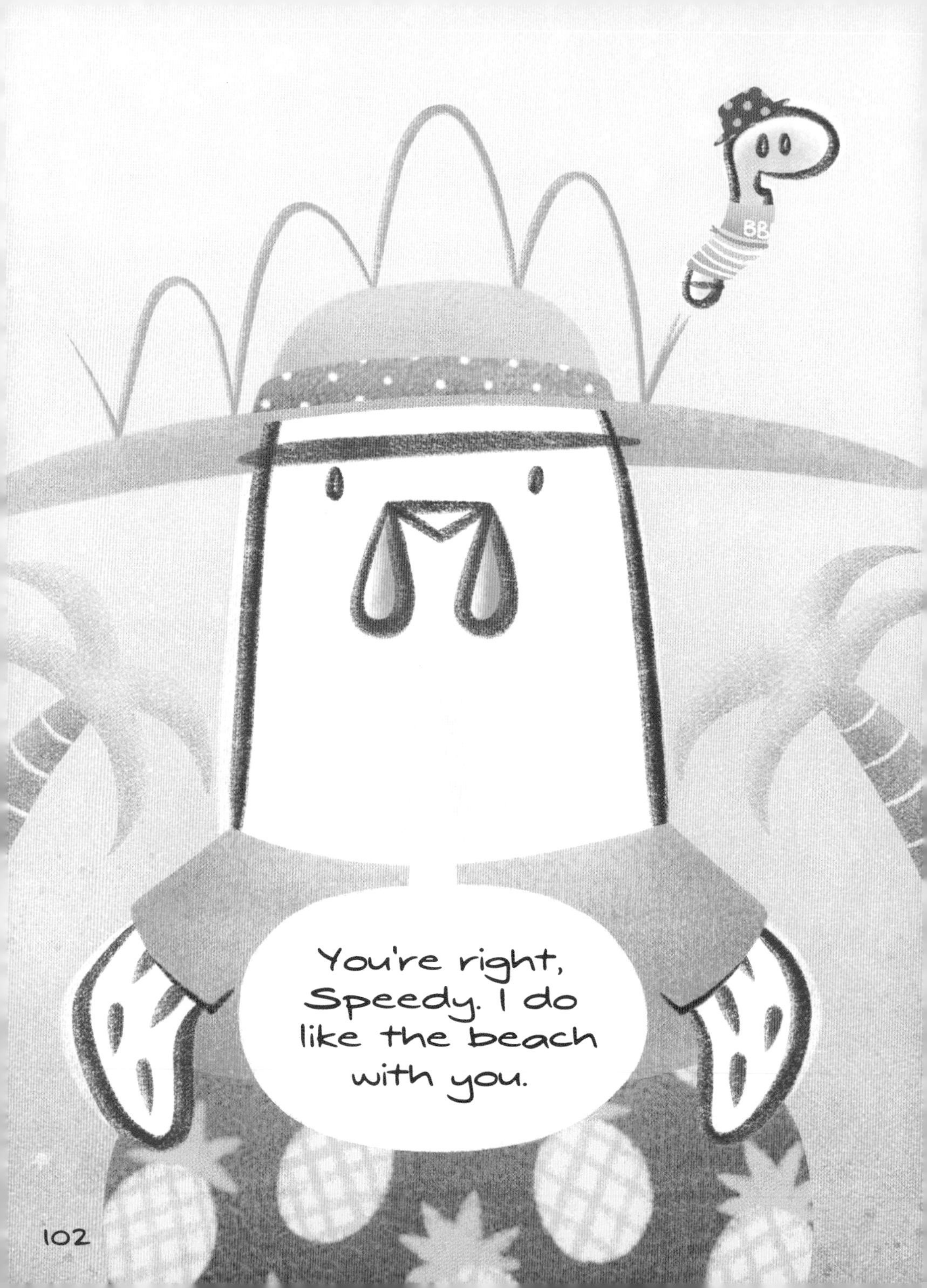
You're right, Speedy. I do like the beach with you.
BB

Best Beach Buds forever!

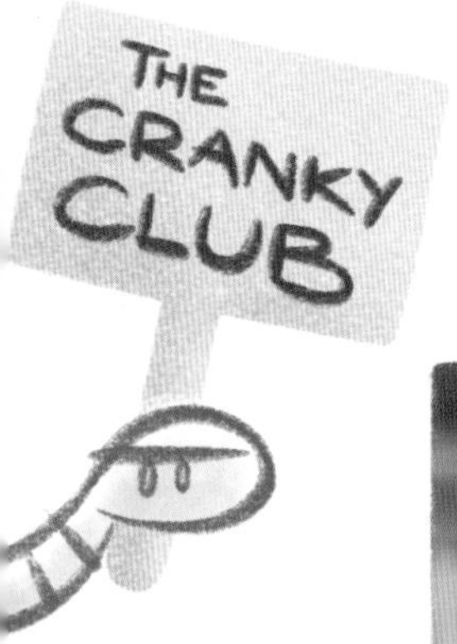
THE CRANKY CLUB

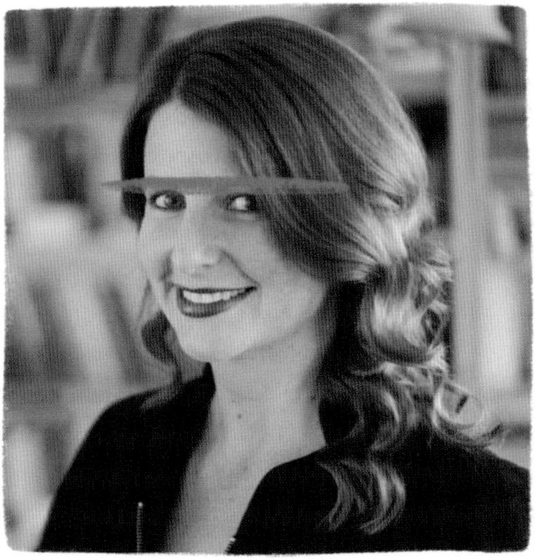

Katherine Battersby

is the critically acclaimed author and illustrator of a number of picture books, including *Perfect Pigeons* and *Squish Rabbit*, a CBC Children's Choice Book. Her books have received glowing reviews in the *New York Times* and starred reviews from *Kirkus* and have been shortlisted for numerous Australian awards. Katherine is president of the Cranky Club and can be found grumbling about bananas, exclamation marks, and windy days. She lives in Ottawa, Canada. Visit her at KatherineBattersby.com.

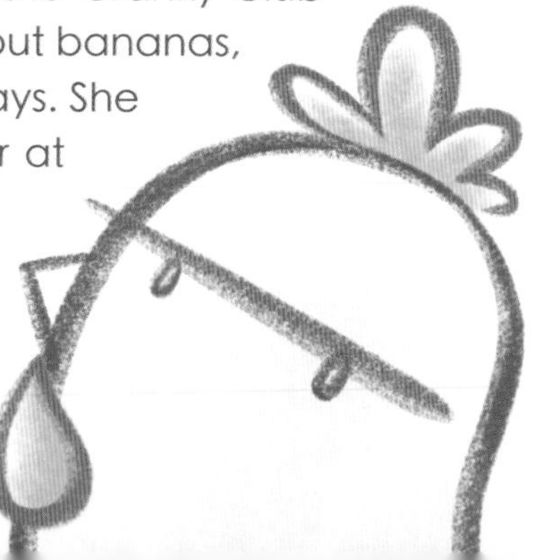

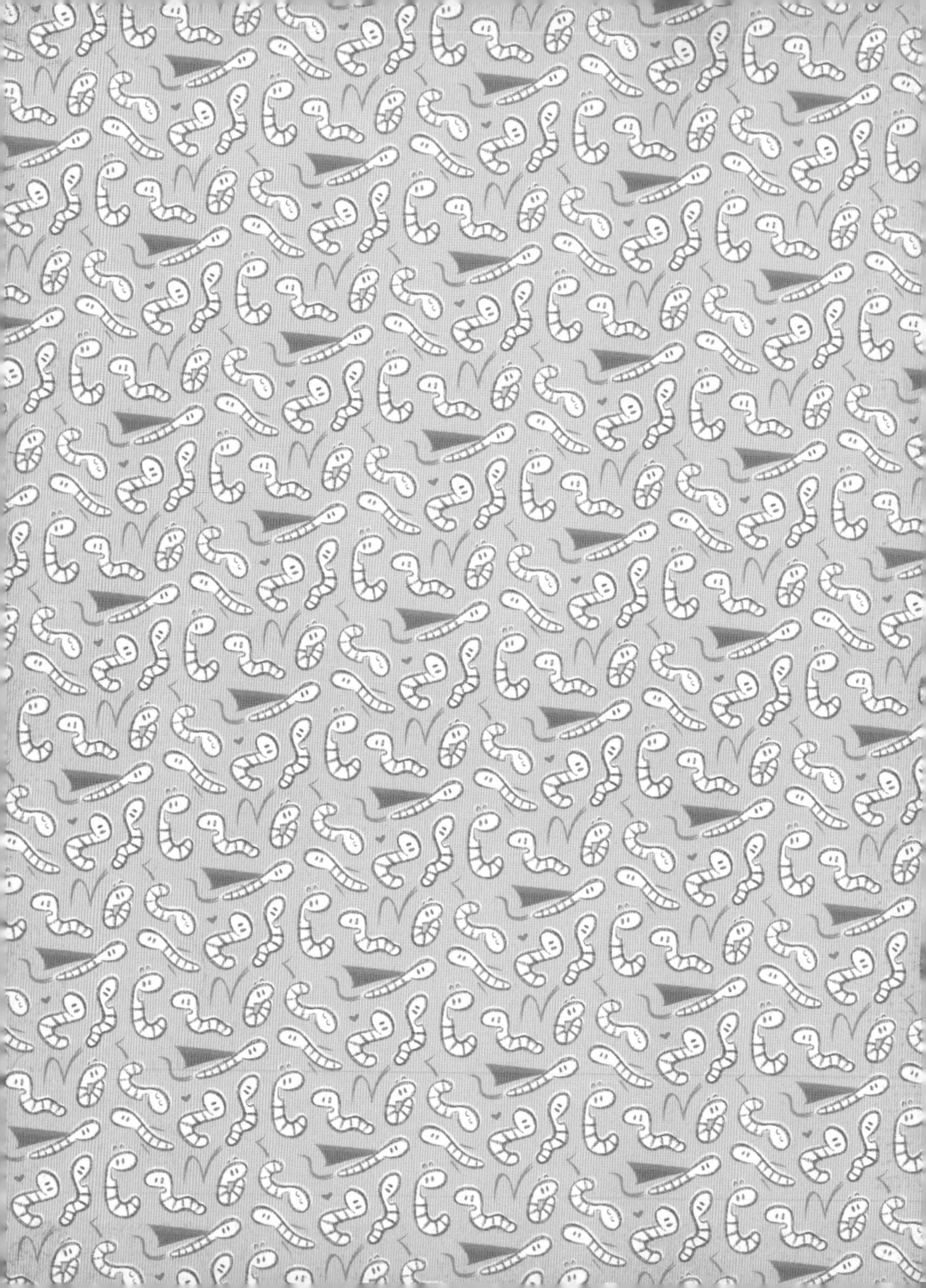